THE WATER CASTLE

THE
WATER
CASTLE

Megan Frazer Blakemore

illustrations by Jim Kay

WALKER BOOKS FOR YOUNG READERS
AN IMPRINT OF BLOOMSBURY
NEW YORK   LONDON   NEW DELHI   SYDNEY

First published in the United States of America in January 2013
by Walker Books for Young Readers, an imprint of Bloomsbury Publishing, Inc.
www.bloomsbury.com

For information about permission to reproduce selections from this book, write to
Permissions, Walker BFYR, 175 Fifth Avenue, New York, New York 10010

Library of Congress Cataloging-in-Publication Data
Blakemore, Megan Frazer.
The Water Castle / by Megan Frazer Blakemore.
p.   cm.
Summary: Moving into an inherited mansion in Maine with their mother and
stroke-afflicted father, three siblings uncover a mystery involving hidden
passageways, family rivalries, and healing waters.
ISBN 978-0-8027-2839-5 (hardcover)
[1. Secrets—Fiction.   2. Families—Fiction.   3. Discoveries in science—Fiction.
4. Dwellings—Fiction.   5. Moving, Household—Fiction.
6. Maine—Fiction.]   I. Title.
PZ7.B574Wat 2013   [Fic]—dc23   2012016442

Typeset by Westchester Book Composition
Printed in the U.S.A. by Thomson-Shore, Dexter, Michigan
2 4 6 8 10 9 7 5 3 1

Manufactured by Thomson-Shore, Dexter. MI (USA); RMA586LS791, December, 2012

For Jack,
because he let me write it

THE WATER CASTLE

ONE

Their mother had tried to make the trip seem fun, like a vacation. "We're going to Maine, dear!" she'd cooed to their father. His lack of response reminded Ephraim, Price, and Brynn that this trip had nothing to do with fun.

It had been three days since Brynn had found their father in his studio and they had gathered at the hospital. A breakdown. Like a car on the side of the road. But it wasn't a car; it was their father. Some sort of misfiring connection in his brain. They'd had to wait several hours in the cheery green waiting room before the official diagnosis had come: a stroke. Their father's life had been full of strokes, carefully placed on canvas. This was nothing like that.

"It was on the left side of his brain," his mother had told

them. "That affects the right side of his body. Also his ability to speak. His nonresponsiveness, though, that's a little unusual."

That word had stayed with Ephraim ever since: *unusual*. It meant atypical. It meant it was something his mother couldn't understand, couldn't fix.

They drove north, up the highway, and then off the highway, through towns and forests with leaves in brighter and brighter shades of orange, red, and gold. It seemed to Ephraim like they were driving through a photo on a calendar.

At the hospital their mother had told them about a former medical-school instructor of hers: "Dr. Winters is an expert in the field. He's a country doctor up in Maine now, semiretired. He said he'd take on your father's care as a special case." Her voice cracked. "I thought we could go to the family house."

The siblings had exchanged looks. The house in Maine was more mythical than actual. Their mother had been contacted by a lawyer years before and told of an inheritance. Their parents drove up to see it, and returned awash with ideas: A summer home! A family retreat! As of yet, they had never been.

In the car Ephraim tried to talk to his mother, though in an awkward and stumbling way, about whether Maine was the place to go when they lived so close to the best hospitals in the world. Her face darkened, and she said, "This doctor is an expert. We're getting the best." He had not pressed her anymore.

The three siblings sat shoulder to shoulder in the backseat of the SUV. Price squeezed a tennis ball. He always kept it with him, tucked into a pocket, pulling it out when he needed something to distract his mind. Brynn read a book so thick she could barely hold it in her small hands. She turned the page. She was nine, slight, with her hair cut in a severe bob that made her eyes look as big and dark as winter lakes. She chewed on her lip as she read. Price, too, seemed untouched. His sandy brown hair flopped down into his eyes. He squeezed the tennis ball, though, fast and hard.

Stuck in the middle, Ephraim had not thought to bring anything with him, so all he could do was look out the window while raking his fingers across the wales of his corduroy pants. It made a *shrift, shrift* sound that he found oddly comforting.

Coming out of one of the forests, he saw the sign:

WELCOME TO CRYSTAL SPRINGS
POP. 1716
A WONDROUS LITTLE PLACE

Wondrous. Ephraim wasn't sure that was even a word.

"You won't believe this place when you see it," their mom said. "I can't believe we haven't made it up here before now. It's amazing. You guys are going to love it, I know it. I wish I'd had a chance to come here when I was your age. It's just perfect for exploring." She drove with both hands on the steering wheel, stealing glances at her husband as she drove. "And the stories—my goodness, the stories my grandfather used to tell me about his great-uncle. Orlando Appledore. Quite a name, huh?" She glanced in the rearview mirror for the response that didn't come. Undaunted, she continued, "He was a hoot, it sounds like. He was always coming up with these crazy inventions, like, oh gosh, I can't even remember, something about changing the weather. A cloud buster or something like that."

No one was really in the mood to hear the stories of the family, not even Brynn, who usually loved such a thing.

A mile or so later, they drove into the main part of town. A church, white and bright as new paper, was the first building they saw. They passed the town hall, a little yellow building with an American flag waving softly out front. The library was a brick box of a building with columns around the front door and a stone lion out front. They rolled past the Wylie Five and Dime, which was advertising a sale on gourds, Ouija boards, and pumpkin-pie filling. Two old men sat on the bench outside. Each wore a polo shirt and a golfing hat. On the other side of the street was a bakery with two café tables outside. A couple sat drinking coffee and holding hands. Another couple strolled by and stopped to talk.

"Isn't it just adorable?" their mother asked. "I don't know why it's not a tourist destination."

It wasn't a tourist destination, Ephraim knew, because it was about three thousand light-years from civilization.

On the edge of the downtown section, they passed a park with a white gazebo decorated with pumpkins. A toddler flew a kite with his father on the edge of the lake, while a group of older boys kicked around a soccer ball.

"Not much farther now," their mother said.

They turned right and started up a hill. About halfway, the pavement ended and changed into a rutted, grassy path. At the top of the hill, the road surface changed again, this time to white crushed gravel. The road looped around in front of a looming stone house that sat atop the hill like a king on a throne.

"Holy cow," Ephraim said.

"Seriously," Price agreed as the family clambered out of the car.

"I told you," their mom said. "I remember seeing a picture of it when I was little and thinking it looked like a magical castle, like I had been stolen away from my life as a fairy princess." She laughed at herself and shook her head.

Ivy ran up the walls of the building and dripped down over the doorway, a rounded stone outcropping that protected a large, wooden door.

"There used to be a hotel, too, a resort, really, with a spring-fed spa. There was a whole water bottling business, too. The hotel burned down in the early nineteen hundreds. But before that it was one of the grand hotels, and people would come from all over to relax and recuperate. They said the water could heal any illness, but of course that's just the placebo effect at best." She looked a little wistful as she spoke, as if she wished she could forget all her medical training and believe in simple cures.

"It looks haunted," Ephraim said.

Price elbowed him and both boys looked to their father. He was hollowed out, white and fragile as a shell. It was improbable—impossible—that their strong father, the one who used to swing them sky-high and onto his shoulders, had shriveled. But, as their mother had explained, some people were just born with weak spots—"kinks in the armor"—and sometimes those spots gave in. She was a doctor, a cardiac surgeon, and her words had weight, but did not make them feel any better.

"I'm going to get your father settled," she said. "Why don't you come in and pick bedrooms?"

She went around to their father's side of the car and, with Price's help, heaved him out and settled him on the driveway. Wrapping her arm around his waist, she led him up the three stone stairs to the gargantuan front door. His right leg slid along behind him. "This way, darling," she said. "We're in Maine now. Isn't it even more grand than you remember?"

Ephraim didn't know how his mother could just go on talking to his father like that. As if he understood. As if he could remember.

Price picked up his backpack and hitched it onto his shoulder. "Let's go," he said as he hopped up the stairs and pulled open the front door with ease. Brynn and Ephraim passed through into the front hall, a wide-open space with ceilings so high they had to crane their heads back to see them.

The tile floor continued into the main part of the home. A large archway opened to a majestic staircase that split into two sides and curved gracefully up to the second story, like something from an old movie where a woman would walk down the stairs, skirt trailing behind, to meet a man in a tuxedo on the landing.

Before the archway, to the right, was an open door and a few stairs that led down to the kitchen. Ephraim wondered why it was tucked away. The dining room faced the bottom of the staircase, and it would be a long walk with the food. Then he realized that of course the owners of the house didn't have to worry about that. They'd have servants to cook and bring them their meals.

Next to the dining room was a large sitting room, and beyond the stairs were still more doors. Each one had a taxidermied animal head above it.

As they walked up the stairs, puffs of dirt came out of the rug. "It smells like no one has been here in years," Ephraim said. Price did not answer. He had jogged up and was already on the second floor. Brynn was a few steps ahead of Ephraim and turned her head from side to side, taking it all in.

At the top of the stairs, two open doors revealed a library. Floor-to-ceiling shelves circled the room, filled edge to edge with books. There were two windows on the far wall, both covered with heavy velvet drapes that made the library dim and dreary as a monastery.

"I want this room," Brynn declared.

"You can't," Ephraim told her.

"Leave her alone," Price said.

"What? It's a library, not a bedroom."

"It's not like anyone except Brynn is going to read the

books. It might as well be hers." He turned to his little sister. "We'll bring a bed down from one of the other rooms."

Brynn smiled for the first time since their father went into the hospital.

The library ran up against the master suite, where their mother talked to their father in low tones.

"You want to wait here or come with us?" Price asked.

Brynn gave a longing look at all the books, but said, "Go with you." She hadn't wanted to be left alone lately, and Ephraim wondered how well she would do in the large, dark library. At home she had been sneaking into Price's bedroom to sleep on the floor.

They wandered to the far end of the second floor, to the back of the house, where they found a set of stairs going up. Though not as dramatic as the main staircase, these were still wider than what Ephraim was used to, and so seemed very impressive. They led to the third floor: a hallway with several doors off it. Ephraim walked into a room with an old brass bed and windows that looked out over the river. It was the attached bathroom, though, that made up his mind. Privacy, finally.

He turned to tell his siblings that he had found his room, but they were no longer behind him. After a moment's hesitation in which he considered the possibility that they had simply vanished, he went out of the room and followed their voices to a small bedroom on the opposite end of the floor. They were coming from what appeared to be a closet. When Ephraim looked inside he saw a set of stairs, plain and skinny, heading steeply up. He climbed them to a fourth floor of the house. He entered a tiny room with low ceilings and windows that jutted out. It was cluttered with odds and ends: a rusty springy-horse, a collection of empty picture frames, and an antique-style sword.

"You found the attic," Ephraim said.

"Actually, this was probably the servants' quarters," Brynn said. "Those stairs down might have led to a nursery."

Price left the first room and headed to the second. The others followed. This room had a small bed with a white metal headboard and no mattress. It was pushed up against the wall, and there was nothing else in the room: just bare floorboards painted gray. Brynn tucked her small, warm hand into Ephraim's, and he was glad to know he wasn't the only one creeped out by the space.

Price moved on to the next room. "Huh," he said.

Brynn and Ephraim came in after him. The room was sunny, but stacked with trunks. What had caught Price's attention was a set of stairs going down. The three descended and found themselves in yet another room. "This isn't the third floor," Ephraim said. "We didn't go down enough stairs."

"It's the third and a half floor," Brynn said.

"My room," Price said.

"You want to go up and then down to get to your bedroom?" Ephraim asked. Of course Price did. He was like a Spartan soldier: the harder something was, the more he enjoyed it.

Brynn walked around the edge of the room. "I just can't figure out where in the house this is. It would have to be sticking out, and I didn't notice any shapes from the outside."

"It's just some architectural trick," Ephraim explained.

"It's cool," Price said.

Brynn said, "It's impossible."

"Clearly it's not," Ephraim told her, although Brynn tended to be right.

Price put his hands on her shoulders. "Why don't you look it up? I bet there's something about it in your library."

"Maybe," she said. She shook free of his hands and went to the window, which offered a view of the postcard-perfect town. "Crystal Springs isn't on the map."

"It's a very small town," Price told her.

"I checked in the *Maine Gazetteer* Mom had. Then I checked online maps. Then I checked with the U.S. Geological Survey."

"Maybe it's not really a town," Ephraim said. "It could be part of a bigger town, like a village or something. You know, like Coolidge Corner is part of Brookline."

"Maybe," she said again. She turned from the window, her hair swinging around her face.

On the center of Price's bed was a small, handmade doll with brown skin and yarn hair that had grayed with age. "Here you go, Brynn," Price said. "Take this doll as a, what's it called, protector of the house."

"A talisman," Brynn said.

"Right."

Brynn regarded the doll for a moment, then took it from her brother's outstretched hand. "Let's go see Mommy and Daddy."

On her seventh birthday she had declared herself too old to call them that, but she had lapsed back into it after their father's stroke. She was the one who had found him. He was sitting in his studio, staring at the painting on his easel. It was of a petal falling off a hyacinth. His own paintings were more abstract, but for work he painted greeting cards. This one had been a sympathy card. Brynn had found him staring at it, moving his lips wordlessly. She had tried to speak to him, but he would not respond.

"Okay, sure," Price said. He dropped his backpack on the bed. "Let's go."

They climbed up the stairs, through the smaller bedrooms, and down the stairs. "Are you sure you want to live so far out of the way?" Ephraim asked.

"What's the matter? Are you afraid to be by yourself?"

Ephraim shoved Price, not that it even moved Price an inch. "It just seems antisocial is all," he replied.

"I can work out and won't bug anybody," he explained.

They clomped through the third floor, and then down to the second. Their mother emerged from the master suite just as they came out of the stairwell. "Your father is sleeping," she said. "I'm going to go to the grocery store we passed to get something for dinner. Can you boys unpack the car?"

"Sure," Ephraim said. Price was already halfway down the stairs.

They unloaded their belongings from the SUV into the entryway. "All set," Price called up to their mom.

She came down the stairs holding Brynn's hand. "Come with me, Brynn?" their mother asked. Brynn nodded.

After they left, Price and Ephraim carried the suitcases upstairs. Ephraim put his down in his room and looked around: brass four-poster bed, window looking out toward the river, small bathroom. He let out a deep breath and tried to tell himself that everything would be okay. That's when he noticed the strange humming noise.

TWO

In the village of Crystal Springs, the return of the Appledore family to the Water Castle did not go unnoticed. The news moved through the town like a ripple of water. The oldest and youngest were the most interested. The oldest because they had hints of memories: a grand hotel, an eccentric old man, a horrible fire. For the youngest, the Water Castle had always seemed haunted, and they whispered together about who could possibly be living there. Vampires? Werewolves? Witches?

Mallory Green heard the news, but she refused to get excited about it. She stretched across her couch and watched a black-and-white zombie movie on TV.

In the adjacent garage, her father, Henry, rolled out from under the car he was fixing. He wiped his greasy hands on a rag, and then walked across his lawn past the rusted-out cars and animal figurines that peeked out of the fallen leaves. Mallory looked up when he walked into the living room, but then returned her attention to the movie.

"I'm going up to the Water Castle to have a look around. Meet the family and make sure everything's in order. You should come with me," he said.

She had no interest in going to the castle ever again. "No thanks."

"You're going to have to go up there sooner or later."

He glanced at the television. What they both knew he meant by this was that sooner or later they were going to have to go to the house together—the place where she had spent so much of her childhood. And between them would be the big empty hole left by the departure of her mother.

Mallory had muted the volume, but the scores of zombies still lurched across the screen.

"I'm not sure what they know," he said. "I don't plan on telling them anything right off. I don't want to overwhelm them."

"Sounds like a plan." He didn't have to worry about her telling tales, because she didn't believe a word of them, and didn't need the new folks in town thinking she was crazy right off the bat.

Mallory's life had always been woven through with stories. Her parents both spun them out like silk, and she'd walked between the worlds of the real and the imaginary as easily as most people walked from room to room in their houses. Her parents had stories about everything, but mostly they were about the Water Castle: the big Appledore mansion on the hill.

Now the stories seemed like taunts: a shadow of a world that wasn't there anymore.

Her dad didn't smile or nod or even say good-bye when he turned to go, and Mallory knew that he was disappointed in her, but she wasn't going to play along with his games. Not anymore. When he left, Mallory jumped off the couch and looked out the window. Her father swung himself up into his old truck. It rumbled and shook for a moment, and then he began to drive.

She hated that house. *The Water Castle.* That's what people in town called it because some said it was constructed from a fortune made selling water. But the castle came first; Mallory knew that from her parents' stories. The Appledores were already rich when they came searching for the water.

It was bad enough that her parents had spent all their free time there when no one was even living in the house. Bad enough that he kept going even after her mother—whose family had been the caretakers of the place for generations—had left. He was cleaning up another mess of hers, fulfilling another commitment. Now, though, some new rich family—or rather, the same rich family, but a new generation—had swept in, and he couldn't wait to get up there and see what they needed.

Shaking her head, she sank back down into the couch. Normally zombies gave her comfort. They were slow. There were straightforward ways to kill them. If they ever showed up, she would know what to do. Too bad the rest of life wasn't like that.

She clicked off the television and navigated around the piles of books, up the stairs, and into her bedroom, where she side-stepped more books and picked up a picture of her parents. It was from right after she was born and they looked so young: fresh-faced and glowing over their young child. Her mother wore straight-legged pants, and her hair was cropped close to her head in soft tufts that Mallory had liked to run her hands over. Her dad wore a flannel shirt and held Mallory close to his chest.

Looking at the picture, she could hear their voices telling her the stories, could feel the wind as they sat on the stone wall looking up at the Water Castle. "Look at it, won't you, Mallory? You can tell it's something special, can't you?"

She had nodded eagerly.

"People will tell you it's haunted, but don't you believe them. Those are just the words of folks who are scared and small-minded. There's a power there, a life force. There's special water here, and if you drink it, it cures your injuries and illness. It slows down your aging so much, it's like you can live forever. You've heard of the Fountain of Youth, haven't you?"

"The Fountain of Youth is in the castle?"

Her dad picked up a smooth pebble and tossed it in his hand. "Not exactly. We need to start at the beginning."

"Once upon a time," her mother said, "there was a young man named Angus Appledore."

"Angus?" Mallory had asked.

"Yes, Angus."

"A fine Scottish name," her dad interjected. "We almost named you Angus."

"Are you going to tell the story or do I need to?" Mallory's mom asked.

"Now Angus, he was taken by the story of the Fountain of Youth. You see, he was a young man in love, and he wanted his love to last forever."

Her parents always exchanged a glance at this point in the story. "An eternity together."

"He was a wise young man, and brave. He read all he could about the Fountain of Youth, and visited all the places it was said to have been. He went to Ethiopia, where the people were so tall and strong that the Greeks felt certain the fountain had to be there."

Mallory pictured tall, dark people like herself drinking from the fountain. Her parents told of how he went to Bimini, a name that always made Mallory giggle, and then to Florida, where Ponce de Leon was supposed to have found the fountain. But always, Angus was disappointed. So he studied and studied. He looked at maps. He read medical journals and science journals and mystical treatises. The circle of possibility got smaller and smaller until he was sure it was in Crystal Springs. He packed up his wife, who was not so young anymore, and their children and they moved across the ocean.

Her mother took Mallory's hand in hers. "This is where the story gets sad. Are you sure you want to hear this part?"

Mallory nodded.

"His wife died along the way. Just when he felt he was as close as he had ever been, his reason for searching ceased to exist."

Her parents exchanged another glance.

"Desolate, he had the castle built as a place to hide and grieve. Angus hired workers from the town, most of whom came from the Darling family, and each night when they went home to their own houses, they wondered why he had it built so strangely, with secret passages and hidden rooms," her dad explained.

"Some people say he was paranoid and wanted places to hide. I think it just reflected the state of his heart," her mother surmised. "Angus left his children to their own devices, raised by your great-great-great-great-grandmother. She had heard the stories, too, and though Angus forbade anyone to speak of the fountain, she whispered the stories to them before bedtime."

"Why?" Mallory asked.

"Because that's how stories survive," her dad said.

Her parents had told the story together, made it up together. They had made everything together. This life, this home. Mallory.

And then her mother left.

She put the picture back down on her bureau, picked up an old book from a stack by her desk, and flopped onto her bed. She flipped through the pages until she got to a nearly blank one and began drawing. She started with the shape of the face, then added curly hair. Moving on to the body, she sketched out a long gown. She didn't always know where the people in her drawings came from. As a child she believed they were real—as real as the stories her parents told her—trapped in some other world. If she could only draw them correctly, they would be free. Now she just drew.

Underneath the picture, she wrote, "October 4th. The Appledores have returned. Dad gone to vow servitude. Still bored brainless." She closed the book. These old books were both sketchbooks and journals to her. Nearly every entry ended with the same line. "Still bored brainless." In a town with only 1,716 people, what else could she be?

August 12, 1908

Nora knew that people could survive without fingers or toes. Why, Robert Peary had lost several of his toes on one expedition, and he was on his way to try again to reach the North Pole. Still, the clothes wringer made her nervous. Her mother used her wrist to wipe stray curls that stuck to Nora's face with sweat. "It won't eat you," she said.

It *could* eat her, though, and, Peary aside, Nora could not imagine life with her fingers crushed and useless.

Her mother blew out a sigh of exasperation. "Since you'll be no help here, go on inside and prepare some lunch."

As Nora walked in the back door of her house, she heard a knock on the front. Drying her hands on her apron, she went through the house, wondering who it might be. Never in a million years would she have guessed right. When she flung open the door, she saw ninety-seven-year-old Orlando Priam Appledore.

She stepped back, then cleared her throat and said, "Hello, Dr. Appledore." Looking past him, she saw her brother Solomon sitting on the carriage, a wry smile on his face.

"Nora Darling?" Orlando asked.

"Yes, sir."

"It has come to my attention that you are a student of Latin. Is this accurate?"

"Yes, sir." Nora regarded him carefully. It was widely reported that Orlando Appledore was mad as a hatter—even some of her family said so—but he seemed relatively normal to her.

He rearranged his gnarled hands on his cane. "And French?"

"Yes, sir."

"How are you at computations?"

"First in my class."

"For the girls? For your race?"

"For everybody, sir."

The features on Orlando's face rearranged themselves. "Well, then, how would you like a job?"

Nora again looked to Solomon, convinced he had somehow cajoled the old man into teasing her, but Solomon looked as surprised as she was. "Sir?" she asked.

"I need an assistant. I have heard reports that you are the brightest child in town, and I need the brightest if I'm to accomplish my life's work before this life is over."

Nora had always known that she would go to work for the Appledore family someday. Her family had been working for theirs as cooks, stable help, nannies, and more as long as the Appledores had lived here; the Darlings had actually built the Appledore mansion. She had always expected, though, to work in the hotel or spa, perhaps as a chambermaid, or to take in laundry as her mother did.

"You'll live in the house. I have a room set aside for you. It is quite private, I assure you. Originally I thought I could use the space as my laboratory, but Mrs. Appledore complained of the scents and I convinced my grandnephew to build me another space. A better space. Of course you will continue your studies under my tutelage. I have set about a whole schedule starting with calisthenics in the morning. Following that we shall have our time in the laboratory, then move on to mathematics. Then lunch, of course. And then . . ." His voice trailed off. He looked into the sky and then made a grasping motion as if attempting to catch a fly, but there were none buzzing around. "Well, I assure you the rest of the day is planned as well, to the minute. I have it all written down in my notebooks. You may start today."

"Today, sir?"

"Today."

"I'm sorry, sir, I'm afraid I don't understand. What is to be my job?"

He looked right and then left. "I shall explain it in the carriage. The walls have ears, you know."

Nora thought of days spent on her hands and knees scrubbing floors in the hotel or above a hot stove boiling sheets, her appendages always at risk, and compared that future to the idea of working alongside strange Dr. Appledore. "I shall fetch my things," she said.

"Right, quite right," Orlando said.

When Nora turned around, she saw her mother in the kitchen. "Mother," she called. "Dr. Appledore is here."

Nora's mother came into the room with a look of concern upon her face.

"He wants to offer me a job."

"I have offered you a job," Orlando said. "An attention to detail and precision shall be of the utmost importance while you are in my employ. I hope that the reports on you have not been exaggerated."

Nora wondered just where these reports were coming from. Her mother gave her a quizzical look before she ushered Orlando into the sitting room and offered him a cup of tea, which he declined.

Nora went into the bedroom she shared with her siblings. She found a satchel and filled it with some of her clothes. From under her bed she took out her box of her most prized and personal possessions. It was old and wooden, stamped with the words *Dr. Appledore's Crystal Water*, though everyone knew that both the water bottling operation and the resort were under the management of Harold Appledore the Second, Dr. Appledore's grandnephew. Many years before, she had written in a careful hand *Property of Nora Darling*. She slid back the cover to see the contents: a tortoiseshell hair clip that she thought too beautiful to actually wear in her hair, a clipping about Henson and Peary's 1905–1906 attempt at the North Pole, and a doll made for her by her mother that she had grown too old to play with, but still loved dearly. She replaced the lid and tucked the box into her satchel.

On the way back to the sitting room, she took a book down from the shelf and placed it in her bag as well.

While she was gone, Dr. Appledore had explained the job to her mother in the scantest of detail. Solomon came and helped Dr. Appledore to the carriage. While he did so, Nora's mother grasped her close. "Do you want this?" she whispered into Nora's hair.

Nora thought for a moment of the life she had always planned: cleaning up for others, doing their bidding. It would be the same day after day. But working for Orlando Appledore, learning from him, that held more promise. She could become more educated. "Matthew Henson started his career as a porter," she told her mother. "And now he is accompanying Robert Peary to the North Pole. Every journey starts by taking a chance."

Nora's mother buried her head in her daughter's curls and kissed her lightly. "Be well, my dear. And don't go leaving for the Pole without giving us notice."

"Of course not," she said, grinning to herself. All of a sudden, such an adventure actually seemed possible.

* * *

The carriage jostled along the road through town, back toward the Water Castle. Orlando cleared his throat. "My great-great-uncle came to this village in search of the Fountain of Youth."

Nora looked down at her lap, unsure of how to react to such a statement.

"Angus Appledore. He never found it. His wife died. He was devastated." He waved his hand in the air as if this part of the story were superfluous. "However, his notes remain. Our mission will be to find what he never could."

"The Fountain of Youth, sir?"

"Please stop calling me sir. It makes me feel like a schoolmaster or a prison guard. Do you know that every Appledore has lived past one hundred years?" he asked. "Additional evidence: the Passamaquoddy used to come up to the hills of Crystal Springs to bathe before going into battle."

"In the lake?"

Orlando shook his head. "Not in the lake. I've tested that water repeatedly and it displays absolutely no unique qualities. Somewhere else. Someplace secret that has been lost. Otherwise, what is the point in searching for it? Nor is it the water that my nephew sells. Dr. Appledore's Crystal Water. I'm the only doctor in this family and I assure you I offer no endorsement of that so-called 'life-giving elixir.' That is just a cynical misuse of the myth. Though I suppose if anyone is foolish enough to buy it, the fault is their own."

The Appledores had grown their fortune in the last generation by selling bottled water. Harold Appledore, Orlando's grandnephew and current head of the family, had opened the Crystal Springs Resort and Recuperation Center—home of the world-famous Dr. Appledore's Crystal Water. People came from all over the country—some even from Europe—to restore their life spirits with the healing water that they drank from leaded crystal goblets or bathed in inside the marble bathhouses. Nora liked to visit her brother Solomon, who worked in the stables and drove the carriage. She would listen to the voices and the accents and wonder what it would be like to live in a city like New York or Paris.

"We shall proceed not with fantastic stories, but through science," he announced. "So much has been discovered in this age of enlightenment, and natural philosophy—or science, as I prefer—is where we shall find the most wondrous-strange discoveries."

Dr. Appledore spoke in circles it seemed to Nora, but she liked the idea of being a scientist. Arctic explorers were scientists, learning about a world that so few had seen.

They had driven onto the Appledore property, and Nora stared out the window at the field. She saw young Harry, Orlando's great-grandnephew, hop the fence and cross over toward the cows. He was home from boarding school in Massachusetts. He had the dark hair, sharp nose, and green eyes of the Appledore family, and Nora thought he might have been handsome if he hadn't always looked so sad and serious. Surely the girls in town spoke about him often.

"Indeed," Orlando went on, "some believe that our new knowledge has hemmed us in by showing us how much is not possible. I maintain that it is only our own ignorance and lack of imagination that keeps us from unlocking all the mysteries of the world."

Harry and Nora rarely spoke, and when they did, their speech was formal. Their distance was not merely because her family worked for his, but because each wanted the life the other had, and neither understood how the other could want his or her own. Harry would gladly spend his days outside working with animals and the land just as Nora's brothers ranged over the fields, occupying their hours with the Appledore sheep and cattle, as well as their own hens and livestock. Though it was perfectly acceptable for Harry to work with the animals as a hobby—a gentleman farmer—it could never be his occupation, and much of his days were filled with lessons and comportment exercises. Indeed he was only allowed to keep the cattle as a means for learning about business.

For her part, Nora would have given anything to go to the boarding school in Massachusetts, even though it would mean being away from her family. She had once overheard Harry's mother talking about all the things he was studying there: Shakespeare and science and geography and geometry. It all sounded so wonderful to Nora that she could almost taste the sour-sweet desire for it on her tongue.

"And when we discover the true elixir of life, my dear Nora, then we shall show the world that all manner of things are possible, isn't that right?"

Nora returned her attention to Orlando. *Possible.* The word rang in her head like a beacon of hope.

THREE

I don't believe in ghosts," Brynn announced. She fingered the dress of the doll Price had given her, then placed it on the windowsill. The three siblings sat in their pajamas in the library. Brynn was in her bed with her sheets drawn up over her lap. She wore a nightgown that was too small for her, pulling across her shoulders and exposing her twig wrists. "It just doesn't make sense. All the time the world has been here, all those people, we'd be overrun with them."

"Did someone tell you there were ghosts here?" Price asked.

"Ephraim said it looked haunted."

Ephraim had been examining his toes, but he snapped his head up when she said that. "I didn't mean I actually thought it was haunted. I just said that it looked that way. Like if this were a movie, this would be a haunted house. But not in real life."

Brynn shrugged. "I was just pointing out that it's not possible."

"You're right," Price said. "But if you do get scared, all you have to do is think about your breathing. You just breathe in and out really slowly, through your mouth. That's what Coach always has us do for a big race and it works every time. Sometimes when I'm really excited the night before, I do it while I'm lying in bed and it puts me right to sleep. Okay?"

"Okay," Brynn agreed.

A gust of wind picked up and shook the panes of the window. It sounded like someone knocking to get in. Brynn took a deep breath in and exhaled.

"Good," Price said. "Now listen. I think we're going to have to start acting more grown-up. Mom's under a lot of stress and we need to help her out as best we can."

He didn't look at Ephraim, but the words felt like tiny little arrows pricking him all over his body. Ephraim shuddered thinking of that night's dinner. He'd asked their mother how long they'd be staying. When she said she wasn't sure, he demanded, "How about a ballpark? A few weeks or months or what?" Ephraim didn't know why he'd pushed his fragile mother. He was angry. Angry about being ripped away from his if not happy then stable existence back in Cambridge. Angry that his dad was not at the table, but instead sat silent in the bedroom upstairs. None of this was his mother's fault, he knew, but he couldn't seem to stop himself.

Then things had gotten worse. "We'll be here long enough for you to attend school," she had told them. "You'll start tomorrow. The caretaker stopped by earlier and we arranged for him to pick you up and drive you in."

Ephraim shoveled his spaghetti into his mouth, fuming at this latest development.

"I've never started a new school before," Brynn said.

Their mom reached out and ruffled her hair. "You'll do just fine, Brynn. I'm not worried about you at all." Her glance quickly darted to Ephraim, then back down at her plate.

"Do you think they have a nice library?" Brynn asked.

"I'm sure they have a lovely library," their mother said.

Ephraim snorted. He imagined a room full of dusty old books, with a librarian who wore a bun and glasses slipping down her pointy nose. It would be nothing like the library at their school in Boston, which was sunny and full of new books and computers.

"We'll make it work, Mom," Price said. Which was easy for Price to say.

In the library of the Water Castle, Price continued taking on the role of head of household. Ephraim wanted to be angry—who had made Price boss?—but it wasn't like he was about to step up. "We each need to pitch in more," Price said. "We need to do the dishes and maybe make dinner from time to time. Whatever we can to make life easier for Mom. I can bike into town whenever we need anything, but you guys will need to help around here."

Ephraim walked over to the large telescope by the window. When he looked through the eyepiece, he saw that the glass on the far end was cracked.

Maybe Price had the right idea, he told himself. Maybe this would be his chance to make things work. Sure he'd never been anything more than mediocre back in Boston, but it was all relative. Compared to the kids in this small, middle-of-nowhere town, he would no doubt seem like an intellectual superstar. Coming from the city, he'd be far more sophisticated, too. Maybe this was just the chance he needed to reinvent himself. For however long they'd be there, he could be a different guy. A cool guy. A smart guy. A guy with lots of friends.

"Okay," Brynn said. "I can keep things organized. I can make the shopping lists, too. Mom always forgets them at home anyway, and Dad just draws pictures when it's his turn to do the shopping."

Ephraim was in a reverie about the potential for newfound popularity when he realized they were both staring at him. "I'll help out, too," he said. "Somehow."

"Good," Price said. "Now I suggest we all go to sleep. It's been a long day, and tomorrow will be another long one."

He sounded like a person trying on his father's clothes, but Ephraim and Brynn both nodded, and Price and Ephraim left for their individual rooms.

The three had always lived in the city, in a large home by

city standards, but still piled on top of one another. Their mother, too, had grown up in a townhouse on Beacon Hill. Only their father had ever lived in the country. The siblings were used to the noise of cars, sirens, and most of all, each other. Spread out about the house as they were, no one felt at ease.

It did not help that everything was different, even the little things—especially the little things. The light switches were two round buttons, rather than an up-down switch. The sinks had one tap for cold, one for hot, and the stopper was labeled, in small script, *waste*. The carpets were threadbare, as if centuries of feet had carried the wool away with them. Each room had a fireplace with a stack of logs, ready to burn, along with giant mirrors, sconces on the walls, and beds so high even Price needed a stool to climb in.

It was not home.

It might have felt like an adventure if they were there for another reason, but none of them could forget why they had traveled to this giant house.

Price did ten sets of push-ups, then lay in bed and concentrated on regulating his breathing and pulse, just like he'd told the others to do. The first night in the house, he was able to put himself to sleep. Brynn removed stacks of books and placed them around the bed that Price and Ephraim had carried down from the third floor. She sat against the rattling windows of the library, reading the books with a headlamp strapped to her forehead.

Ephraim tried to do as Price had said. He closed his eyes

and focused on breathing in and out, but before he knew it his eyes were wide open and his mind was racing. He was stuck in this town, in this creepy house, for an indefinite amount of time. He was going to have to start at a new school. And, of course, he could not forget that his father had had some sort of brain malfunction that kept him from speaking, reacting, and, Ephraim feared, feeling and remembering.

Ephraim got out of bed and went to the window. The moon, thin to the point of being barely visible, hung over the river. Though the light was dim, Ephraim made out a cluster of bats on the opposite shore. He shifted his gaze to the grounds of the house. He could make out shapes but wasn't sure what they were—bushes, statues, walls.

There were two large oaks, and from each hung a swing. One of them swung back and forth, while the other was dead still. He wondered who had put them there and who had used them. It seemed inconceivable to him that a family had lived here.

He heard the humming—like a piano hitting one note and holding it for an impossibly long time. Below it was a sort of skittering noise. Ephraim was normally not the type of boy who investigated strange sounds in the night, but he figured if some sort of violence befell him, at least he wouldn't have to go to school the next day.

The sound seemed to be coming from the far end of the house. He walked down the hall with his hands trailing along the textured wallpaper. At the end of the hall was a large window that overlooked the driveway up to the house, and he could almost imagine the people who had lived here before him standing where he stood: waiting, surveying.

The sound was definitely louder here, and higher pitched—one key up on the piano. He ran his hands along the wall, checking for vibrations. He had about given up when he noticed a blue glow. It seemed to be all around the house, growing brighter and brighter. He leaned against the window, his palm flat against the cool glass, turning his head from side to side to try to find the source of the glow. Just when he determined that it seemed to be coming from up above, there was a flash of light bright enough to blind him. The whole world seemed to turn blue. Ephraim's eyes burned and he blinked until he could see again.

The humming subsided. It was still there, but barely discernible, and the skittering was gone completely. His vision glowed around the edges with the memory of the flash. He stood and waited. Waited. Nothing happened. He just stared out the window. Beyond the driveway was the town. A smattering of lights remained lit. He kept waiting for another flash, and when it didn't come he wondered if he had imagined the whole thing, or if it was some trick of the eye.

Either way, he was finally starting to feel tired. He started back down the hall and stopped at a small alcove that held, on a pedestal, a bust sculpted out of bronze. He leaned in to read the inscription: ORLANDO PRIAM APPLEDORE, KEEPER OF THE FLAME. The statue was dusty, so he blew on it. The dust sparkled in the scant light. It was a very lifelike sculpture, especially considering it was made of bronze. The eyes were closed, but Orlando seemed to be lost in thought, as if he might open his eyes at any moment and reveal his grand idea.

"Well, Orlando," Ephraim said softly. "I hope you don't mind us being in your house. It's not exactly where I want to be."

Orlando had no reply.

FOUR

Ephraim watched Price hop onto his bike and coast down the driveway while he and Brynn sat on the stoop, shivering and waiting for the caretaker to come and pick them up. Some caretaker. The ivy was threatening to smother the building, and inside, everything was covered with a thin layer of dust.

The temperature hovered around forty degrees, which he gathered was not that cold for a fall morning in Maine. Price hadn't seemed to mind the brisk air. He wore wool long underwear and wind pants with a light jacket. The purple of the jacket faded as he went around the corner.

Brynn picked up a stone and scraped it against the granite steps. "Did you hear the house singing last night?" she asked.

Ephraim thought about telling her how he had followed the sound and seen the flash of blue light, but he didn't want to worry her. "I did hear a humming," he said. "I think it's just an old-house sound."

Brynn gave him a look like she couldn't quite believe him. Then she hefted a large book out of her bag and began reading.

Ephraim looked up to the window of his parents' room. He thought he saw the silhouette of his father; it looked just like him, tall and thin. His heart beat faster. He turned to Brynn to tell her. "Look—" he began. When he looked back up, though, all he saw was glass and drapes. His stomach sank.

"What?" Brynn asked.

"Nothing," he said. "I thought I saw an eagle, but it was just a crow."

They'd filed into the room the night before, Price, Brynn, and Ephraim. Their father looked paler and smaller than when he was in the hospital, like the stroke was shrinking him. He'd blinked when Brynn squeezed his good hand, but that was all. Price had stood a few steps off, squeezing a tennis ball. Ephraim, though, took a deep breath and leaned in to kiss his father's papery skin. His bravery was not rewarded with a response: no flick of a smile, no blink of his father's eyes.

Ephraim heard the rumble of a diesel truck. He stood up and hitched his backpack onto his shoulders. "That's our ride, I guess," he said to Brynn.

The truck slowed to a stop and coughed out a purple-gray cloud. A man emerged, blowing on his knobby hands. His white cheeks were streaked with red patches and his green eyes shone out like fireworks. "Good morning. I'm Henry Green." He extended his hand to Ephraim, which Ephraim took and squeezed. The man looked young but tired. He smiled at Brynn and Ephraim, who said nothing. So Henry kept going: "Brynn and Ephraim, I presume? I met your mother last night while you guys were off exploring the house." He leaned in a little closer and said, "Floors and floors to explore, aren't there?" He gave a little wink and Ephraim wasn't sure if he was hinting at the third-and-a-half floor or something else entirely. Henry blew on his hands again. "Well, then, your chariot awaits."

Henry pulled open the passenger door, and Brynn climbed in. After a moment's hesitation, in which he considered turning tail and running right past the house and down the hill behind it, Ephraim followed her. As he did, he noticed the girl sitting there. She wore camouflage pants and a white tank top with a sweatshirt over it. The sweatshirt was covered with patches and pins. The top half of her hair was pulled back from her face, and braids stuck out in all directions like porcupine quills. "Oh," he said.

"Oh," she said back to him. He looked at her, confused, and she said, "I'm sorry, I thought that was the standard greeting wherever it is that you come from."

"Cambridge," he said.

"Cambridge, England? Cambridge, Maine?" she challenged.

"Massachusetts," he said.

"Of course."

"You could introduce yourselves," Henry suggested, grinning.

"I'm Ephraim."

"Mallory," she replied.

"That's a nice name," he said.

"It means 'ill-omened.'"

"Oh," he said.

"Oh." She smirked.

Ephraim thought that she had pretty eyes, dark as walnut, but she was mocking him, he knew.

"We weren't really baby name book people," Henry explained, and started the truck.

Mallory surveyed Ephraim's khaki pants and wool pea-coat. "Most people wear jeans," she said.

"Okay," he replied. There wasn't anything he could do about it now. Anyway, he wasn't going to be like most people in this podunk town. He might as well send that message from the get-go. He was different: smart, sophisticated, urban. And he wasn't going to be here for long.

While Henry started around the driveway loop, he stole a glance at Ephraim. "You look like the Appledores. It's in the nose," he said, tapping his own long nose. "They call a nose like that a smelling nose. Able to smell bull—" Henry stopped him-self with a sound between a chuckle and a clearing of his throat. "Well, you know."

Ephraim couldn't keep from rubbing the bridge of his nose, which elicited a tiny flick of a smile from Henry. He dropped his hand back in his lap.

"Everything okay up at the house?" Henry asked. Before Ephraim or Brynn could answer, he said, "I have to admit we haven't been around the place as much as I would like. The will was a bit strange. Nothing could be changed physically. I couldn't even cut the ivy. It was very explicit that all we could do was fix things that were broken: windows and the like."

"You've been taking care of the house all this time?" Brynn asked.

Henry nodded. "The Darlings have always taken care of the Water Castle, ever since the first stone was laid in the ground."

Mallory shifted in her seat. "Dad," she growled.

"Before your mom's great-uncle died, we signed a contract saying we'd keep being the ones to take care of it. It's part of the will that the contract must be renewed in perpetuity as long as there's a Darling willing to take the job."

Mallory snorted.

"But you said your name was Henry Green," Brynn said.

He smiled. "I married into the deal. Mallory's mother is the Darling."

This made Mallory squirm again, digging her sharp elbow into Ephraim's side.

"So," Henry said, "if there's anything you need help with, you just let me know."

"The house sings," Brynn said from the backseat.

"It's more like a hum," Ephraim said. He glanced over his shoulder at Brynn and decided to come clean and tell the whole truth. "Actually, I followed the sound, and then there was like, this glow and then a big flash of blue light."

"A flash of light?" Brynn asked.

"Not a flash," he backtracked. "A glow, really. Like from a glow stick. And then it got brighter. And then it was gone."

Mallory bit her lip and willed her father not to start in on his tales. "Probably just the watchtower," she said quickly.

The light had been above and around the house, not away from it, but Ephraim was afraid to argue with Mallory, especially since her lips were set in such a thin line. Plus he didn't want to worry Brynn any more than he already had. So he asked, "Watchtower for what?"

"Zombie apocalypse," she quipped. The comment stopped the conversation, and each disappeared into his or her own thoughts.

Brynn resumed reading in the small backseat. Henry navigated the truck along the river for a time, then turned and drove past a lake, before turning onto a small street that led to the school.

Ephraim tried to look at Mallory sideways, sure some violence would come to him if she caught him staring at her. She wore combat boots with mismatched kneesocks sticking out of them. She had five or six rubber bands around her wrist, which she occasionally pulled at, snapping them against her skin. As he took in her appearance, he realized it would be a very bad thing to come into a new school by her side. He didn't need to know the particular ins and outs of the social world of Crystal Springs to know that Mallory was an outsider. Arriving at school with her would mark him with a scarlet *L* for loser.

He began to sweat.

The school was an old brick schoolhouse, complete with a tower with a bell to call them to class in the morning. Next to it was a smaller building with yellow clapboards. The bus circle was nearly full, and some kids were milling around the front door. Ephraim's heart began to race. Henry swung the truck into a parking place. "You sure you're all set?" he asked.

"All set," Ephraim said. "Thank you for the ride."

The three climbed out of the truck.

"The brick building is the middle school. Main office is just inside the door," Mallory said. "Want me to show you?"

He shook his head. "I was thinking maybe you could just point me in the right direction. I could go there and you could take Brynn over to the elementary school. I don't want to be late on my first day."

"Sure, whatever."

"Is that okay with you, Brynn?" he asked.

Brynn looked at him with her wide, dark eyes, then reached out her hand to Mallory.

After a pause, Mallory took it. "Please," Brynn said. "I'd like it if you went with me."

Ephraim let out his breath. "If you need anything, Brynn,

Price and I are just over in the other building." Then he strode toward the school, trying to emulate Price's confident gait.

Price's very expensive racing bike was locked into the rack by the front door, perfectly straight. Ephraim was surprised Price was willing to leave the bike outside, and he was even more surprised that Price had managed to beat them on the bike though he'd barely had a head start.

Inside the school, a swarm of bodies crossed paths. They wore jeans, as Mallory said, with heavy wool sweaters or sweatshirts. Ephraim knew he was dressed wrong. His earlier confidence started to waver. Had he really thought he could fool all of these people? He looked like a dork, not a trendsetter. He heard snatches of conversation:

I got stuck on number seven, but then I realized I was thinking like Fermat, not Newton.

My dad said I can stay up for the lunar eclipse. Want to come over?

Can't decide if I want to do Robotics or Deciphering Shakespeare's Sonnets for my elective next trimester. What about you?

Ephraim shook his head. Just pretending, he told himself. Maybe they were even trying to impress him. But he'd be the smartest kid there, of that he was still certain.

He pushed through the throng toward the front office. Price emerged in front of him, and he was relieved to see a familiar face. "Checking in, Eph?" Price asked.

Ephraim nodded and pushed open the office door. The

secretary, a young woman with cat-eye glasses, looked up. "You must be the Appledore boys," she said.

"Appledore-Smith," Ephraim corrected.

"Right." She pulled out two folders—one blue, one red. "These are your orientation packets." She handed the blue one to Price, the red one to Ephraim. "Student handbooks, schedules, forms for your parents." Ephraim pulled out his schedule and read it over. He was on team Acadia, whatever that meant, and was taking English, earth science, math, Latin, world history, PE, and drawing and painting. He knew that his only way to make it here was to be in class with the other smart kids. They would recognize him as one of their own; he might even be a leader to them. "Is it possible to meet with a guidance counselor?" he asked.

"Is there a problem?" she asked.

"I'd like to be placed in the honors sections."

Price rolled his eyes.

"All of our classes are taught at the honors level. No tracking," she said. "We don't need it. All of the children in Crystal Springs are very bright."

Now Ephraim rolled his eyes. He looked to Price for support, but all Price said was, "Come on, let's go." Then he turned to the secretary and said, "Thank you," because, in addition to being strong and good-looking, he was also unfailingly polite.

Out in the hall, Price said, "You don't have to be so obnoxious."

"I wasn't being obnoxious."

The few students who passed them in the hall didn't even try not to stare. The girls' glances skated over Ephraim and landed on Price.

"If you need me—" Price began.

"I'm not a baby. I don't need you."

"Fine. But if you do, you can come find me."

"Fine," Ephraim agreed. He made his way down the hall to the open door of room nineteen. It was a science lab, but nothing like the science labs at his old school. This was the real deal, like he had walked into a classroom at MIT or the offices of a major chemistry conglomerate. A bank of computers was in the back of the room with computations running nonstop. Along the side wall were a series of instruments that looked like they belonged in a science fiction movie, shining silver and ominous. The only thing familiar was the faint odor of chemicals and smoke. The kids sat at the lab tables chatting.

When Ephraim entered the room, the teacher, who had lab glasses perched on her head, called out, "Welcome!" Then she turned to the room. "Guys, our new student is here." The other kids stopped their talking and looked up at him—curious, wary, but mostly smiling. "It's Ephraim, isn't it?" She pronounced it the old-fashioned way: *Eff-ra-heem*.

"Eff-rem," he corrected her. "Just two syllables."

"I'm Ms. Little. Also two syllables. I think you're gong to be very happy here in Crystal Springs."

"This is a really nice classroom," he said.

She looked around the room as if seeing it through a

stranger's eyes. "I wouldn't mind a new particle accelerator, but it will do for now." She winked at him, but he wasn't sure if she was joking or not. "Have a seat anywhere."

Mallory sat alone at a table in the back of the room, but he took a seat at an empty lab table in the second row. Immediately a lanky boy with dark brown hair sat beside him. "I'm Ian," he said. "Nice to meet ya."

"Ephraim," Ephraim replied.

"I heard that. So where'd you move here from?"

"Boston. Well, Cambridge, actually." Out of the corner of his eye, he could see another boy watching him, surveying him, sizing him up.

"Uh-huh. So you got a ride in with Mallory Green."

He felt himself blush. His ride had been noticed after all. "Her dad is kind of a friend of the family."

He glanced back over his shoulder at her. In Cambridge, his class had been so diverse that skin color had barely been more noticeable than hair or eye color. Here, though, Mallory's brown skin was striking amid a sea of white.

"Right, of course." Ian rubbed his head. He was a bundle of energy. He introduced the other eight members of the home-room so quickly that it was just a rush of names to Ephraim: KatyTobyChelseaBeckyBrendanDaveJoshandWill. Will was the one who had been eyeing him earlier, and when Ian said his name, he tipped his head toward them, but unlike the other kids did not say hello.

FIVE

Mallory walked behind Ian and Ephraim on the way to social studies. Ian was blathering all about the time he went to Boston and went to the Museum of Science and on the Duck Boats. "Have you been on the Duck Boats?"

"Locals don't really do that. It's more of a tourist thing," Ephraim replied. Mallory winced for him.

"Oh," Ian said, shrugging it off. "So you live up in the Water Castle? What's it like up there? I heard it was haunted."

"I don't think so. It's just a big old house. There are lots of dead animal heads."

"That is so weird and cool. I mean, think about it, those heads have been there longer than we've been alive."

"I guess."

"How come you all never came up before?"

"My parents came up once." Ephraim shrugged.

"It's kind of funny that your family built this town and you've never been here."

There was a stomping sound behind him and Ephraim turned to see Will rushing by. "They didn't build this town," he muttered as he passed.

Ephraim looked at Ian and said, "What's his deal?"

"Don't worry about him. He's just like that. I mean, sure, maybe he has it out for you—"

"Me?" Ephraim asked, staring at Will's broad back as he clomped down the hall in his work boots. Someone that big could do a lot of damage if he had it out for you. "Why me?"

Ian smiled and shook his head. "Man, you are too much."

Ian opened the door and held it for Ephraim, who pretty much let it close in Mallory's face. She grabbed it and threw it open. If the rest of the Appledores were anything like him, she didn't know how her family had managed to work for them for so long.

"Ephraim Appledore?" Mr. Wright asked. He straightened his perpetually wrinkled tie.

"Appledore-Smith," Ephraim said.

Mallory rolled her eyes. Ian was right: this boy was too much.

"All right, Appledore-Smith. We're headed to the library to do research. You've joined us just in time for our annual sixth-grade explorer research project. We're pretty big on explorers around here, but of course I wouldn't have to tell that to an Appledore."

"Of course," Ephraim agreed, though he had no idea what Mr. Wright was talking about.

While they walked down the hall to the library, Mr. Wright consulted a list, and then he sighed. "My usual topics are all taken. What do you know about Admiral Robert Peary?"

"Well, I love military history. But what does an admiral have to do with exploration?"

Mallory sucked in her breath along with the rest of the class. She could practically hear her classmates giving up on him. But then Ian, after a moment, threw his arm around Ephraim's shoulder. "Oh, he's just messing around. He's a funny guy."

Of course, Mallory thought, an Appledore *would* get endless chances.

"Yeah." Ephraim laughed. He could be the funny guy. That was an okay thing to be. Better than being the weird guy. Or the scrawny guy. Or Price's kid brother. These were the ways he'd been known at his previous school. "But seriously, who was he?"

"You really don't know?" Ian asked. Ian let his arm fall off of Ephraim's shoulders. "Oh, man." He shook his head again. Ephraim was pretty sure he could only mess up so many times before Ian would abandon him completely.

"In that case, I think he's the perfect subject for you. He's not normally on my list of approved explorers since the kids here all grow up hearing the stories of the great Peary expeditions. Folks in Crystal Springs have always been wild about explorers—the Appledores most of all—and he is Maine's most famous explorer. As this has somehow been a gap in your education, it will be a chance for you to do some catching up," Mr. Wright said as he stepped aside to let Ephraim go into the library in front of him.

Ephraim stopped short inside the doorway. He'd been as wrong about the library as he'd been about his assured sudden rise to popularity. The sunny room had a bank of gleaming computers against one wall. Low bookshelves were topped with sculptures labeled with things like *Sixth-grade Motion Project* and *Eighth-grade ceramics*. The work looked like something out of the Museum of Fine Arts—nothing like the lopsided pieces that his mom had displayed on their mantel back home. The spines of the books were shiny and inviting. And behind the circulation desk stood a young woman, close to six feet tall, with a tattoo of a hummingbird sticking out of her sleeve.

"That's our librarian, Ms. Topplesworth," Mr. Wright explained. "She can get you sorted. You also might want to check in with Mallory. She's doing Henson."

Ephraim and Mallory glanced at each other quickly, then just as quickly away.

"Or Will," Mr. Wright said. "He chose to do Frederick Cook." He shook his head. "In my seventeen years of doing this project, I've never had anyone choose to do Frederick Cook."

Ephraim looked at Will, who was hunched over a book taking notes. There was no way he was going anywhere near Will.

Mallory took her things to a table at the back of the library. She had a couple of pages of notes already, but her heart wasn't in the project. She was still annoyed that Mr. Wright had assigned Matthew Henson to her. He just assumed she would want to do him, because Henson was black too. She had wanted to do a woman like Sally Ride, the first American woman in space.

Ms. Topplesworth showed Ephraim how to log onto the computers, and showed him the online encyclopedia. According to the article, Peary was someone who claimed to have been the first person to get to the North Pole. Though some people contested that claim. Big whoop. "So, he explored the North Pole?" he asked Mr. Wright.

Ephraim looked around the room and again it seemed like everyone was staring at him. Everyone but Mallory, who was taking notes frantically, and Will, who now sat at a computer smirking.

Mr. Wright asked, "Do you have your student planner?"

Ephraim dug through his backpack and got out the small spiral-bound book that the secretary had given him that morning. Mr. Wright put his finger on the silhouette on the front. "Peary," he said.

Ephraim read the name below the picture. "Robert Peary." And then the motto: *"Inveniam Viam Aut Facium."*

"Do you know what that means?" Mr. Wright asked.

"I don't read Latin." Ephraim wasn't even sure it was Latin.

"'I shall find a way, or make one.'" He cocked his head to the side. "Not a bad motto, wouldn't you say?"

"Okay."

"Like I said, I don't let anyone do Peary because his legacy is an integral part of this school. We're the Crystal Springs Explorers and we all know about him. You, my friend, have a lot of research to do." Then he looked past Ephraim to where Mallory was sitting. "Like I said, check in with Mallory Green. She can help you."

Ephraim had absolutely no intention of checking in with Mallory. And as she sat writing in her notebook about the first person to actually set foot on the North Pole—Peary's assistant Matthew Henson—she knew it as well as he did.

SIX

Mallory held her paper lunch bag in her fist as she made her way through the cafeteria to her normal table in the back. She sat so she could see everyone, which, her dad had told her, was something mobsters always did so they could avoid attacks from the back. Same for her.

She surveyed the groups in the cafeteria. There were the pretty girls who had called her Mallory Makebelieve as a child—and probably still did. She had stopped listening. There was Will sitting alone just like she was, just like always. On the other side of the room was Ian's table, where Ephraim sat looking dejected.

She pulled out her sandwich and one of her books. She had begun a sketch of an ice-covered tree in English class—before she'd been distracted by the Ephraim debacle. He'd made one mistake after another. It was like he'd been trying to make himself seem stupid: mispronouncing words, speaking out of turn, and making statements like, "Clearly the author is obsessed with her own death," when everyone knew that *Tuck Everlasting* was not about death but about choices.

Combining English class with how he'd embarrassed himself in social studies by not knowing something so basic as who Robert Peary was, well, she was surprised he was even allowed to sit with Ian and his crowd.

She held her sandwich in her right hand and drew with her left, adding needle upon needle to the tree.

She actually felt a little bad for Ephraim—he hadn't known what he was in for, what Crystal Springs School was really like. On the other hand, he was treating her like dirt. He'd practically run from the truck that morning, and then even though Mr. Wright had told him twice to go to her for help, he'd avoided her.

She took a bite of her sandwich: roast beef, Swiss cheese, and mustard on rye. It was what she had for lunch most every day, but she never grew tired of it.

With a black pen, she added some sparkles of snow to the sky around the tree, starting to cover the words. She wasn't thinking about what her pen was doing. How, she wondered, had Ephraim known that she was unpopular? Did it emanate off her like some sort of foul odor?

She knew she dressed differently, but that was because

she'd given up trying to fit in and had decided to wear what was comfortable. Why wear silly little shoes, when boots kept your feet warmer? It wasn't how she dressed, though. She knew that. It was the stories that had started it. The stories her parents had told her about the house—which she had believed. Stories that the others had grown out of; stories she had clung to for far too long.

So that's how the circle had been drawn with her outside of it. It still didn't explain how Ephraim had known before even meeting anyone else that she was a loser as far as the kids of Crystal Springs were concerned.

"That's a great drawing."

She looked up. In front of her stood Price Appledore-Smith. His long-sleeve T-shirt pulled across his broad shoulders. His green eyes stared down at her picture while he polished an apple on his pants.

"Kind of odd to draw in a book," he added.

"Thanks." She meant about it being a good drawing, not about being odd. She blushed at the mistake. She had heard the other girls whispering about Price Appledore-Smith, about his bright green eyes and shaggy hair, but she had not expected to be impressed. She was not usually the type to have her heart go all pitter-patter.

"You're welcome." He threw one leg over the bench at the table and sat down across from her. "My dad's an artist. Well, he was."

"What kind?"

"Painter." He took a bite of the apple. "Modern stuff that I don't understand. And greeting cards. Your dad has been taking care of our house?"

"Uh-huh." Of course he didn't want to get to know her or talk about her artwork—it was about the Water Castle. It didn't really matter. He was a jock—undeniably good-looking, but probably stupid, so what did she care what he thought?

"So you've spent a lot of time there?"

"I guess."

He took a large bite out of the apple. "It's kind of . . ." He paused to chew some more. "It's kind of a weird house."

She closed the book using her finger to mark the page. "Weird how?" She had her own thoughts on the house, but wanted to hear his.

"It's never quiet."

"It's an old house," she replied.

"Not like creaks and groans. More like a hum."

Mallory thought of the story that Ephraim had told that morning about the hum and the flash of light. "I never noticed," she told him.

He shrugged. She looked past him and realized that every girl in the room—and a good portion of the guys—was staring at them. She grinned. "I can ask my dad to look into it—"

"No. I don't think it's mechanical or anything."

"What do you think it is?" Her smile faltered. She scanned the faces in the cafeteria to look for snide smiles and snickers. Someone who knew what her parents seemed to believe about the castle—what she had once believed—had put him up to this.

He shook his head. "I'm not sure."

"This isn't a very funny joke."

"I'm not making a joke."

Price honestly looked confused at her accusation, but she still didn't trust him. "There's nothing special about the house," she hissed. "Nothing except that it's ostentatious and sucked up way too much of my parents' time."

"Sorry," he said. "I didn't mean to upset you."

"I'm not upset. Anyway, what are you even doing here? Eighth graders don't eat this lunch."

"I have a free period." He leaned in. "Don't ever tell him, but I kind of wanted to check in on Ephraim. He seems to be doing okay."

"Sure," she lied. "He's super."

She flipped open her book and started to draw the moon above the tree. Price stood up and backed away from the table.

August 19, 1908

"Nora!" Orlando called from the library on the second floor. The rest of the Appledores had little use for the room, and preferred for Dr. Appledore to be out of sight, so the library had become his study. He had built a tube that went down to the kitchen through which he could shout his orders.

Nora heard the barking voice come through a cone-shaped speaker on the wall as she prepared the tea. Her aunt Patience, the Appledores' cook, shook her head and made a *tsk, tsk* sound, but didn't say anything. Nora took the tray and hurried up the stairs.

He sat at his large oak desk, papers and a typewriter pushed aside. A small ceramic elephant was perched precariously on the edge of the desk. When she arrived, he did not say anything. He noted her presence, and then he returned his attention to his papers, while she stood in the doorway and admired his new telescope. It stood on a tripod nearly as tall as her. The thick brass tube was as long as a tree limb. You could see all eight of the planets through it. Orlando had a young scientist visit the week before, and she had found him looking through that telescope. Nikola was his name; she liked the way it sounded all round and exotic. He showed her how to look through the single eyepiece, and in an accented voice told her of the planets she was seeing. "There are creatures living on those planets," he told her. "Wise ones. Not like here, where wisdom is a rare thing indeed." He had chucked her on the chin then, and she wasn't sure if he was telling the truth or just a story meant to entertain her.

She would like it to be true, and she would like to think that people might go up to the planets someday to meet them, and that she might be one of them. She would be an explorer like Matthew Henson. Working with Dr. Appledore was teaching her that all manner of things were possible that she had not considered before.

"Fetch the book," Orlando said, snapping Nora out of her reverie.

These were the types of orders that Orlando gave: urgent and nonspecific. This time, though, she knew exactly what he wanted: Angus Appledore's journal. It was a daily recounting of his search for the Fountain of Youth, including maps, charts, and interviews. Dr. Appledore studied it at least once a day. Reading it had been one of her first assignments of the job, and it had taken her nearly a week.

Angus Appledore had first been taken by the legend of the Fountain of Youth while on a trading vessel to Ethiopia. Some of the sailors there had spoken of a place where the water ran clear and all those who bathed in it lived an eternity, like gods. At first he had dismissed the story as native superstition, but the men's eyes shone with truth, and Angus had a reason to believe them: Persephone Winsor. He had fallen deeply in love with her, and before he left on the mission he had asked for her hand in marriage. He would get his answer upon his return.

As much as he loved Persephone, he also loved his life exploring new worlds. The thought of eternal life, with time for both love and exploration, answered all of his desires. With that, he knew he would be happy. The pursuit of happiness, it turned out, could be a dangerous thing.

He wrote down everything the sailors told him and traveled to where the fountain was supposed to be. Instead he found a village in the midst of a drought. He followed the path of the conquistador Ponce de Leon, who claimed to have found the fountain, but once again was disappointed. From there he searched the nearby waters for the island of Bimini. He found many other treasures and met many strange and wonderful people, but the Fountain of Youth remained elusive.

He kept a map that he covered with *X*'s. For him, these crosses did not mark treasure, but rather the lack of it. As he journeyed, the number of *X*'s grew and grew, the open spaces became fewer and fewer.

Ten years passed and he realized he was circling around to a place in the colonies. He was in favor with the court and asked for a land grant. His request was granted, and he began to build a home for Persephone, whom he still loved with all of his heart. They had three children, and he wanted the home to be a castle for her and for them. He wanted his love to be made manifest in the building.

The journal then went on to detail some of the plans

for what would become the Water Castle. It noted the metal frame and the granite floated down the river when it iced over. Nora skimmed past much of this—though her own family was mentioned as the builders of the house. She wanted to get again to the part where he discussed the water.

Angus detailed his difficulties with a local group of French traders who wanted to know why an Englishman was so interested in their small part of the world. In his journal he wrote that they set a shed holding building materials on fire, but conceded that it could never be proven.

Before the house was completed, but complete enough that they could live there, the family set sail for the New World. It was an arduous journey. Persephone took ill and, without proper medicine on board, she did not survive. She was buried at sea, and Angus arrived on the shores a broken and bitter man.

The journal did not end there, though, as subsequent generations of Appledores had added to the lore. One reported meeting a man who claimed to be one hundred twenty years old, but looked no older than forty. Another told of sustaining an injury while horseback riding: "My leg bent at such an angle it made me ill to look upon it." A man, "wild as the forest itself," found him in the woods, brought him some water, and led him home. By the next morning, his leg was healed.

"If only he had noted his location!" Dr. Appledore said, shaking his head. It was not the first time that he had bemoaned this particular ancestor's lack of specificity.

He checked his pocket watch and said, "The papers."

"Yes, sir," she replied.

She hurried from the room, out the side door of the Water Castle, and into the morning fog. She walked down the carriage lane and into town each day to fetch the out-of-town papers that Orlando had sent to him and which arrived a day late. As she crested a gentle rise she saw Harry Appledore tending to a calf in the field.

"Good morning," he said as she drew near.

"Good morning. I'm off to town. Can I pick anything up for you?"

"I've sent an order in with your father."

"Of course," Nora said.

Just as usual, they never knew quite what to say. So Nora cleared her throat and said, "Good day to you then."

"And a good day to you as well."

She continued down the carriage lane to the train tracks and walked along them into town, where the post office had the papers set aside for her.

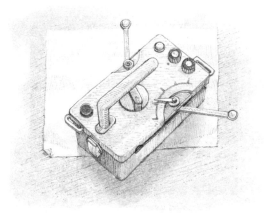

SEVEN

Ephraim's final class of the day was earth science, which he had been dreading even before the social studies debacle and a lunchtime conversation in which he seemed to have alienated or offended just about everyone. He decided he would remain silent; it was the only way to avoid further embarrassment.

Ian walked with him back to their homeroom, though he was distinctly less chatty. When they got to the classroom, Ephraim chose the same seat he had that morning, while Ian took one in the back.

Ms. Little sat down at the lab table next to him and passed him a textbook. "We're on chapter ten," she told him.

They were only on chapter six back home, but it was a

different textbook, and perhaps Ms. Little's class had gone out of order. He opened the book to the table of contents.

"What have you covered?" she asked him.

"The history of the earth, um, minerals and rocks."

"Great. What else?"

He tapped his fingers on top of the lab table. "We did a lot with measurement."

She sucked in on her lower lip. "Well, I'm sure we can get you caught up. I'm always available after school for extra help."

Will lumbered into the room and stopped at the edge of the lab table. "Will, it seems you got yourself a lab partner," Ms. Little told him.

"Great," he said in a flat voice.

Ephraim's stomach dropped. As if this day could get any worse, now he was going to be lab partners with the school thug who already hated him for unknown reasons. Ms. Little stood up and Will took her place. He smelled like wood chips.

"You're in good hands. Will is a star student. And maybe it will finally be time to bury the hatchet," Ms. Little said. "Now if you'll excuse me, I've got a surprise for the class in the back room."

"Great," Ephraim said. "Thank you." Once Ms. Little turned her back, Ephraim asked, "Bury the hatchet? What is she talking about?"

Will just glared at him and took out a binder from his bag—it was black and he had drawn an elaborate, swirling design on it with a silver pen.

"That's cool," Ephraim said. Maybe he could win Will over with kindness.

Will gave him a slow look up and down. "It's a fractal."

"What's a fractal?" Ephraim asked.

Will shook his head. Completely dismissive.

"Why do you have it out for me? What's your problem?" Ephraim asked.

"My problem?" he scoffed. "Nothing. I've got no beef with you—unless you sink my grade."

"I'm not going to sink your grade," Ephraim said, though there was a significant likelihood that he would.

"That's right. You come from some fancy prep school. Well, let me tell you, that school ain't nothing compared to Crystal Springs, so—"

"We learn proper grammar."

"Too bad you don't have anything interesting to say with it."

Ms. Little rushed back into the room carrying a small device. "It's a Geiger counter!" she cried. "I borrowed it from a friend at UMaine and we only have it for today. We're going to measure radiation." She was filled with glee. She turned to the chalkboard and drew a picture of a cylinder. "Okay, so this is how the device works. There's a tube with an inert gas inside—typically helium, neon, or argon. Why would these be good choices?"

Every hand in the room shot up, arms straight as arrows. All but Ephraim's. She called on Will, who gave a lengthy explanation of which Ephraim understood precisely nothing.

"Right," Ms. Little said, nodding. "Now, when the gas is in the presence of radioactivity, it produces a reading. In this case, the little arms on the side of the Geiger counter will flash and go up, higher with more radioactivity. Got it?"

The class nodded. Ephraim, though, didn't follow her. He tried to write down what she was saying in his notebook, but he didn't even know the words to take down and make sense of later. He felt hot and uncomfortable, like the time he had gotten off the train at the wrong stop. He had come up from underground to find the whole world around him unfamiliar and strange.

Ms. Little walked over to the corner of the room where she had a small microwave. She set the time for twenty seconds, and pressed start. When she held the Geiger counter up to the side of the microwave, the arms went up to the side, perpendicular to the body of the device, like a cross. It let out a steady stream of short beeps. "So there's a good base reading for comparison. Now let's do some tests."

Okay, Ephraim thought, so when there's some radiation, the arms go up. In his notebook he wrote: "Arms up = radiation = bad." Will read over his shoulder and shook his head.

She tested a potted plant, a piece of coral, and the window shade, all with little to no effect. A lab table drew a slight reaction. The floor of the room pushed it up even higher, almost as high as the microwave reading. She held it up to the window, and the arms rose above ninety degrees. "Huh," she said. She pulled it back and looked at it. "Maybe I overwhelmed it. I'll just reset it." She held the device back up to the window, and it performed in the exact same way.

"That can't be good," Becky said. Ephraim nodded. Radiation in the air was definitely a bad thing. He didn't write it down, though, for fear of Will's reaction.

"It's probably why we have all those four- and five-leaf clovers on the soccer field," a girl named Alice replied. "Crystal Springs is radiation city."

"Try me," Ian said, jumping to his feet.

Ms. Little walked over to him and held the Geiger counter in front of his chest. He gauged the same as the microwave. Ms. Little frowned, but said cheerily, "It seems we have a very sensitive counter."

"What about me?" Becky asked. Her reading was just above Ian's.

Amid a chorus of "Me next," Ms. Little went around the room, checking them. They all ranged right around the level of the microwave. "It's a very well-insulated microwave," she explained. "It's not like there's a lot of radiation escaping." But she didn't look convinced.

"Not all radiation is bad, though, right?" Mallory asked as Ms. Little took her reading, which was as high as the rest of the class. "There are positive effects, too, aren't there?"

"Sure," Ms. Little said, but she was distracted, looking down at the Geiger counter with a frown.

"That's right!" Ian cried, placing his hands on his hips and thrusting his chest forward. "It gives us super powers!"

"Idiot," Will mumbled, rolling his eyes.

Will and Ephraim's was the last table she reached. Will barely registered, just making the arms lift up a fraction, and the lights barely shone. Ms. Little looked relieved. Then she pointed the Geiger counter at Ephraim. The beeps were so fast they almost ran together, and the arms of the counter went almost all the way up—much higher than anyone else's rating. He felt his cheeks flush. *Arms up = radiation = bad.* She pulled it away from him.

"Whoa, man, you're radioactive," Ian said. "I knew cities were bad for you."

"There must be something wrong with this machine," Ms. Little said.

"If there was something wrong, wouldn't it be consistently wrong?" Becky asked. "Wouldn't we all be getting the same reading?"

"I'll have to talk to my friend. He might be pulling a prank on me."

Ephraim could see his classmates exchanging glances, raising eyebrows, wrinkling noses. Bad enough to be new, and not as smart as everyone else. Bad enough to not know who the local hero was. Bad enough that before he even arrived, he seemed to have an enemy in Will Wylie. But now it seemed he was also radioactive.

EIGHT

"D id everything go okay today?" Mallory's dad asked her as they waited by his truck for Ephraim and Brynn.

"Sure," Mallory said. "Ephraim made all sorts of friends. You don't need to worry about him."

"I wasn't asking about Ephraim."

Mallory picked at some peeling paint on the side of the truck.

"I was thinking with the arrival of the Appledores, and Ephraim being your age, maybe this would be an opportunity for you to reach out and make some new friends."

"I don't want friends."

To his credit, her dad did not tell her that everybody wants friends. Instead he took his wool cap off his head and rubbed his hair, which, Mallory knew, meant there was something he needed to tell her, but didn't want to.

"What is it?" she asked.

"Your mother called."

Mallory pressed her lips together and looked away.

"She misses you," he said.

"She left."

"She left me," he said. He rubbed his hand hard against the top of his head.

"Same difference."

"She'll come back. Your mother has left again and again, but she always comes back. I thought having a child would keep her—" He stopped, realizing what he had implied. "Not that you weren't enough for her. You're her world. This isn't your fault." He tried to catch her eye. "I'm doing a terrible job of this, aren't I?"

"Yes."

"I've never been good at putting the right words to things. The long and short of it is, she'd like you to go visit her."

"No chance," she replied.

"She said she has a bed made up just for you with special sheets and everything." Her dad winced as he said this, with good reason. All of this made Mallory feel like her mother thought she was still a small child, able to be convinced that something was special when really it was just different. "Just think about it, okay?"

A plane flew overhead. "Turboprop," her dad declared. "ATR-42." He identified planes the way others identified birds.

Mallory watched the plane disappear over the horizon, then looked back at the school. "They're coming."

Ephraim and Brynn came out of the east wing. They walked across the parking lot with leaves swirling around their feet. Ephraim's shoes scuffed along the pavement.

Ephraim helped Brynn into the jump seat, and then climbed in himself. He sighed.

"Rough day?" Henry asked as he dropped the truck into reverse.

"No, it was peachy." Ephraim rested his arm against the cool window.

Mallory's dad eased the truck into first gear and pulled out of the parking lot. "I'm sure it wasn't so bad."

"Sure," Mallory said, grateful to have such an easy target to lash out at after the discussion with her dad. "I mean, that thing in social studies wasn't terrible. And you did the problem right in math. Eventually."

"Thanks for pointing out the eventually part."

"Here's the thing about Crystal Springs," she said. "Everyone's a little bit smarter, a little bit stronger."

"I didn't peg you as a town-pride person."

"I'm not. It's just the truth. We win all the athletic championships. All the Quiz Bowls and chess tournaments—whatever it is, we just win."

"Why?"

"Who knows? Good genes and inbreeding. Maybe there was a beneficial mutation and now we're all brilliant." Mallory wished she had not started this line of conversation. She could see her dad leaning forward, ready to explain about the Fountain of Youth and the power of this place.

"So you're brilliant now?" Ephraim asked.

"I was just trying to make you feel better. You don't have to be such a jerk about it."

"Okay now," Mallory's dad said. "That's enough."

Ephraim settled down into his seat and actually seemed to pout.

"What about you, Brynn?" Henry asked. "I hope you had a better day."

"We're adding fractions!" Brynn said joyfully. "We won't do that until next year back home."

Mallory couldn't help but raise her eyebrows and mouth the word *See* to Ephraim. He glowered in return.

They drove through town, past the Wylie Five and Dime, where her great-uncle Edwin and his friend Edward were stationed, as usual. Henry raised his hand in greeting. Then he cleared his throat.

"Ephraim, you know, I think I understand what you're feeling."

Mallory tightened her fists.

"I was born in Crystal Springs, but then I moved away. When I came back, it was like something out of an H. G. Wells novel. Everything was normal, but everything was also a little off. Is that what you're feeling?"

Ephraim turned his head from the window to look at Henry. "Something like that."

He rubbed his chin. "There is an explanation, of course. There's always an explanation."

"Dad," Mallory said, the tone of her voice a warning.

"There is something different about Crystal Springs. Something special." He took his eyes off the road to look at Ephraim.

In the backseat, Brynn had stopped reading and was looking forward. "What kind of special, Mr. Green?" she asked.

"Please, call me Henry."

"It's just a story," Mallory said. "A silly story."

Her dad pushed his glasses up the bridge of his nose. "There's no such thing as a silly story. Every story serves a purpose."

As far as Mallory was concerned, the purpose of this story was to mortify her. She pulled her hood up around her face and sank down into the seat. Her dad drove the truck up the driveway and stopped it in front of the Water Castle. "I guess, though, that it's a story for another day."

NINE

Will didn't tell his dad that the Appledores were back in town. He didn't have to. When he got home, his dad was already there, slamming around in his workshop in the basement. That had once been a magical place for Will, watching his dad take a few slabs of wood and transform them into chairs, bedframes, and cabinets. The bitter and hard thing in his dad's chest, though, had grown instead of shrunk until he was consumed with people that Will had always thought of as ghosts.

Only now the ghosts were real and one of them was his lab partner.

Will got a glass of milk and a bag of Fritos and went back out of the house. He crossed the dirt driveway, kicking stones out of his way, and climbed the stairs to the room above the garage. His dad had built it saying it would be an apartment they could rent out. There was a kitchenette with a stovetop and a minifridge. They'd put a sign up at the Wylie Five and Dime and even took out ads in *Uncle Henry's*, the classified magazine, but no one ever rented the place. Will had taken over the space, making it his own science lab.

On the way in the door he noticed a textbook on the coffee table and picked it up. He put it back into the right place on his bookshelf. He was particular about his books. One bookcase for fiction, one for nonfiction, with the fiction divided into classics, modern, and fringe: all sci-fi.

The textbook was on particle physics, something he'd been toying with for his World's Science Fair project. The competition had been going on for fifty years and kids from Crystal Springs had won seventeen times. When he was a senior in high school, he intended to earn grand prize as well. He just had to come up with the perfect project.

That thing with the Geiger counter could be a start. Why were so many of the kids getting such high readings—especially Ephraim—and why had his been so low? Maybe there was something radioactive in Crystal Springs that he could investigate. Maybe it was like one of those corporate ecological disasters, something the Appledores had done long ago that was still affecting the town.

His dad would just eat that up, but it probably wouldn't mean much to the judges of the World's Science Fair.

He heard footsteps on the stairs and his body tensed. He saw the doorknob start to turn, but then a knock came instead. "Come in," he said.

His dad pushed open the door, walked in, and gave a look around before settling himself down on the old couch that was pushed against the near wall. "I suppose you've heard," his dad said. The couch had no springs left, and his dad sank down so far that his knees were up to his chest.

Will thought about pretending he didn't know what his dad was talking about, but instead he said, "Yeah."

"Al down at the hardware store says they got kids."

"Yeah," Will said again. If his dad knew that Ephraim was his lab partner, he'd march down to the school and throw a fit. Will liked Ms. Little and didn't want her to have any trouble from his dad.

"I don't have to tell you to stay away from them." He tugged his cap down low over his eyes.

"You just did."

"What?" He lifted his head and stared at Will with his clear blue eyes, clear as Crystal Lake itself.

"Nothing," Will said. He picked up his glass of milk and then put it down again.

"They're dangerous, Will. Nothing good has ever come of the Appledore family."

"I know." He picked up a glass petri dish and examined it for a moment. He hoped his dad would take the hint and drop the subject. His dad was starting to sound as obsessed with the Appledores as his great-aunt Winnifred, a bitter woman who wore ribbons until the day she died at ninety-seven.

"If it weren't for them we—"

"Dad, I really need to get to work."

"You think I don't want more for you? You think I don't want better than this?" He spread his arms out wide.

"I like this, Dad," Will said. "I'm happy."

His dad shook his head. "It's only because you don't know better. That house on the hill, *the Water Castle*"—he said it so snidely that Will thought his dad would have spit if they hadn't been inside—"that life should have been ours, not that we'd be so over-the-top. A nice, comfortable life is what we should have had."

Will glanced over at the poster for the World's Science Fair. The grand prize was a full ride to college. He wanted to go to MIT or maybe out to California somewhere. He'd make all the dreams his dad ever had come true, and then his dad would be proud of him. "I know," he said again.

"Okay, then," his dad said.

"Hey, Dad," Will began; then he cleared his throat. "You ever hear anything about Crystal Springs having high levels of radioactivity?"

His dad rearranged his Red Sox cap on his head. "There were some scientists from UMaine who came through a few years back. Well, more like twelve years ago, I suppose. Your mom was pregnant with you. Said they were getting some high readings. I can tell you, that got your mother scared. They did a few studies and couldn't find any ill effects. Why?"

"Ms. Little brought in a Geiger counter today and the ratings were a little high. That's all."

"I remember those UMaine folks said it must be just one of those quirks of nature. No explanation. No harm, no foul was how they saw it."

Will nodded, though he thought that if he were on that research team, he wouldn't have stopped after a few tests.

"You thinking of working on that for your project?"

"Not sure yet."

"Well, what are you working on these days?" he asked.

"I'm kind of between projects."

"I'm working on an armoire for the Baudelaires. It's giving me a heck of a time. I could use an extra hand."

"I've got a lot of homework," Will said.

His dad nodded. "Sure, of course." He nodded again. "I'll probably be down there all night. You just call out for a pizza, okay?"

Will glanced at the pile of empty pizza boxes by the door. "Sure," he agreed. He didn't mind getting pizza again. It was the routine he had, and, like all great scientists, he liked routines.

September 3, 1908

Harry Appledore lay in the field on the south side of the property staring up as the clouds went by overhead. His father would want him to come in soon so that they could have their daily conversation about the family businesses: Dr. Appledore's Crystal Water and the Crystal Springs Resort and Recuperation Center. Harry thought that was a whole lot of words to not say anything at all, not that he had ever told his father so. As far as his father was concerned, Harry was next in line to take over. With no siblings, there was no other choice.

The cloud shapes made him think of icebergs shifting and cracking, and he wondered what it would be like to be out walking on that ice with it never firm beneath your feet.

That's when it came to him: how to fix the wagon wheel. He jumped up and began jogging to the stables. One of the wheels on the primary carriage for transporting guests from the train to the hotel had cracked the day before. His father was putting in an order for a new one, but that would take nearly two weeks to come from Concord. Harry was sure he could fix it himself. And now, thinking of the sledges the Arctic explorers used, he knew just how to do it.

As he raced up the lane he saw Nora Darling coming in the opposite direction with her determined stride and braids bouncing. She'd been working for his great-uncle for nearly a month now, and he was tremendously curious as to what they were up to. They spent a good deal of time in the library, but they would also disappear down into the tunnels below the house for hours at a stretch. He raised his cap to her, and she nodded in return, and that was the whole of their interaction.

Harry's solution to the wheel problem was so simple, it was a wonder he hadn't thought of it before. The sledges that Peary and the others used had wooden rails covered by steel shoes. He would cover the wheels in the same way. The metal would be strong enough to hold the repaired wheel together.

As he passed the house, he glanced at the doorway, half expecting to see his father standing there and beckoning for him. But of course his father never beckoned for anyone. He told you when to arrive and you did. Harry always had.

The sun shifted and the house seemed to shimmer. It made Harry think of the stories that Orlando had always told him about the house and the land being a magical place.

Once upon a time—Orlando never began that way, but Harry liked stories to start in a traditional manner—there was a man named Angus Appledore. He was certain that the Fountain of Youth was real and that it was in this very spot. He had the house built and moved his family over from England. Before he could find the Fountain of Youth his wife, his reason for wanting to live forever, died. The bitter twist to the story, though, was that Angus lived to be 103. His children, too, Harry's grandparents, lived to see their hundredth birthdays. Indeed, everyone who lived in Crystal Springs had an exceptionally long life. So perhaps they had not found the Fountain of Youth itself, but one that engendered good health and longevity nonetheless.

That was Harry's father's claim, but Harry knew he didn't really believe it. That was just one of the reasons he didn't want to go work for his father: he despised the deceit of it all.

In the stable, he picked up the wheel and examined it. The crack went all the way through the rim of the wheel. He would have to nail it first, then put the metal on top. There was an old barrel nearby, broken down, that some of the donkeys had claimed as their own. Harry figured they wouldn't mind if he took the metal bands from around it. If his idea worked, he could get more bands from the blacksmith in town.

What he needed was small nails. He searched the stables, but found nothing, not even nails for horseshoes. That meant one thing. He sighed, but it had to be done. He would have to go to the Wylie Five and Dime, and that meant seeing Winnie Wylie.

As he walked down the lane into town, he hoped that she would not be there, but as he neared the store he could see her just outside sweeping the stoop. She saw him almost immediately, and began waving her arm in the air. "Harry Appledore," she called. "Yoo-hoo!" Her voice trilled. It was said that she had a lovely singing voice.

When he neared, he took off his hat and said, "Good morning, Winnie. How are you today?"

"Just fine, Harry. And how are you?" She gripped the broom tightly in her hand as she spoke, leaning in close to him. He took a step back.

"Fine, thank you. I've come for—"

"I'd heard you'd gone back to school already, but I knew you wouldn't leave without saying good-bye to me. I don't see why you need to go to school all so far away in Massachusetts. The school here in Crystal Springs is very good."

She spoke like sugar, but there were few people in this world as vile as Winnie Wylie. Her family had been here even longer than the Appledores, or the Darlings, for that matter, and they acted like they were royalty because of it. They'd started out as fur traders with the Indians, and now they owned the five-and-dime, and her father was a councilman, always trying to thwart his father's plans for expansion.

According to Orlando the Wylies had been looking for the Fountain of Youth at one time, too. When Angus Appledore had started building his house, they figured he must be up to something and sussed out what it was. That's the way they were: always working one angle or another. He couldn't figure out what Winnie was up to in that moment, but he knew she was up to something.

She straightened one of the flouncy ribbons on her dress. "I think it's time for you to spend more time around Crystal Springs. You're going to take over that business from your daddy and it seems being there by his side and running it would be the best education you could have."

He looked down the street, where he saw Nora leaving the post office with a stack of newspapers.

It was true that he would like to spend more time in

Crystal Springs, but not more time at the hotel and bottling plant, and certainly not in his father's study. He would like to see all the seasons on the farm, to help plant and to help cultivate.

"I've come to fetch some nails," Harry told her.

"What?" Winnie asked. Then she smoothed her dress. "Why, of course, come right on inside."

He found the nails quickly and brought them over to settle up. Mrs. Wylie was behind the counter, and she looked at Harry and then at Winnie, who had followed him around the store like the horses did when they knew he had sugar cubes in his pockets. Once those sugar cubes were gone the horses paid him no mind, and he imagined that Winnie would be the same if Harry weren't to inherit the Appledore fortune. Mrs. Wylie smiled. "How lovely to see you, Harold. Won't you stay and have some tea with us?"

"I'm afraid I can't," Harry said, grasping for an excuse. "I told my mother I would pick up some biscuits from the bakery."

"Don't you have staff who could make biscuits for you? Why, I thought one of the Darling women worked in your kitchen."

"My mother has her working on other things," he said. "Could you add these to our accounts?"

"Certainly."

As he turned to go, Mrs. Wylie said, "Winnie, why don't you accompany Harry. I could use some of those biscuits myself."

Harry wanted nothing less, but could think of no polite way to refuse.

"Of course, Mother," Winnie said gleefully. She moved toward Harry and tried to hook her arm through his, but he sidestepped her.

They walked out into the bright light of the fall morning. "When do you leave for school?" she asked.

"Next week," he replied. "We move into dormitories on Saturday."

"I heard the boys play awful pranks on each other in the dormitories." She giggled and put her hand over her mouth.

He imagined that if girls were allowed at the school, she would be the cruelest prankster of them all. "Some do. I try to stay away from all that."

The grin faded from her face. "Of course."

They arrived at the bakery and he pushed open the door. Right away he saw Nora Darling. She was bent over a newspaper, a sweet roll in one hand. Of course she had come here for a treat! Orlando had strict food guidelines that he learned from Dr. Kellogg in Battle Creek, Michigan. He called it "biologic living" and it included a slew of nos: no alcohol, no tea, no coffee, no meat, no chocolate, no tobacco, no milk, no cheese, no eggs, and no refined sugars. He expected Nora to share his diet of whole grains, nuts, and fruits, and so Nora liked to sneak treats when she could.

As Harry drew near he saw that Nora was studying a map that he would recognize anywhere: the Arctic. "Peary's expedition?" he asked.

Nora looked up, surprised, and swallowed hard. "Did

Orlando send you? I'll be going back to the Water Castle in just a moment."

Winnie stepped out from behind Harry, her true self revealed, wolf grin and dark, darting eyes. "Why, hello there, Nora."

Nora nodded. "Good day, Winnie."

"It's Ms. Wylie to you, please. Why haven't you been in school?"

Nora sat up straight. "I'm employed now."

Winnie smiled, smug and satisfied. "Oh. Such a pity."

Harry stepped forward to intercede, but the words just stayed in his mouth as hard and cold as pebbles. He raked his fingers through his hair and wished that words came easier to him.

Nora, though, did not seem to need his help. She continued on confidently. "Plus I'm receiving private tutoring."

Winnie narrowed her eyes.

"On account of my advanced intellectual gifts," she added.

Harry grinned.

Winnie put her hands on her hips. "Who is tutoring you?" she demanded.

"Dr. Appledore," Nora said.

Winnie slapped her knee and guffawed to the sky. "That old coot?" she managed to blurt out. She pretended to be tottering around with a cane. "You'd be better off tutoring him. Actually, maybe somebody could teach both of you some common sense."

"I'd prefer to be uncommon."

Winnie's face darkened then. "Oh, but you'll always be common, Nora."

Harry froze as he watched the two girls. None of the three moved. Finally, Harry said, "Does the story say where Peary is?"

Nora shifted her gaze from Winnie to Harry. "There's a full report. I'll leave the paper for you once Dr. Appledore is finished with it." She stood up and sidestepped Winnie. "I must get back to the castle. I don't have time for your tomfoolery today."

*　*　*

Nora walked quickly, carried by her annoyance. She tried to tell herself that it did not matter what Winnifred Wylie thought. Who was Winnie to make judgments? To call her common? When she was a famous inventor or explorer like Matthew Henson, Winnie would still be nothing, and then it would be Nora's turn to laugh.

Her pace slowed a little. She'd had her own concerns about Dr. Appledore, but now she could see that his mind worked in different ways from most people's: more complex and indirect. They could not even begin to imagine the things that he knew.

In the pasture, the cows calmly chewed their cud in the morning sun. Most people, she decided, were like those cows, chewing on grass and never leaving their fenced-in pasture. She and Dr. Appledore, why, even the moon was in their reach.

TEN

The rain started falling that afternoon and pelted against the house. Ephraim's window had a tin awning on it, and sitting on his bed it sounded like he was trapped inside a metal garbage can while stones were pelted at it. This was not a fate that had ever befallen him, but it was one he could readily imagine, especially at the hands of a thug like Will Wylie.

He flipped open his science textbook. Ms. Little had said she would stay after and help him whenever he needed it, but it would take twenty Ms. Littles and a year of afternoons for him to catch up on the month of her earth science class that he had missed. Mallory had said everyone was a little bit stronger, a little bit smarter, but as far as he could tell he had wandered into some sort of school for the gifted elite.

He held his hand out in front of him and looked at it. Radioactive. He half expected to see wavy lines coming off it like in the comic books. If his dad were well, he'd tell Ephraim that he had nothing to worry about. He'd make some silly joke like, "A little radiation never killed anyone, Ephraim. Not anyone who lived to tell about it." Ephraim would groan, but it really would make him feel better. Now Ephraim's dad was sitting like a statue in the bed down the hall, and he was the one who should be making his dad feel better. He didn't know how, though, didn't even know where to start. He could try to tell a joke, but his father wouldn't understand and Ephraim had never been very good at joke telling anyway. It seemed that all Ephraim could do around his father was stare helplessly.

The pounding on the metal was too much, so he slipped off his bed, eschewing the little step stool, and made his way down the hall. His foot hit a floorboard that gave a creak like a crypt opening in a horror movie. He seemed to hit that board every time he walked, and it spooked him each time.

At the far end of the hall he found Brynn staring at a closed door, muttering to herself. He froze. Was this how she had found their father? "Brynn," he called softly. He kept walking toward her. "Are you okay?"

"There's another set of stairs through that door. I want to go and see, but I'm afraid to go by myself. Only I know I shouldn't be afraid, so I've been standing here trying to convince myself to go alone."

"Oh," Ephraim said. He knew he should offer to go with

her, but he wasn't interested in exploring any more of this strange house.

They heard the main door open and shut and then Price was clambering up the center stairs. He looked at Brynn, and then at Ephraim, then back at Brynn again. "You okay, Brynn?" Price asked. His voice was soft and kind, just like their father's, only their father didn't have to put it on like a costume.

"I'm just getting myself psyched up to explore this side of the house."

"We'll go with you," Price said.

Ephraim wasn't sure why Price hadn't just offered to go himself, but now that there was a "we," he couldn't very well back down. "Right. I was just about to offer to go with you."

With a deep breath Brynn put her hand on the doorknob and pulled the door open. Each door here seemed to have its own symphony of creaks and moans.

Price went first, of course, and Ephraim last, with Brynn sandwiched between them. The stairway was narrow and steep. "Definitely a servants' stairway," Price said.

But when they got to the top of the stairs, they found a wide-open, unfinished space. It was cut through with thick, roughly hewn beams. Leaning against one wall were six or seven headboards, each ornately carved. A chair with its stuffing spilling out sat in a corner. There was a single, fogged-over window that had a small bird's nest tucked into its corner, one perfect blue egg resting inside it.

"It's just storage, I guess," Brynn said.

"There's a door," Price said, pointing across the way. They clomped across the floor, kicking up dust. Price pushed open the door, which was barely as tall as he was. They stepped down into another room that looked like their attic back in Cambridge. The room had two windows, one of which was cracked. In between stood a hulking wardrobe. The ornately carved top almost reached the ceiling. In a corner there was an old-fashioned bicycle, the kind with a big front wheel and a small one behind. "Maybe if I rode that one to school you could actually beat me," Price said.

Brynn walked over to a desk and picked up a small bag that sat on top. She peered inside. "Jacks," she said, dumping the starlike pieces out onto her hand. "I love jacks. Annemarie is going to be the champion now, I suppose."

Price put a hand on her shoulder. "You'll just have to be the champion of Crystal Springs then." He helped her pour the pieces back into the bag and tug the strings closed.

Ephraim rubbed his nose and then sneezed.

Brynn picked up a fountain pen with a crooked nib. "I wish I had some ink for this."

"I'm sure we could get you some," Ephraim said before Price had the chance to jump in and be a hero again. His gaze glossed over a stack of wooden crates and landed on a steamer trunk that was covered with stickers from all over the world.

Brynn made her way over to the wardrobe and tugged on one of the doors. It opened with a pop and revealed a stunning array of clothing for both men and women. There was a shimmering gold dress resting next to a pair of worn pants with faded striped suspenders. Brynn let her hand drift along the length of a silk gown.

Ephraim lifted the top of the trunk. Neatly stacked were mementoes from what seemed like hundreds of journeys. Right on top was an etching of the Eiffel tower next to an African mask that looked at him with surprised eyes. He reached in a little deeper and unearthed a small white teapot decorated with blue drawings just like the kind his grandmother collected and kept in a locked china cabinet.

"Can you get that down for me, Price?" Brynn asked, pointing to a hatbox on a top shelf in the wardrobe. Price had to stand on his toes to get it and even then he had to prod it along with just the tips of his fingers before it fell to the ground, spilling out a man's and a woman's hat onto the floor.

Brynn picked up the woman's hat, a swirly affair decorated with bright blue and green peacock feathers. She placed it on her head, then handed Price the black bowler.

"Why, good day, madam, what a lovely hat."

"Good day, sir," Brynn replied, giggling. "So kind of you to say so."

Ephraim found a stack of postcards tied together with a faded green ribbon. He shuffled through them and found they were from every World's Fair from 1915 in San Francisco to 1939 in New York. None of the postcards had been written on or mailed.

Next he pulled out a framed photograph that showed an

old airplane. Two women stood in front of it. One was white, her short curls tousled and her grin mischievous. She looked so familiar to Ephraim. Next to her was a young African American woman, still wearing her leather flying helmet. In the background a young man in a suit examined the cockpit. Written in neat script on the corner were the words *Me and Amelia, 1937.* Ephraim held up the picture. "Look at this!" he called out.

Brynn and Price, who were still exchanging pleasantries in fake aristocratic accents, looked over at him. "Yes, sir, how can we be of assistance?" Price asked.

"It's Amelia Earhart," he said, holding up the photograph.

"A photograph of Miss Amelia!" Brynn said. "How lovely!" She hurried over and took the photograph from Ephraim's hand. "She's an old friend, don't you know."

Ephraim shook his head.

"Ephraim seems rather out of sorts," Brynn said to Price, her voice high pitched and wavery like the people on PBS specials.

"The problem is clear, my dear Brynn. Ephraim does not have a hat."

"Indeed!" Brynn agreed. "We must find a hat for Ephraim!" She hurried back to the wardrobe, her peacock feathers flopping. Ephraim wondered what kind of woman would have worn such a hat seriously. After a moment of digging in the mammoth space, she emerged with a leather, fur-lined cap. "This will do."

She tossed it to Ephraim, who caught it in one hand. It smelled of mothballs, but he put it on his head anyway.

"Why, it's the explorer back from the great north. How was your journey, sir?" Price asked.

"Cold," Ephraim replied.

"Delightful!" Brynn exclaimed, giggling.

Ephraim realized he had not seen Brynn acting silly since their father's stroke. He tugged the hat on tighter and stood up. "Well, my lady, as you know I have been accompanying Robert Peary on his mission to the North Pole and I am happy to report that we have found it."

"Splendid!"

"Indeed," Ephraim said. "And such wonders we found there. There was a polar bear dancing on top of a ball and a, uh, a band of seals that barked out the National Anthem for us."

"I have heard that seals are quite musical," Price said. He grabbed the handlebars of the bike. "Anyone fancy a ride?" he asked.

Ephraim looked at the flattened tires on the wheels and doubted the bike would roll more than a few feet. Brynn, though, said, "I would love one, sir."

Price lifted her up onto the seat, told her to hold tight, and then began guiding the bike around the room. Even with his hands on the handlebars, she wobbled side to side, but laughed the whole time.

As the bike rolled it made a creaking sound like crows screeching in the early morning. "What a remarkable piece of machinery you have there," Ephraim said. "Top of the line. Top of the line, indeed."

"Nothing but the best in our family," Price said.

Ephraim peered into the wardrobe to see what else was in there, perhaps a hat with a little more dignity and a little less of an odor. Tucked into a corner was a small wooden box. When he opened it he found a gold pocket watch. Inscribed on the back were the words *For my love Harry, now, forever, and always.* He popped it open and saw the wide blank face looking at him. When he wound it, it started ticking away, and so he tucked it into his pocket just like a proper gentleman.

He heard a crash and turned just in time to see Price catching Brynn as the bike fell. They tumbled to the ground, but instead of crying out, they were laughing. Ephraim rushed over to them, and as he did, he saw the strangest thing in the window. "Are you okay?" he asked.

"We're fine."

He looked again at the window, unsure he had seen what he thought. "That window doesn't go outside."

"What do you mean?"

He peered more closely and sure enough, instead of the outside world, he saw another room, much like the one they had started in. "It's another room." He reached down and tugged on the window sash, but nothing happened.

Price joined him and they pulled together until the window creaked upward. "Well, sir and madam, I feel it is our responsibility to investigate," Price said, throwing one leg over the ledge. Ephraim and Brynn followed him through the window into the next room. They had to step up and when they got inside, they each stopped in amazement.

"This looks just like the first room," Brynn said.

"This *is* the first room," Price replied.

Ephraim looked at the beams and then at the bird's nest and the blue egg. "But that's impossible. We didn't go in a circle."

"We must have," Price said.

"But we didn't. We came in one door from this room and went out the window and here we are."

"Dear sir, a great explorer such as yourself must know that it can't be impossible, because it's happening," Price said.

Ephraim turned around and poked his head through the window into the second room. Bicycle. Wardrobe. Trunk. All was in place. He crawled back through the window, crossed the room, pulled open the door, stepped inside, and was next to his siblings.

"See," Price said. "Possible."

"Splendid!" Brynn said, though with less enthusiasm than before.

Price stepped closer to her. "It's obviously just another one of those architectural tricks. Like the way it seems there's not enough space for my room to exist. People were crazy about this sort of thing back in the day. It's like that house we went to out in California, the one that kooky lady had built."

"The Winchester Mystery House," Brynn reminded him.

"Right, where the woman just kept building it and building it for thirty-eight years and adding on to it."

They had taken the trip out West a few years before. Their tour guide, a middle-aged man with thinning hair and Coke-bottle glasses, had told them ominously not to separate from the group or they might be lost for hours.

"A medium told her that her dead husband said that she would live as long as the house was incomplete," Brynn said. "That's why she kept building it."

"She was building it for ghosts," Ephraim said; that much he remembered from the tour. She thought she was being haunted by the ghosts of all the people killed by firearms manufactured by her husband's company. "The passageways were so she could escape from the evil spirits."

Price frowned at Ephraim. "I don't believe in séances or running away from ghosts or any of that. I just think she was cuckoo. But, having secret rooms and strange staircases and all of that, that was what eccentric rich people did. And from all Mom has told us, this house has held a lot of eccentric rich people."

"Maybe," Brynn said.

"I'm certain of it," Price said. "Look it up. You'll see. In the meantime, madam, what do you say we go downstairs and play some jacks. Maybe *I'll* be the champion of Crystal Springs."

Brynn laughed and followed Price to the stairs.

Ephraim stayed behind. He crossed the room and looked at the egg, blue as a summer sky. He reached down to pick it up, but as soon as he touched it, it crumbled to dust.

ELEVEN

The second day of school was as bad as the first for Ephraim. In English, he'd misidentified and mispronounced every vocabulary word he was asked to define, to the titters of his classmates. In science he had knocked the scale they were using off the lab table. It fell to the ground and shattered into its composite parts. Will hadn't even bothered to glare at him.

He said nothing to Mallory or Henry Green in the truck on the way home, which was fine with Mallory. Brynn filled the space chattering about the robotics team she had decided to join.

When they pulled up the driveway to the house, Ephraim looked at his father's window. A dull light shone from behind the curtain, and he could see the silhouette of his mother and someone else moving around.

"Thanks, Henry," Brynn said cheerfully as she got out of the truck. Ephraim, though, had his eyes on the car parked there: a rusting gold Mercedes with whitewall tires and a pine-tree deodorizer hanging from the rearview mirror.

"Whose car is that?" he asked.

Brynn just shrugged.

Inside, they found out who drove the unfamiliar car: Dr. Winters, their mother's old teacher.

Dr. Winters looked exactly like someone named Winters should. He had pale, white skin, watery blue eyes, and a shock of white hair. He stood about six feet tall and had small wire-framed glasses. His clothes were rumpled, but of good quality: khaki pants, wool jacket, a burgundy-colored vest.

Ephraim and Brynn saw him as they passed by the open door to their parents' bedroom on the way to her library. Ephraim would have just kept going, but Brynn stopped.

Dr. Winters and their mother stood next to their father, who sat in bed looking, if possible, even more tired than usual. "I'd like to see him making more progress. It's possible he's in something like a state of shock. He's locked himself away inside his body."

"Is that typical?"

"Frankly, no, but I have seen it happen before. There was a long time between the stroke and when he was found, right? That sort of delay in treatment can have all sorts of ramifications."

Beside Ephraim, Brynn stiffened. "It's not your fault," he

whispered to her. "If you hadn't gone down there, it would have been even longer."

"I'm not overly concerned yet," Dr. Winters concluded.

Ephraim tugged Brynn to the side and held his finger to his lips, as they crouched down, out of sight. Their mother coughed. "What else should we be doing?" she asked.

"You're doing everything right. But you knew that already."

Brynn snuggled in closer to him. "Ephraim," she whispered.

Ephraim shook his head.

Dr. Winters continued. "You never did like it when patients didn't respond right away to treatment. You can't control every little thing, you know. Medicine is as much an art as a science."

"I didn't believe that in med school and I don't believe it now," she replied.

"The best thing you can do is to take care of yourself. You won't do anyone any good if you wear yourself out."

"If you think I need to be more aggressive, I can do that. I've read that the worst thing you can do with a stroke patient is to coddle them—"

Dr. Winters interrupted. "Emily, please. He's not your patient. He's your husband. You love him. You hold his hand. You tell him about your day."

Brynn tugged on Ephraim's sleeve. "Ephraim—"

"Let's let them finish up," Ephraim whispered back.

"What are you doing?" It was Price, taking the last of the

steps two at a time and coming down the hall. His hair looked wet and mussed, and his cheeks were flushed. He looked like he'd stepped out of some catalog aimed at happy, healthy teenaged boys, the kind who played pickup games of soccer and hiked mountains for the fun of it. The kind of catalog that wouldn't send a copy to Ephraim even if he offered to buy every item in it.

"Kids?" their mother called.

Ephraim and Brynn stood up and all three went into the bedroom. Ephraim kept his eyes off his father.

She smiled at them. "These are our children: Price, Ephraim, and Brynn. Kids, this is Dr. Winters."

They all said hello and Price even went over and shook the old doctor's hand. "How's Dad doing?"

"Quite well," Dr. Winters said.

Ephraim and Brynn exchanged a look. Ephraim hated when adults lied to kids. Plus it made him sure that their dad was even worse off than they'd thought.

"It's really nice of you to come out here and check on him," Price said, as if he were a grown-up.

It was all too much—the way Price was acting, Dr. Winters lying to them, the dark circles under his mother's red-rimmed eyes—and so Ephraim cracked. He knew he was saying the wrong thing as he said it, but he didn't stop himself. "What's for dinner?" Even to him, his voice sounded whiny.

Price glared at him. Dr. Winters coughed. Ephraim swore he felt his father's eyes on him, but he wouldn't check to see.

"Oh, um," his mother said. "I was thinking of trying to make chili."

"Have you ever made chili?" he asked as he pulled out the old pocket watch to check the time. He had never made chili either, but felt sure it was one of those things that had to simmer for a long time, and it was already after five o'clock.

"I have a recipe. And really, how hard can it be? Cooking is like chemistry. You just have to follow the directions."

"We can get it started," Price said. "And you can finish up here."

Ephraim felt red anger pressing in around him.

"I'm pretty much done here," Dr. Winters said. "The visiting nurse will come the next few days, and a physical therapist. I'll come back on Monday if that works for you."

"That's perfect. Let me show you out."

Their mother walked around the bed with Dr. Winters just behind her. Once they were past the children, Price elbowed Ephraim hard in his side. "What is wrong with you?" he hissed.

"What's wrong with *you*?" Ephraim retorted. "Dad's sick. He's not gone, so stop acting like you're the man of the house now or whatever."

Price rolled his eyes and trotted to catch up with Dr. Winters and their mother. Ephraim and Brynn followed behind, and he noticed that she kept a good distance from him, too. No one wanted to come near his radioactive loserdom.

"So," Dr. Winters was saying to Price as they went down the stairs. "Your mother tells me you're joining the swim team."

"First practice today," Price replied.

"I was a swimmer in my day. I still go to the Y three times a week. What's your event?"

Price shrugged. "Today we were doing time trials for the fifty free and I set a pool record. It wasn't an official meet, so it doesn't count, but that was pretty cool."

"Pretty cool indeed!" Dr. Winters said.

"That's wonderful, Price." Their mom wrapped her arm around his shoulder. "You must have a natural ability in the water. When's your first meet?"

Ephraim watched the conversation with incredulity. "You beat the pool record?"

"Yeah," Price said without looking back over his shoulder at Ephraim.

"But you've never trained."

"I know," Price said.

"They must have made a mistake," Ephraim said.

Price smirked. "Like Mom said—I have a natural ability."

It didn't make any sense to Ephraim. His brother was a gifted athlete, sure, and after a few practices his record-setting might be believable. But just jumping into the pool and being spectacular—it seemed impossible. Then again, most of what Price did seemed impossible to Ephraim, who, while not clumsy, was not by any means an athlete.

They walked through the entryway, and their mother gave Dr. Winters a hug. "Remember what I told you. Take care of yourself." Then he turned to the children. "Price, Ethan, and Brynn, you take care of your mother."

"Ephraim," Ephraim corrected softly. But his voice was drowned out by Price promising to do just that.

After Dr. Winters left, their mother went into the kitchen to make the chili. Price came up to Ephraim and, without saying anything, punched him hard in the arm. "I know it's monumentally difficult for you not to be a tool, but for the sake of Mom and Brynn, you'd better try."

When Price left, Ephraim rubbed the sore spot on his arm. He felt pretty sure that he deserved the hit.

TWELVE

On Ephraim's fourth day of school, Ms. Little announced that they were going to visit the Van de Graaff generator. Ephraim's face lit up. A Van de Graaff generator meant they were taking a trip to the Museum of Science in Boston to see the machine that re-created lightning. There couldn't be one any closer than Boston—that meant going home. As he was reaching up his hand to ask when the field trip would be, his classmates were getting out of their seats. "Where's everyone going?" he asked Will.

Will shook his head. Maybe Ephraim had some sort of attention deficit disorder, Will thought, and that's why he was so dim. "To the Van de Graaff generator."

"Right now? Don't we need permission slips or anything?"

Ephraim hadn't packed a lunch, and he didn't think he would have enough money on him to buy anything at the museum cafeteria.

"It's not like it's dangerous," Will said, stuffing his notebook into his backpack.

Mallory walked by and said, "It's here. In the school."

"You have a Van de Graaff generator in the school?"

Mallory liked the way it was so easy to surprise Ephraim. He might have been the one from the city, but he sure was a bumpkin. "Sure. It's right next to the planetarium. Will built it."

Ephraim's eyes grew even wider as he swiveled his head back toward Will. Will didn't say anything. He had built it, it was true, but it was from a kit paid for from an alumni grant, and Ms. Little had helped him. At the time he'd thought that maybe his World's Science Fair project would have something to do with electricity, but now he felt he needed to do something more ambitious.

The rest of the class had already gone ahead, leaving the three to follow behind. They didn't walk together, though, but staggered themselves, each making sure not to get too close to the others.

The Van de Graaff generator was at the far end of the school. They went down a narrow set of stairs and then into a room that opened up several stories high. In the center were two large poles, each with a ball on top, the two balls pressed together. A pole with a smaller ball was in between them. At the base was a station with a control board, all surrounded by a metal cage. Will dropped his bag by the bleacher-style seats and went to the command center.

"Ephraim, why don't you join your lab partner," Ms. Little suggested.

Ephraim shook his head. "No, that's okay."

"Yeah, Ms. Little. I got it," Will said, his eyes fixated on the control panel.

"I don't know the first thing about Van de Graaff generators," Ephraim said. That wasn't entirely true. He had seen the show at the Museum of Science seventeen times. His favorite was the one he'd seen about Nikola Tesla. The presenter had pretended to be Tesla, and talked about how he was always in Thomas Edison's shadow. Ephraim could relate to that.

"See. He doesn't know anything about it," Will agreed, and even though he was only saying what Ephraim had said, it still annoyed Ephraim.

"The best way to learn is by doing. Hop on up there, Ephraim."

Ephraim, miffed and out to prove himself, did as he was told. He shut the door and locked himself into the cage with Will. The array of dials and buttons was dizzying. He tried not to get too close to anything.

"As I'm sure you all remember, a Van de Graaff generator is an electrostatic generator able to produce high voltages of electricity. We use it to study how electricity works. Why don't we review how it functions just so we're sure we've all got it before we start our experiment for the day?"

Everyone, Ephraim included, knew that Ms. Little was only reviewing for Ephraim's benefit. Ephraim tried to listen carefully as Will explained.

Looking bored, Will pointed to the tower that held the two large spheres. "So there's a rubber belt in there that goes around."

"At sixty miles per hour!" Ms. Little interjected.

"Then there's an adaptor there that sprays electricity onto the belt."

Ephraim nodded, though he had no idea how electricity was sprayed.

"Then the belt brings it up and the spheres get a negative charge all around the outside. Then when you bring the neutral point close"—he pointed to the small ball on the pole—"it's like the negative charges jump over to the neutral and you get the lightning bolt."

"You got that?" Ms. Little asked. "It's as if the negative charges are all bottled up and when that small ball comes close, it pops the cork, and out spills the lightning."

Ephraim nodded. This all sounded vaguely familiar from his visits to the museum. His dad had told him it was just like when you got a static shock. The charge built up on you and then you touched another person or something metal and the electricity jumped. He and Price had spent whole afternoons rubbing their fleece sweatshirts and chasing each other around trying to zap one another. The Van de Graaff generator was like a really big version of that.

"So let's see a few test trials before we get down to business," Ms. Little said.

Will started fiddling with the dials and the machine purred into action. Ephraim had never been so close to the generator before. It loomed above him, and the vibrations seemed to go all around and through him.

Will pushed a button that raised the small ball a little higher. A lightning bolt jumped from the large spheres to the small one. Ephraim rocked back. Will snickered at him.

Ephraim set his jaw. "I just didn't realize it was all warmed up and ready to go," he explained.

"It's ready," Will said. He moved the ball on the pole around, and soon another bolt shot out. This time Ephraim managed to keep himself still, though his insides were quivering.

"Want to see something really cool?" Will asked.

"Sure," Ephraim said, though he had serious doubts about what Will might think was really cool.

"Hold on," Will said.

Slowly the cage started to rise.

"What are you doing?" Ephraim asked.

"We're going to shock the cage."

"What?"

"It's completely safe. We're in a metal cage; it's just like being in a car."

"Except we're not in a car. We don't have any rubber wheels."

"That's not actually what makes a car safe. Rubber is a

good insulator, but it's not that good." He looked at Ephraim's perplexed face. "Never mind. If this were dangerous, Ms. Little would be stopping me, wouldn't she?"

Ephraim looked down at Ms. Little, who was smiling up at them. She probably thought that she had brought Will and Ephraim together. He turned toward his classmates, none of whom looked concerned. A little jealous, maybe, but not concerned.

The hum was getting louder and louder. It sounded an awful lot like the house.

"You're sure this is safe?" Ephraim whispered.

Exasperated, Will said, "Yes. You could just reach right out and grab the lightning bolt if you wanted to."

It sounded like a dare to Ephraim, a chance to prove he wasn't a wimp—or an idiot. He reached out his hand.

Will turned just as Ephraim's wrist passed through the bars of the cage. "Ephraim, no!"

The bolt jumped from the cage to Ephraim's hand. Ephraim stumbled backward, slipped, and hit his head on the metal floor of the cage. The last thing he saw was Will's face hovering above his own. "Ephraim? Ephraim? I didn't mean it." Then he closed his eyes.

Will knew that everyone thought he had shocked Ephraim on purpose. Probably even Ms. Little, who was Will's favorite teacher. His dad would be proud of him. This gave him a sick feeling.

He weaved through the fallen leaves as he rode his bike home that afternoon.

Even if he had done it on purpose, like if there were some deep, dark part of him that actually wanted to hurt Ephraim, how would he have known that he'd fall down and hit his head? That's what had knocked him out: not the shock but the fall.

The truth was he didn't think anyone was stupid enough to actually reach out and try to touch a lightning bolt. It was Ephraim's own fault for being just so plain dumb.

He rode over the leaves now, liking the noise they made when they crinkled under his bike's tires.

No one else saw it that way, and he guessed he didn't really either. It was his fault. It was that simple.

At the end of his driveway, he turned at their crooked and dented mailbox; the *y* in their name had turned upside down. People drove by and saw the mailbox, the broken-down cars and tractors, and shook their heads. Will pedaled hard and wondered if he would always be "that Wylie kid."

October 26, 1908

When Nora went to fetch the morning newspapers, the postmaster handed her a letter addressed to her. She had never before received mail and tore into it as soon as she was outside.

The letter was from Harry.

Dear Ms. Darling,

I hope you do not find me too forward for writing to you. I noticed when we met in the bakery that day that you were reading about Robert Peary.

Nora pursed her lips. That day in the bakery, when he had just stood there while Winnie Wylie insulted her and his great-uncle.

I did not get a chance to tell you that I, too, am an aficionado of Arctic exploration. I keep a map in my dormitory room on which I mark the progress of the expedition. I imagine that you do something similar.

He was right. She kept a map down in the laboratory, and Dr. Appledore allowed her to keep all the newspaper stories related to the expedition. She had them pasted into a scrapbook made from an old history book that Dr. Appledore said was of no value.

> *As no one on this campus seems to understand the import of this journey—perhaps they lack the intellect—I hoped that you and I could correspond about their progress. I am sure that in this attempt they will be successful. I hope you will not laugh when I confess that I actually dreamt of it.*

Nora, too, was certain that this would be the time when Peary and Henson finally made it to the Pole.

> *The last I heard they were still in Greenland. Preparing for such an endeavor must be a monumental task. I should like to see the inner workings of the boat. Such a machine it must be to cut through the ice off Greenland. I would like, even, perhaps, to taste the pemmican.*
>
> *I hope to hear from you. Please share any news you hear of the journey, and I shall do the same.*
>
> > *Sincerely,*
> >
> > *Harold Appledore, Junior*

Nora held the paper in her hands as a smile warmed her face. He wrote as formally as he spoke, but for the first time she felt she saw beneath his surface and she admired what she saw there.

Before she could revel too long in this moment, the letter was snatched from her hands.

"What's this? Reading your master's mail?" It was Winnie Wylie, of course.

"I have no master. My family never has." Her family had arrived as free blacks in the 1760s, working on steamships. They'd traveled up the river from Portland and settled in Crystal Springs.

Winnie, though, was no longer listening to Nora. She was looking at the signature. She looked up with her eyes flashing. Winnie had all sorts of names for Nora, most of which did not bear repeating. She chose some of the worst on that day. They buzzed around in Nora's head like angry wasps. "You're nothing, Nora Darling, and never will be. Don't let those foolish Appledores let you believe anything else. Harry is a sap, and Dr. Appledore is an old coot!"

Nora clenched her fists so hard her nails dug into her palms. She would not rise to Winnie's bait. She would not sink to Winnie's level. "Dr. Appledore is a renowned scientist who is at work on a very special project."

"Is he? What sort of a project?"

"His work is confidential."

Winnie laughed. "Oh yes, his work is certainly confidential. My mother says the family keeps him locked in a room so he doesn't embarrass them."

Nora knew that Orlando's reputation was that of a wealthy eccentric. It was true that Orlando Appledore had several interests outside of his quest for the fountain, and some of these experiments had ended poorly or in near disaster. As Dr. Appledore explained it, though, great science did not happen without great risks.

"Orlando Appledore is a very wise man, and when he makes his latest discovery, you'll be thanking him."

Winnie raised her eyebrows. Then a smile spread across her face and she leaned in close. She whispered: "My family knows what Orlando is looking for. We've always known. We already found it."

Nora watched as Winnie dropped the letter, pivoted on her heel, and walked away with determined strides. As Winnie's curls bounced on her back, Nora's heart sank to her feet.

* * *

Orlando Appledore was also a cautious man, some might say paranoid. What he feared most was that someone would find the Fountain of Youth before he did. So, when he decided to build a laboratory to test the properties of the water he found, he had it built under the house. Harold—Harry's father— thought it was an unnecessary expense, but realized it meant his uncle would be out of the public eye. The tunnels were already in place for the water operation, so all that was needed were some adjustments and the carving out of space.

Nora popped open the door and walked slowly down the stairs. At the bottom she found a kerosene lamp, lit it, and made her way down the tunnel.

Nora had a key, one of only two copies, that she used to

unlock a door with no handle or knob, and then she pressed on the door and let herself into the lab. It was lit by electric lamps designed specifically for the laboratory by Orlando's friend Nikola Tesla, the one who believed in life on other planets. Orlando stood behind a long black table and watched as water filtered from one set of glass bottles through glass tubes filled with a variety of substances and into another set of glass bottles.

"Winnie Wylie says they found it."

Orlando looked up from the filtration apparatus. "It?" he asked.

"The Fountain of Youth."

Orlando put down his pen, but he did not yet look concerned. "What did she say precisely?"

Nora made sure she was telling it to him exactly as Winnie had. "She said she knew what you were looking for, and that they already found it."

Orlando picked up his pen and began writing. "Has your Mister Henson found the Pole yet?"

Nora didn't understand this shift in conversation, but she answered, "Not yet. I believe they are still in Greenland."

"And when they do find it, how will they know?"

"By the latitude," she explained.

"A very scientific process."

"It is a scientific expedition," she said, still confused.

Orlando put down his pen and looked Nora in the eye. "Here is something that I am sure Peary and Henson understand. It's all very well and good to say that you've found it, but without proof, what's the bother? It's not enough to find it—or claim that you have—you need to understand it. Understanding is something we never have to fear from the Wylies." He turned to his large oak desk, the surface of which was strewn with papers that she would have to organize later. "Copernicus, you will recall, was one of the world's greatest scientists. He understood what the Wylies never will. To wit, nature can be controlled by man, but only through observation and experimentation. You cannot simply bottle it up and claim it is so."

"But they will bottle it, and sell it. Just like Mr. Appledore and his Dr. Appledore's Crystal Water, only they will claim that it is actually from the Fountain of Youth. Then when you truly find it, no one will believe you."

He inspected his bottles again, noting how quickly the water passed through each filter.

"Perhaps the Wylies will try to sell this new water," he said. "But it will fail."

"How can you be so sure?"

"This is the age of enlightenment and science! A new century has begun and we shall all be awakened to possibilities of our world. A man is going to find the North Pole, is he not?"

Nora nodded, though she still wasn't sure what Henson and Peary's expedition to the North Pole had to do with the Wylies and the water. What she did know was that Henson and Peary weren't the only ones looking for the Pole, and if they didn't find it soon, someone might steal their glory from them.

Orlando reached out his hand and placed it on her shoulder.

"You are a lucky girl, to have been born into such a wonderful age. Fallacies will fall by the wayside."

Nora wasn't sure what the word *fallacy* meant, but she could tell by his tone that it was something Dr. Appledore disdained.

"We are entering a new Renaissance. And with your help, my dear, I will be there to see it all!"

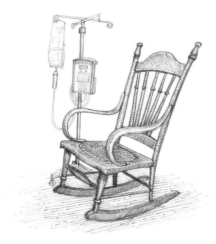

THIRTEEN

It had taken a week for the lump on the back of Ephraim's head to recede. He could still feel it when he reached back and rubbed it, as he did while standing outside his parents' bedroom. His mother had told him to go check on his father, though what he was checking for, he was not sure.

He hesitated, tucking his hand into his pocket and rubbing the engraving on the watch. Since they had moved to the castle nearly two weeks before, he had hardly seen his father. His dad could not walk. He could not speak. He sat in his room. Sometimes Brynn read to him, her voice a steady cadence. Their mother spoke with him, and asked him questions as if he could answer. Even Price went in and helped to move his father's limbs, saying that exercise could help the brain.

Ephraim, though, stayed away, unsure of what he could do to help his father.

He put his hand on the decorative doorknob, the whirls and patterns pressed into his palm. Then he pushed open the door.

The room was dark, slashed through with large rectangles of light from the windows. It took him a moment to locate his father in the corner of the room. He sat in a rocking chair, guided there by Ephraim's mother. His IV stand was next to the chair, giving off a faint glow. Ephraim shivered, then took a few steps into the room. "Hello," he said. "Hi, Dad."

The bands of light between him and his father made his father seem to be moving, rocking in the chair. It was wooden and oversized, the back reaching up above his father's head, making him look even smaller.

"I, um, I just came up to check that you were okay." He went over to the IV monitor and looked at the dials, as if he had some idea how to operate it. "Was there anything that you needed?"

He paused, though he did not expect his dad to say anything.

Ephraim ran his palms along his jeans. "I just, well, I hope you are doing okay."

Okay? Okay? Why couldn't he think of a word other than *okay?* Clearly his father was not okay. He was as far from okay as a person could be.

Ephraim took a few more steps. The skin on his father's face was pale and slack. His hands, which had been able to do such fine work with a paintbrush, lay flat on the arms of the chair.

This was not his father. This could not be his father. His father told corny jokes. His father drew pictures for Ephraim and his siblings of strange creatures like two-headed squirrels. His father sang opera off-key. His father laughed. This man was a shell: a taxidermy like the animal heads on the first floor.

He rubbed his head again. He had not yet told his father about the accident. How could he? He didn't want to have to tell his dad that after Ms. Little had brought him to the nurse, none of his classmates had come to check on him. Once Price had gotten a concussion on the soccer field and it was like the whole school took up a vigil outside the nurse's office. Ephraim had only had Mallory there, tapping her foot and telling him that her father was waiting to take them home.

Then again, his father had always been the only person he could tell these things to.

And suddenly the red rage came over Ephraim. It wasn't fair. *Fair* was such a little word, but there it was. He needed his dad to talk to, and that was one thing his father couldn't give him.

He wanted to tell his dad how the past weeks had been. How all the kids seemed to think he was dumb. It started with his not knowing who stupid Admiral Peary was, and it was cemented when the Geiger counter deemed him radioactive. They still tried to be polite, especially Ian, but now Ephraim knew that Ian was just one of those people who wanted everyone to like him—even if he didn't like them very much in return.

He wanted to tell his father about how Will had hated him, even before their family had arrived, though Ephraim wasn't really sure why. Will certainly thought he was an idiot and had maybe tried to kill him. Now in science class Will basically did the work for both of them with minimal conversation.

He wanted to tell his father how he'd been mean to Mallory and how it made him feel small inside, and yet he couldn't manage to apologize or make himself any nicer since she was so prickly herself.

He wanted to tell his dad how he ate lunch outside every day and it was a little cold, but the sun was beautiful and the light was clear and how those things made him think of his dad and when they used to go outside to paint: their dad with his easel and oil paints, Ephraim and Price sitting on the ground with watercolors. Brynn had been too little.

But his father wouldn't hear and the words would just be lost in the air.

Ephraim started to cry, and then ran from the room.

He ran right into Brynn, who asked, "Do you hear that noise?"

FOURTEEN

"Do you hear it?" Brynn asked again.

It was the humming and skittering sound that he had heard on the first night. It seemed to be coming from the walls, all around them. "Yeah," he said. He wiped at his eyes, and she pretended not to notice that he'd been crying.

"It seems stronger that way," she said.

Ephraim put his hand on the wall, expecting to feel a vibration, but there was nothing. They walked toward what seemed to be the origin of the noise. Price came down the stairs from his floor. "Do you hear that?" Ephraim asked.

Price nodded. "I've heard it a few times before. Never this loud."

They kept going down the hall, then up the second set of stairs to the third floor. The noise seemed even louder, the skittering more urgent. Brynn tucked her hand into Price's. "It's probably nothing," he said. "It's an old house. It could be the plumbing or the wiring or anything really."

"What is it then?" Ephraim asked. "Anything or nothing?"

Price glared at him. "Come on. It's louder this way."

They passed Ephraim's room, and then they were creeping along the red and green carpet in the same direction he'd gone that first night. Once again they ended in the small alcove with the statue of Orlando Priam Appledore. Ephraim cleared his throat. "Our first night, I followed the noise here and—"

Before he could finish, the blue glow started. The three children leaned toward the window. Cool air emanated off the glass and their breath made three little puffs of white on the pane. Then, the flash.

Brynn tumbled backward, pulling Price with her. Price threw his hand up and let loose the tennis ball he always carried. The ball smacked against the wall at the same time the two fell to the ground. Ephraim stood beside them.

"What the heck was that?" Price demanded.

"That's what happened before," Ephraim said. "And see, now the noise is almost gone."

Price got up and then extended his hand to Brynn, helping her to her feet. "That was intense," he said.

"But what does it mean?" Brynn asked. "I mean, what was it? How did it happen?"

"Mallory said it was a watchtower, but I don't know. That was all around us, right? All around the house?"

Brynn nodded. Then, behind them, Price said, "Hey. Look at this."

The tennis ball had dislodged one of the wooden panels of the wall. Price shifted it farther aside and looked inside. It was hollow back there. He peered in. "I think there's something in there."

"Like what?" Ephraim asked.

"Boogey man!" Price yelled. He turned and lurched at them, arms raised.

Ephraim and Brynn jumped together.

"I'm just kidding."

"Obviously," Ephraim said. "There's no such thing as the boogey man."

"Or is there?" Price asked. "Seriously, I think it's a box or something. I'll go get a flashlight. It's probably just some more old stuff."

He trotted off, leaving Ephraim and Brynn alone. "What do you think it is?"

Brynn shrugged. "This house has been around for a long time. It could have been hidden at any time. I mean, maybe it's some letters. Or a special store of money, in case of an emergency. People hide things for all sorts of reasons."

"Maybe it's a treasure map!" Ephraim suggested.

Brynn shook her head, but said, "I guess anything is possible."

Price returned with a flashlight and shined it down into the hole. "Yep, it's a box. It looks wooden." He reached his hand down into the hole. "I can just about get it." They could hear his hand wiggling around in the empty space. He leaned so his whole body was right against the wall. "Got it," he said, his voice muffled.

He pulled it out and they all looked at it: a small wooden box with a hinged lid. The top was branded:

DR. APPLEDORE'S CRYSTAL WATER CRYSTAL SPRINGS, ME

Written below were the words *Property of Nora Darling*. Price flipped open the top. A hair clip tumbled out and fell to the floor with a clattering sound that made Brynn shiver. Inside the box there was a small glass bottle, a photograph, and a handful of sand. An old and yellowed newspaper article was folded up. Ephraim took it out and carefully smoothed it. It showed a map of the Arctic and had a first-person account of the Peary expedition. "Holy cow," Ephraim said, holding out the article. "This will be perfect for my history project." It was the first stroke of good luck that he'd had related to school.

Brynn took the photograph and carried it closer to the sconce in the wall, while Ephraim took the amber bottle out of the box. It was empty, but had a label on it.

RADITHOR
Reg. U.S. Pat. Off.
CERTIFIED RADIOACTIVE WATER
CONTAINS RADIUM *and* MESOTHORIUM
in TRIPLE DISTILLED WATER

"Whoa!" he said, dropping the bottle back into the box. "That's radioactive."

"Well, don't give it to me," Price said. He snapped the box closed.

"Impossible," Brynn said.

"We can't play with radioactive materials," Ephraim said. "I'm already teeming with radiation. The last thing I need is another dose."

"What are you talking about?" Price asked.

"Look at this picture," Brynn told him.

"Ms. Little brought in a Geiger counter. I was off the charts. And now I just held that bottle . . . was there any water left in it?" Ephraim stared at his hands as if he expected them to shrivel up and fall off just from touching the bottle.

"Look at this picture," Brynn said again, holding it out to him.

"What?" Ephraim asked.

"It's you."

*　*　*

Brynn led her curious brothers back to the library. Then she put the photograph down on a desk full of other papers and shined a light onto it. "Look," she instructed.

The photo was of a large group of people standing in front of the castle. Judging by their clothes, it seemed to have been taken at the turn of the century. She put her finger down by a child in the front row. Ephraim blinked his eyes, because the girl was Mallory, and next to her was Ephraim.

"But that doesn't make any sense," Ephraim said. He picked up the picture and looked more closely.

"Let me see," Price said. "Well, this is a family house. And her family has always been the caretakers. It's probably just a family resemblance thing."

"Maybe," Ephraim said. But even the way the girl in the picture was smirking was just like Mallory. And he feared that he had a confused expression like the boy in the photo. He took the photo back. He could start to see some differences between the boy and him. The boy had a narrower face, and Ephraim's eyes were bigger and wider. The girl, though, he could see no differences from Mallory beyond dress. She wore an apron type of a thing that looked dirty and maybe torn.

"It's another piece of the puzzle," Byrnn said. "I found a book about the Appledores. I guess it was common at the time to have books published of your family history. Anyway, it got me started on some research in here." Brynn had laid out many of the things she had found in the library that were of interest to her. There were some oversized, rolled-up papers, and she spread them out. "Look at these. They're house plans."

"What are these?" Ephraim asked. He pointed to some boxes on the first floor with lines extending from them straight out of the building.

"Exits?" Price suggested.

"They're in the floor," Brynn said.

"Maybe it's like a secret passage," Price said. "Crazy rich people always had secret passages in their houses."

Brynn tugged on her ear. "Henry said there were quirks about this place. It's special. I'm trying to figure out if it's good special or bad special." Her fingers lingered over the plans, tracing the lines.

"It's just a house," Price said. "A big, weird humming house, but in the end it's just a house."

"A big, weird humming house that flashes," Ephraim said.

"There's more," Brynn said. From a stack on the desk, she pulled out a leather-bound book. "The guest book," she explained.

Ephraim opened it up and read through the names. Most of them sounded like old New England families: Adams, Ricker, Warren. Brynn reached her arm under his and pointed to a name: Nikola Tesla. That had been someone he'd enjoyed studying: he'd invented just about everything interesting, like the remote control and wireless and he'd wanted to build a death ray.

Michael Faraday.

"The physicist. I looked him up. He studied

electromagnetism." She pointed to another name: James Clerk Maxwell. "Him, too."

"So why did all these scientists come here?" Ephraim asked.

"That's what I was wondering. There's something weird going on here, but maybe it's something scientific and they wanted to witness it."

"Or maybe," Price said, "there was some rich old guy here and he invited scientists up here to amuse him."

"I was going through this section last night," Brynn said, leading him over to a set of books in the corner. "You want to take a look? I'm going to keep reading through the papers."

Ephraim scanned the titles, while Price looked over his back: *Strange New England, Mystical Maine, Magical Places of the World*.

"Brynn, come on, I know you don't believe in all that magic stuff," Price told her.

"I don't," she said. "But before people had science, they used magic to explain it. Maybe there's something in there that will help us figure out what's going on here."

"Well, you guys have fun with all this. Enjoy the weirdness while it lasts. We'll be going home soon."

Both of his siblings snapped their heads up to look at him. "What do you mean?" Ephraim asked. Maybe their mother had told Price something.

"This place is nice and all, but we're not going to stay here forever. Dad's getting better and—"

"No, he's not," Ephraim interrupted.

Price glanced quickly at Brynn, then glared at Ephraim.

"Yes, he is." He said it firmly, not giving Ephraim space to argue, as if saying it could make it so, or at least make Brynn believe it.

"Like I said, enjoy it while it lasts. I for one am going to play pool. Don't get swallowed up by a trapdoor or anything." As he left, he made spooky noises.

When he left, Brynn and Ephraim exchanged a look. "Do you think Dad's getting better? Even a little?"

He couldn't stand to lie to her, so he said, "You think there's something strange going on here? Then let's figure it out. You take the science and I'll look through these magical-mystical ones and see if we can find anything about this place. If there's anything strange or special, there's bound to be a record of it, right?" She nodded, and he picked up a book and scanned the index. No mention of Crystal Springs or the Appledores. He turned back to the title page, where he found a check mark and a date: *7 April 1939*. "This is an old book!" he exclaimed.

"They all are."

He scanned several more books, looking in the tables of contents and indices for Maine, Crystal Springs, Appledore— and found nothing. Each book, though, had a small mark and a date. He showed it to Brynn. "Do you think someone was checking off when they read them? Like, so they didn't read it again by accident."

"If it's a good book, you can read it again."

"Or maybe they were checking for something," he said. "Maybe they were looking for the same thing we are, some explanation, but it's not in there."

"Maybe they didn't want it to be in there. Maybe they were trying to keep it a secret. So they checked off the books that were safe."

He pulled a slim volume off the shelf. It fell open to a page as if it had been studied.

Au Clair, also known as Crystal Springs.
This sleepy hamlet masks a deep secret. Deep indeed! The springs are rumored to be the source of great power and vitality. Drinking from the source enhances the natural assets of the imbiber. Could it be the elusive Fountain of Youth?

The Fountain of Youth? Ephraim knew such a thing was impossibile. A myth. But then he picked up the picture with the people who looked just like him and Mallory.

He turned back to Brynn, who had returned to the house plans. She stared down at them with a serious expression, chewing on the tip of her pinkie. "What's wrong?" he asked.

"It's just that with all of these books, you'd think that there would be some explanation. Some reason why this house is so strange. Some book in here should tell us what's really going on in this town." Brynn looked lost, this tiny girl in a giant library, the shelves three times as tall as she was. Price thought that he could protect them all by lying and making believe things were better than they really were. Well, Ephraim could do better that that. He'd find out the truth.

FIFTEEN

When Ephraim sat down next to Mallory in the library, she narrowed her eyes at him. "What?" she demanded.

"I need to talk to you," he said. "It's urgent."

"I'm not going to give you all of my sources if that's what you want." Ephraim, she knew, had been struggling with the explorer project. Mr. Wright was giving them another day to work in the library, and Ephraim was probably scrambling to get more books and articles.

"It's not about that, it's—"

He felt in his pocket for the picture, but before he could pull it out Ian plopped himself down in a third chair at the round table. "You are so lucky," he declared. "I wish I could do Peary. I was Peary for Halloween when I was seven."

"Half this class has been Peary for Halloween," Mallory said.

"He went someplace no one else had ever been before. I think that is just the coolest. I mean, can you imagine discovering someplace totally new?"

Mallory shook her head. "You know, Matthew Henson was actually the first one to get there, not that anyone ever gives him any credit."

Ian tugged his sleeves up over his elbows and said, "It was Peary's expedition, Mallory. That's what matters."

"If the point of the expedition was to be the first person to step on the North Pole, then what mattered was who stepped first."

Suddenly Will was looming next to the table. His thumbs were hooked through his backpack straps. "Actually, neither of them was first," he said. "Frederick Cook was."

Ian threw up his hands. "No way. Frederick Cook lied about getting to the Pole, just like he lied about climbing Mount McKinley." He turned to Ephraim. "Have you noticed that there are no Freds in this town?"

"Um, I hadn't, actually," Ephraim said.

"That's because no one would name their child the same thing as that liar."

Will shook his head. "He wasn't lying." His tone was flat, but his eyes flashed and Ephraim was reminded once again that Will was a *big* guy. A big guy capable of administering electric shocks. Ephraim rubbed the back of his head where there was still a small nub of a bruise. If he were Ian, he'd stop pushing back against Will.

"You know how Frederick Cook said he was the first one to climb Mount McKinley? Well, the guy who supposedly went with him said it was all a lie. He signed a paper saying so," Ian said. "Everyone knows that. And if he lied about climbing Mount McKinley, then he lied about reaching the Pole."

Ephraim blushed. This was yet another thing that he did not know, but he was learning to keep his mouth shut.

"That man was *paid* to sign that. By Peary. Peary had all the money and all the influence. People always believe the people with the money." Will stared right at Ephraim as he said this, as if he were arguing with Ephraim rather than Ian.

"He made up a story of where he was in the Arctic. And you know what, he stole that, too," Ian said. "My dad said the route he claimed to have taken came right out of a book by some lady Julia something or other."

"Jules Verne," Mallory corrected. "Who was a man."

"Whatever. The point is, Frederick Cook was a thief and a liar," Ian said. "It's no wonder you chose him."

Will rose up to his full height. "Say that again, Sanderson."

"What are you going to do?" Ian asked. "Electrocute me? I'm not that stupid."

Ephraim looked down at the table.

"Whoa, what's going on here?" Mr. Wright asked.

Will put his finger down on Mallory's agenda book, right on the picture of Robert Peary. "'I shall find a way or make one.' Sounds like a confession to me."

"That's not what he meant at all," Ian retorted.

"What did he mean?" Mr. Wright asked.

"Well," Ian began. "Well—"

Will smirked.

"Ephraim?" Mr. Wright prompted. "Care to clarify your subject's motto?"

"I think he meant that even if the route wasn't clear or easy, he would forge ahead."

"Go on," Mr. Wright said, nodding.

"If there was no trail to follow, he'd create one."

"Good," Mr. Wright said. "Now that we have that sorted, I suggest you all go back to work on your projects."

Will slinked away. Mr. Wright turned his attention to Ephraim. "How is your research coming along?"

"Okay," Ephraim lied. He really hadn't gotten very far. He was distracted by his father and the things he'd found in his house.

"Don't forget you need both print and online resources."

"Sure," Ephraim said. "Of course."

Ephraim desperately wanted to talk to Mallory about the photograph and how she could be sitting here one hundred years later looking exactly the same. Ian, though, stayed at their table after Mr. Wright moved on, pulling out his laptop to start his work as if he hadn't just insulted Ephraim. "See, Ephraim, I told you about that kid. Bad news."

Ephraim shrugged. "Maybe he just feels passionately about exploration."

"We *all* feel passionately about exploration. We're the Crystal Springs Explorers."

Ephraim glanced at Mallory, and she shrugged.

"All I'm saying is watch your back," Ian said. "The Wylies have had it out for the Appledores for who knows how long, and I don't see it stopping anytime soon."

Ephraim took out his notebook and said, "Thanks, but I think I can handle myself."

Ian looked him up and down. "If you say so. But remember, he did already try to kill you once."

November 13, 1908

Nora sat with Nikola at the table in the laboratory, wrapping wire around blocks for the polyphase motor he was building for Dr. Appledore. Nora liked working with him. While it was true that he had exhibited some strange qualities during his visit, like requesting that she wash off everything he was to touch, he was dashing with his black hair and mustache. He said the most rash and ridiculous things. Best of all, he treated her the same way he treated everyone else. He called her Ms. Darling and asked her opinions, which he either considered or dismissed based on their merit, rather than her young age.

"Orlando tells me you are an aficionado of Arctic exploration," Nikola said.

"My friend Harry and I are tracking their progress." She had never before used the word *friend* to describe Harry, but she supposed that's what they had become. They were exchanging letters while he was at boarding school, sharing whatever information they could glean about the expedition. She kept a map in the laboratory where she tracked the progress. "I believe they are still in Greenland," she said, pointing to it.

Nikola tinkered with a contraption he had brought with him. "That seems an admirable hobby, Ms. Darling," he told her.

Nora frowned. She did not consider her interest in the North Pole to be a hobby. It was an education. She was going to be a great explorer, like Henson, and so she was learning from the best. "What do you think Henson might find when he arrives?"

"Henson?" Nikola asked.

"With Robert Peary."

Nikola put down one block, then examined one that Nora had completed. "Good work," he said. He held the block for a moment longer, a twinkle in his eye, as if he were considering telling her a fantastic story. "The Arctic is all sheets of ice, I believe. There is not much to discover."

"But no one has been there. They might find anything!"

"You think Peary might discover the Fountain of Youth?" Nikola asked. "That would rub Orlando raw!" He gathered the blocks and began inserting them into the contraption he had brought along with him. He glanced at Nora. "What, dear, do you think might be there?"

Nora looked down at her work, suddenly shy. "Creatures, maybe. Perhaps they would find the remains of a dinosaur, only, instead of just the bones, it would be the whole thing, muscle, skin, and everything, frozen solid in the ice."

"They could bring it back and thaw it in Orlando's water to reanimate it." Nikola held his arms out and lurched about the way he imagined a dinosaur might.

She almost asked him, then, what he thought of Orlando's quest, but she waited too long. Nikola went back to assembling his motor. He turned a switch and the machine roared to life. Nikola looked around and then found a nail that he held out to the machine. It hovered there when he let it go. "It creates a magnetic field," he said. "An apparatus like this is the best way to move electricity over long distances."

"What does this have to do with the water?" Nora asked.

Nikola shook his head, his black flop of hair turning to and fro. "Orlando has not completely explained his line of reasoning to me. Only that he is interested in the electromagnetic field."

"Can an electromagnetic field affect water?" Nora asked.

"Water is a magnificent conductor of electricity," Nikola said, then, seeing her confused expression, he clarified: "Electricity travels very easily through water. More easily than through air."

"But why would he want to send electricity through water?"

"That is a very good question, Ms. Darling. I am not sure that even Orlando knows the answer to that."

"But he works away at it anyway," Nora said.

"It does represent a new direction for him."

"How so?"

"There are two approaches to science, Ms. Darling. There are those who endeavor to discover new things."

"Like the Curies discovering the new element."

"Precisely. And then there are those of us who seek to create new works from what exists already—from what we know of the world." He finished wrapping another block. "Then there are those who simply take the work of others as if it is their own. Like Edison."

Nora knew never to speak of Thomas Edison with Nikola. "So you think Dr. Appledore is trying to create something?"

"It does seem the case that your patron, with my invention, is considering ways to work with the water that is so plentiful here."

"You do not sound convinced. Do you think it's the wrong path?"

"It's not so much about the right or wrong path, Ms. Darling. It's about what you see along the way."

* * *

That afternoon, Nora made tea and brought it to the library, where Nikola was in deep discussion with Dr. Appledore. They had been there for hours.

As she approached, she heard raised voices. After she put the tea down on a side table, she tucked herself into a corner with a pen and notebook. Part of her job was to record all comments of note made by Orlando's guests, but, of course, especially by Orlando himself. Often when a guest was present, he would turn to her with an idea, yell it out, and then go back to his conversation. It was up to her to suss out what he'd meant and record it so he could go back to it later.

"If you are not going to take my advice, then why did you invite me here?" Nikola demanded.

"You are an expert in your field, but your conclusions here are invalid."

"My conclusions are invalid? Why, you sound just like Edison when he took my idea and made a million off it."

"Always with the Edison!" Orlando threw up his hands. "You well know that Edison's work is not applicable here."

"Ah, but if it were, you would have him."

"I will speak with any great mind who might help me on my quest."

"Traitor!" Nikola cried. Standing, he threw his glass onto the tile in front of the fireplace, where it shattered into thousands of sparkling pieces. When he stormed out he did not so much as glance at Nora. She watched as the back of his trim suit disappeared down the hall.

Orlando turned and his rheumy eyes focused on her. "There are no opposing sides in science, Nora Darling. Remember that. No sides, only truth." He used his cane to push himself to standing. "No sense wasting the day. Let us go now to the laboratory."

Nora put her pen and paper away, and then took his arm.

"I ought to remember," Orlando said as they puttered down the hall toward the door in the floor. "You ought to remind me how grating that man is, and how it distracts me from the real work to be done. That bit about the death ray? Honestly! A death ray. It is the exact inverse of my work, and yet he asked for my help. Can you fathom that? He wants to destroy life while I want to extend it."

"It does seem a rather strange direction for such a brilliant mind."

"Brilliant, mad, and bitter," Orlando said. "We'll have none of it!" They entered the small study at the back of the Water Castle. "What's this? Are you sad, child?"

"I did rather enjoy his company."

He smiled. "You oughtn't let that mustache cloud your judgment. I once had a mustache, you know. A fine one, too. It curled down to my chin."

Nora smiled at the thought of Dr. Appledore with a ridiculous mustache. She rolled back the carpet and lifted the trapdoor. Together they descended to the lab.

SIXTEEN

After class, Ephraim went into the bathroom and waited for the bell to ring. Once the halls were cleared, he snuck out a side door and made his way to the space capsule that was on display in front of the school. The capsule was shaped like one of the glass flasks they used in chemistry class: a cone-like bottom that narrowed up to a cylindrical spout.

He'd finally managed to talk to Mallory at the end of the period, telling her he knew about her past, and she, ashen, told him to meet her outside. She appeared a moment later. "Come on," she said. She pulled on a latch on the side of the capsule, and a door creaked open.

"We're going in there?" he asked. He wasn't sure if going

into a small confined space with someone who had potentially managed to live for at least a century was such a good idea.

She crawled in without answering. He had no choice but to follow her.

Any equipment or furnishing that had been in the capsule had been removed so it was just an empty vessel with the walls painted a pale blue. They crouched down on the cold metal ground, their knees nearly touching in the small space. Air came from their mouths in white puffs.

"So?" she asked.

"So," he replied.

She huffed. "You told me you needed to talk to me about something private and confidential, so here we are. Talk."

"How old are you?"

"Twelve. Why?"

"No, really. How old are you?"

She started to lift herself up. "You are crazy. Certifiable."

He put his hand on her arm to stop her. "I'm not going to tell anyone your secret. I just want to know how you did it. To help my dad."

She stopped and looked at him. He looked sincere, but you never could tell with people. That had been her experience anyway. "What are you talking about?"

He pulled the picture from his pocket and shoved it at her.

It only took her a moment to find herself. There were other black men, women, and boys, but only one girl. Her hair was plaited down close to her head, and she wore an old-fashioned dress and stained pinafore, but it looked just like her. There was an old man with a hand on her shoulder, and both were smiling broadly. Next to them was a boy who looked remarkably similar to Ephraim.

"Where did you get this?"

"In the house. Behind a wall board. With an empty bottle of radioactive water. I'm probably cancerous as we speak."

Her mind tried to make quick calculations, to determine what was actually happening. She studied the picture carefully. It was old and in shades of brown, and it felt like looking at one of those photographs you can get taken at amusement parks: there they were all dressed up in old-fashioned clothing. She scanned the rest of the people, but no one else looked familiar.

"Anyway," he said. "All I want to know is how you did it. How are you in that picture?"

"That's not me."

"Of course it's you."

"Next you're going to say that the boy is you."

"No. The boy just looks kind of like me." He had studied the picture and there were small differences between that boy and him: a longer nose, darker hair. "That girl looks exactly like you."

"It's probably some relative or something, so—" A low and terrible thought came to her. "Are you messing with me? Did Will put you up to this?"

"Will?"

"It's not funny, you know."

Ephraim leaned back and cracked his head against the metal wall. "Shoot!" he cried out, his voice echoing around the space capsule. "What is this thing, anyway? Why is it here?"

"I'm not really sure. Someone from the town who was an astronaut or something donated it. Listen, if you're messing with me, just tell me, okay? Just tell me and we'll forget about it."

"I'm not messing with you. Why would I be?"

Mallory turned away from him. "I don't know what's going on. I don't know who this person is."

"It's not just this. This whole town is weird. You have to tell me." His voice cracked on the last word. "If you've found a way to live—my dad really needs this. I need to help him."

She looked at the way his face crumpled.

"All I can tell you is what my parents told me." She unbuttoned her coat. "But they were just fairy tales. Myths. About your house, and your family, and my family. When I was little, I believed them. Everyone thought I was a nut job. I was the big joke around school." She kept her gaze on her hiking boots.

"So tell me the stories."

Mallory tugged on the laces of her boots. "Basically, the story goes that Crystal Springs has always been a magical place. The people that live here, live longer. They're smarter, stronger, faster."

Ephraim thought of his brother, who had set a pool record in his first time trial, and his sister, who had announced the night before that she had memorized the periodic table of the elements.

But not him. Coming from the city, he'd thought he'd be a

standout here in Crystal Springs. He was, but not as the sophisticated, smart star he had hoped—just the opposite, and in this town his averageness was thrown into high relief. Will's mind wrapped around scientific concepts like his brain was a microscope, instinctively seeing how each piece worked and fit together. Mallory's mind was quick as a mousetrap—and often as pinching. The other kids made being smart and successful appear so easy. Ephraim was the only one who seemed to struggle.

His father, too, remained a shell.

"Tell me everything," he said.

Mallory sighed and leaned back. "Your great-great-however-many-times-great-uncle Angus was obsessed with the idea of finding the Fountain of Youth. He traveled all over the world. Ethiopia, Florida, Bimini." Without meaning to, she smiled over the name Bimini, just as she had when her parents had told her the story. "Through years of searching he finally determined that it was right here in Crystal Springs. There've been these myths around Crystal Springs forever. The Passamaquoddy, those were the people that were here before everyone else, they used to bathe in the springs before they hunted. The legend is that if you drink it, it's not that it makes you immortal, but it slows your aging so much you might as well be. And if you're sick or hurt, it cures you."

"Any kind of sickness?" he asked.

She hesitated. She didn't want to feed him false hope. "That's the myth."

"Go on," he prompted.

"Well, so Angus decided to move here and have the house built. The Darlings, that's my mom's side of the family, they already lived here, and he hired them to build the house. No expense was spared. One winter, the river froze and so they sent all the granite down on ice barges."

"Get to the water part," he urged.

"I'm telling you the story the way I know it. If you don't want to hear it, I'm perfectly happy to go back inside."

"No, no," he said. "Tell it your way."

"My parents' way, actually. So he came over but on the way, his wife died. That's why he'd been looking for the Fountain of Youth, so he could be with her forever. When she died, he sort of lost interest in the whole thing. He actually forbade anyone to talk about the Fountain of Youth. But he kept my family on. They kept building the house. He was always coming up with ways to change it and add on. Sometimes they would build a wing one summer and tear it down the next. The Darlings also cooked and cleaned and took care of the kids. And I guess some of the women who took care of the kids told the stories of the fountain to them."

"Even though it was forbidden."

"Even though it was forbidden. It became a family legend. Every once in a while an Appledore would look in earnest, but none of them ever found it. Then along came Harold Appledore and he started bottling the water and selling it. He called it Dr. Appledore's Crystal Water even though he wasn't a doctor.

He never actually said it was the Fountain of Youth, but he said it gave people strength and vitality and all that. He built a resort, too. There used to be a whole hotel up there and everything."

Ephraim had seen the pictures around the house: the hotel grand and lit up for Christmas, a dance in the ballroom with men in tuxedoes and women in long elegant dresses, workers in starched white uniforms filling bottles of water, and a group of men soaking in a marble tub of the supposedly miraculous water.

"That water Harold Appledore sold, did it really make people healthier?"

"I don't know."

"Well, where did it come from?"

"I don't know that either. Springs, I guess. There was a fire at the hotel and spa. The bottling plant survived, but not the packaging building. Harold Appledore moved on to other things. He became a congressman. He ran for governor, too, but he didn't win. No one really talked about the water after that."

"When was the fire?"

"1909," she said.

Ephraim flipped over the picture, where the year 1909 was written. "That's a strange coincidence."

"Not really. It was the last year they would have had a huge staff like this."

"And there were no records of where the springs were? Nothing at all?" Desperation edged his voice.

"It's just a story, Ephraim."

"Except that maybe it isn't."

"It's just a story," she repeated.

"But what if it isn't?"

"So you're saying you believe in magic?"

Ephraim had never really formed an opinion on magic. It was something he'd read about in books, and that had been nice enough, but whether or not it actually existed in the real world, he'd never given it much thought. But stories always had some basis in truth, didn't they?

An idea was forming in Ephraim's mind the way a pearl formed in an oyster shell. A little sliver of an idea that was growing and shaping itself into something shiny and solid. If there was something magical about the house and this town, then that could explain everything strange that had happened since he arrived.

The more he thought about it, the truer it became.

Mallory handed the picture back to him. "For the record," Mallory said, picking up the picture, "that person looks much more like my mother than me. I don't have that dimple."

"Sure," Ephraim agreed without really thinking about it. There were magical springs somewhere in this town. He was going to find them, and they were going to save his father. If his father got better, then they could go home. He just had to figure out how. "So that's all you know?"

She wasn't sure what she knew, really. "Yeah."

A voice came from outside the capsule, tinny and bent: "There's more to the story."

Mallory pushed open to door, and there was Will. "What are you doing here?" she demanded.

"I followed you."

"What's the rest of the story?" Ephraim asked.

Will smirked.

"You're not funny, William Wylie," Mallory told him.

He stooped and came into the capsule with them.

He looked through lowered eyes at Ephraim. "Angus Appledore came here looking for water all right, but it wasn't some grand, organized search that brought him here. My family has been here for centuries. They knew about the water, and he came to steal it."

Mallory rolled her eyes. "Yes. I did leave that part out. The whole time the Appledores were looking for the water, the Wylies were trying to get in their way." She turned to Will. "If your family knew where the water was, why didn't they bottle it up? Why weren't they the ones with the hotel and the castle on the hill?"

This was a question Will had asked himself many times, but he didn't let it show. "Not everyone is interested in making money. Maybe my family didn't want to exploit the natural resource."

"Sure," Mallory said. "That sounds just like your family."

Will didn't want to admit the next part, not after what Mallory had just said, but he knew he had to tell them the whole truth. "Actually, at one point in time there was a Wylie who wanted to sell the water and have a resort of our own. We used to own land from my house right up to Crystal Lake. But then there was the fire at the Appledores' and everyone blamed our family, so I guess the person decided not to do it after all."

Mallory gave Ephraim a meaningful glance.

"So that just proves that we didn't start the fire. If there hadn't been a fire, we could have sold the water, too."

"So who set the fire?" Mallory asked.

"I don't know. Maybe the Appledores started the fire themselves. The point is, the people in my family, they really believed in the water. They might have been foolish, but they weren't lying. Harold Appledore, he was nothing more than a charlatan."

"A what?" Ephraim asked.

"He sold people something that didn't work to solve a problem they didn't really have."

Mallory felt her back bristle. True, she also believed that the whole story was a lie, but hearing someone else tear down her parents' stories twisted her insides.

"His water was nothing special. Just healthy spring water that was way better for people than the dirty stuff they were getting in cities, so of course they seemed to be healthier when they drank it. Harold Appledore knew it was a sham, but he didn't care. He told a story that he didn't believe just to make money. He built his hotel around the magic and mystery."

"I already said that," Mallory said.

"But you didn't say anything about the tunnels." He turned to Ephraim. "That's where the water came from. He had this whole series of tunnels underneath the different buildings of the resort so no one would see that the water actually came from the lake."

"Really?" Ephraim asked.

"I can show you," Will said.

"They're still there?" Ephraim asked.

"After the hotel burned, they stopped bottling water, but they left the tunnels. And the tunnels go right down to Crystal Lake. There never was a spring. He just took the water from the lake and carried it up to the house. Not him personally, of course." He glanced at Mallory.

"That's totally ridiculous," Mallory said.

"I thought you didn't believe the story," Will said.

"I don't. It's just a story. But if you're going to tell it, you'd better tell it right."

Will shrugged as if none of it mattered to him one way or the other. But then he said, "Meet me after school. I'll show you."

After an exchanged glance, Mallory and Ephraim agreed. It wasn't like they could say no.

SEVENTEEN

After school, Ephraim and Mallory met Will by the space capsule, and he led them down a path through the forest away from the school. He had his bike with him, pushing it along beside them as they walked.

"It's down by the lake, sort of. At least that's the entrance I know about. I bet there are hundreds of them, all over town," he said.

Mallory scoffed but didn't say anything. Why hadn't her parents ever told her about the tunnels? Was it possible they didn't know about them? Or maybe they were trying to keep her from finding out something. She chewed her lip.

"Why did they need so many if they were just getting water?" Ephraim asked.

Will looked back over his shoulder. "They were paranoid."

Ephraim thought of the blueprints and the strange lines on them. There could be miles and miles of tunnels crisscrossing the town. And he thought of what wasn't on the blueprints: the entire floor where Price's room was and the impossibly interlocking rooms. It seemed like this family—his family—liked to make things complicated and elaborate.

They walked for what felt like miles to Ephraim until the lake shimmered in front of them. Will stopped and looked around, then nodded his head and went toward a willow tree that bent over the water from a small rise on the edge of the pond. He swept aside the willow's branches and stepped under. It was cool and damp, smelling of old rotted leaves. He bent over and pushed on the ground until suddenly his hand seemed to be swallowed up by the earth. "Here we go," he said, and spread his arms wide, revealing a small hole.

Will crawled in first, then Ephraim, then Mallory, who still wasn't sure about the whole escapade.

The ground was soft and wet against Ephraim's hands and knees and he couldn't see anything. Sounds seemed muffled, too, and time slowed down. There was a clicking noise followed by a tiny light. Will's face was almost visible behind it. He retrieved a large flashlight and turned it on, which still only provided scant illumination. It was enough, though, for them to begin walking. As they did, the tunnel expanded, and soon they could all walk standing up, side by side.

"How did you find this?" Ephraim asked.

"My dad was always telling me these stories. About the Appledores and the water and the tunnels."

Mallory shivered. She wasn't used to anyone else being the child of storytellers, and certainly not to hearing twisted versions of her own stories.

"And we spent a lot of time at the lake, so I guess I was just always looking for it. One day I thought about it and asked myself, if I were going to hide a tunnel, where would I hide it. Under the willows seemed to make the most sense. So I started looking, and then I found one with a big hole under it—it wasn't all covered up then."

"So you covered it?" Mallory asked.

"Yeah."

"Why?"

"Don't know. I just did." He scratched his chin.

"Did you ever find the springs?" Ephraim asked.

"There are no springs," Will said.

"Did you look for them?"

Will shook his head. "I just follow this one path nice and straight. I figured if my dad's stories had been kind of right, they could be all the way right, and if these tunnels went back and forth and round and round, well, I didn't want to be caught up in them. So I went straight and straight and straight and then the tunnel started to go up, and then there was a door, and when I pushed it open it was a trapdoor up into this cold, dark room, totally covered with leaves. There was another door and it was bright sunshine. You've never felt anything like that on your eyes, from this dark to that sun. And then I turned around and there was your house. I looked on a map. Three miles."

Being in the dark seemed to turn a switch in Will that made him talk like he never had before, and neither Ephraim nor Mallory was quite sure what to make of it.

He shone the light on the side walls, which had ropes running along them, thick and heavy. "I figure this was how they got the water into the hotel," he said, and pointed out a large wheel. "It's a pulley system. They must have hooked buckets on it and dragged them back."

"We should be listening for running water," Ephraim said. He ran his hand along the wall, which was damp, but not flowing as he imagined a spring would be.

The air felt heavy enough to separate them, so they walked in silence, each with their own thoughts and ideas.

Ephraim thought about his father, alone and still in his bed. He thought of his mother's face, which seemed so pale and fragile now. The Fountain of Youth had to be real. It had to be. It was the only way he could save his father. He watched Mallory's back as she walked in front of him. That she could be the same girl as in the picture seemed implausible, but much of Crystal Springs seemed to be implausible. His brother setting records in a sport he had never tried before. His sister, always brilliant, seeming to grow smarter by the second. He was certain that something strange was going on here, and that the cure for his father was somewhere down here in the dank of the tunnels.

Will thought of his father's stories. How everything that had ever gone wrong for the Wylies was the fault of the Appledores. Now here he was in an underground tunnel chasing after a myth with the son of that family. His father would never forgive him if he knew.

Mallory wondered about generations past from her family who had walked these tunnels, hauling water for the Appledores and their hotel. They must have hated being underground all day. She wondered, too, if her parents knew about these tunnels, and how they might have wound them into their stories if they had—or why they had left them out.

"Just a little farther," Will said.

They walked on and soon, just as he described, came to a door. When they opened it they were in a marble room. The floor and the counters, all of it, was silvery-white and glowed like the moon. Empty iron light fixtures hung from the walls. Around the edges of the room were contraptions that Ephraim didn't recognize. They looked almost like barbecue grills, but instead of a grate, each had a grid of square slots. The windows were mostly grown over with ivy, but through them, he could see his new home.

"This was the bottling house," Will said. "They said the water was piped in from the springs but, well, you saw where we came from."

"It seems like a lot of work to haul the water from the lake," Ephraim said.

"Not for the Appledores," Mallory replied.

Ephraim glanced at her, trying to read the malice in her voice. "So they hauled the water up from the lake. So that means the lake is the source? The Fountain of Youth?"

"There is no Fountain of Youth," Will said. "It's a myth. You know, as in not true."

Mallory was more patient. "If it really were here, that's not it. We aren't all living forever in this town, and everyone swims in Crystal Lake. This was just where they got the water for the bottling and the hotel."

"To scam the people," Will added.

Ephraim ignored him. "So we haven't proven that the magical springs *don't* exist yet?" he asked.

"Just listen to yourself, would you? Magical springs? Come on, are you still six or what?"

Will's teasing echoed the way kids had picked on Mallory, and stung almost as much. "Ephraim, it's just a story. We aren't going to find any magical springs. We aren't going to find any magical anything. It's impossible."

Impossible, Ephraim thought, until they found it.

EIGHTEEN

When they came out of the door of the building, stone animals surrounded them. The sculptures towered over them, as if the children had been shrunk or wandered into an alternate world where everything was oversized. Some of the sculptures were grown over with lichen, and almost seemed to glow a green-silver in the afternoon light.

"Holy cow," Ephraim said. "This is amazing."

"You haven't been out here yet?" Will asked.

Ephraim shook his head. Most of his exploring had been inside the house as, in general, he preferred the indoors to the outdoors.

"My parents used to bring me out here," Mallory said. "They

said that Angus Appledore had all of these built after his wife died. She was fond of mythical animals, I guess."

"That's kind of creepy," Ephraim said. "Let's say instead that he had them built for the kids to play around since he wasn't really there for them. That's a nicer story."

Mallory shrugged. She was all too familiar with people making up stories so that real life was easier to deal with. "We'd play freeze tag and you'd have to freeze like the sculpture near you."

Will grinned, then reached out his large hand, tapped Ephraim on the back, and said, "You're it!"

Ephraim hated tag, ever since he'd stopped being able to catch Price. Mallory took off in one direction, and Will in another. Ephraim laced around the sculptures after them. He came close to Mallory and she stopped, holding her arms out like wings and pressing her neck forward. "I'm a griffin!" she called out. He looked up at the sculpture above her, which had its beak open as if it were about to snatch up its prey.

Ephraim turned in the other direction. He saw a flash that was Will and he snuck up behind him. Just as he was about to tag him, Will held a finger up on his forehead and made a sort of prancing pose. "I'm a unicorn."

Ephraim couldn't help but laugh at giant Will trying to be a graceful unicorn. "If you're a unicorn," he said, "I'm a Pegasus."

Will laughed, too, but didn't come out of his unicorn shape, so Ephraim went in search of Mallory. He thought of playing games like this with Price when he was younger. There was a time when he'd been able to keep up with Price, or when Price had let him stay close, but no longer. And now he seemed so much faster, so much older. Without hesitation Price had stepped into their father's place, looking out for Brynn, especially, while Ephraim kept messing up again and again.

He heard a thunk and turned around. There was Mallory, just feet away. If he lunged, he could tag her. Her eyes grew wide and she looked up at the sculpture above her. She was contorting herself into a gargoyle, when Ephraim tagged her. "Mallory's it!" he cried.

"I'll give you ten seconds to get away," she declared, and Ephraim was off racing through the park. The sculptures were in concentric circles that got tighter and tighter. Ephraim, Will, and Mallory snaked around them. Their laughter rang up to the sky. It was such a change from the cold, dark tunnels to be out in the sun in this strange and magical place.

Will found the base of a sculpture with no animal. He scrambled up and held his arms out. "Look. I'm a sculpture! I'm the Will-de-bird!"

Mallory laughed. Then she reached up and grabbed the arm of a nearby lion mixed with a scorpion. She lifted her feet so she hung from its paw. "I'm the Malbatross!"

Ephraim smiled at them, at the strange faces they were making.

"Your turn, Ephraim," Mallory called as she let herself drop down to the ground.

He felt himself start to redden. Creativity was another thing that was not his strong suit. "I guess I'm a, a—" He took a big step forward and leaned over his knee.

"You're Ephrasiastic," Will said. "Determined even in the face of obvious defeat. Like a dog."

"Ha-ha," Ephraim said. "What's your power, Will-de-bird, doubt and sarcasm?"

"Those are just bonuses," Will said. "My gift is extreme intelligence, outside the realm of human comprehension. The Will-de-bird absorbs information through the air as he flies."

"You might think you know everything, Will-de-bird, but the Malbatross can tell truth from fiction without fail."

"But she's cursed because no one will believe her."

Mallory blinked: what he'd said was like the inverse of the truth. For so long she had mixed up fact and fiction, believing her parents' silly stories, and everyone thought she was crazy. Now she saw the truth about her parents' tales, and along came Ephraim so eager to believe them.

"Wouldn't it be great if we actually had magical powers?" Ephraim asked.

"I'd fly right out of here," Mallory said.

"I'd absorb all the world's knowledge and put it to good use."

"I'd fix my dad."

They walked on silently, each lost in thoughts of the things they really wanted. They were coming to the center of the circle now. Will laughed and said, "Hey look, here it is, Eph, your Fountain of Youth."

At the center of the circle was an old stone fountain grown over with ivy and moss. Standing on top was an angel. Not a chubby Valentine's Day cherub, or a beautiful woman in a long flowing dress. This was an avenging angel. He wore knee-high boots with a knife tucked into the laces of one, and he held a sword out in front of him. With the water bubbling out of the fountain, it would have looked like he was standing above it, floating in the water.

Now though, only a thin stream of green water trickled down below his feet.

"I wish," Ephraim said. And he really, really did. But maybe that's all it was. Maybe they were right and his wishes were foolish, as foolish as the idea that they were each some kind of mythical creature. Maybe it was time for him to just give up the fantasy.

Will jumped up onto the edge of the fountain. "I declare the discovery of the Fountain of Youth!" he proclaimed. "The Fountain of Youth has been discovered in the name of Frederick Cook!"

"No!" Mallory cried as she jumped up as well. "In the name of Matthew Henson!"

"Fie!" Ephraim yelled. It was the first old-fashioned word that came to his mind. "The Fountain of Youth is hereby the discovery of one Robert Peary!"

They each struggled to keep their footing atop the crumbling fountain.

Mallory looked from one of them to the other. "It kind of seems silly, doesn't it?"

"What do you mean?" Will asked as he sat down on the edge of the fountain.

"Maybe it doesn't matter who was first," she said.

"I'm pretty sure it mattered to Peary and Cook," Will said.

"No, I think I see what you mean," Ephraim said. "I guess they were so caught up in finding it, the reasons they were looking kind of got lost. It's like this water. Everyone wanted to use it for their own purposes. My family was trying to sell it. Your family wanted to sell it, too, and they burned down our hotel since we wouldn't share—"

"We didn't burn down your hotel," Will said.

Ephraim waved his hand. "The point is, if they'd just found the water for real, and shared what they found, think how much better everything would be now. We wouldn't have to worry about cancer or strokes or anything."

"Except for that the world would be totally overpopulated and we wouldn't have enough resources for all the people," Will replied.

Ephraim scratched at some moss on the edge of the fountain. "It just seems like instead of racing or fighting each other, if they had just, you know, worked together, then maybe everyone could have found what they wanted."

"You're right," Will said, and Ephraim and Mallory both

looked at him with surprise. "Why don't we all do our project together?"

"What, like a debate?" Mallory asked.

"Sure," Will said.

"Or maybe we tell all of the stories and how each one could possibly be right—how each one *is* right," Ephraim suggested.

"You're talking about settling a century-old controversy here, Ephraim," Mallory said.

"I know. Don't you think it's about time?"

Will patted him on the back. "I like it," he said, and he reached out to shake Ephraim's hand. Mallory stuck hers out, too, and they held them together like the spokes of a wheel, ready to get rolling in a brand-new direction.

December 22, 1908

Nora sat outside wrapped in her overcoat, reading *Franken-stein,* a book her mother had sent over with her brother Little John. She usually only came to this spot in the warm months, but Orlando, who was perpetually cold, had a fire burning in the library, and the air had been so warm and dry she felt as if she were suffocating. So she'd decided to take her book outside. They read literature for half an hour each day. Orlando said it was important for scientists to have minds kept open by litera-ture, and souls touched by the creativity of art. "It is impor-tant to remember not only the what but the why of what you are seeking."

Nora turned another page. Dr. Frankenstein had just awak-ened to find his creation staring down at him. A snapping twig made her lift her head; the hairs on her neck stood up. She heard feet stomping though the dry leaves. No one ever came to this part of the property. Not the Appledores, who thought the twisted roots and silver green moss on the rocks were ugly. And of course the hotel guests never ventured so far. A moment later, Harry emerged. He grinned when he saw her, and she grinned in return. In their letters back and forth they had tracked Peary and Henson's progress as best they could, and discussed issues such as what shaped sledge was best for going over the ice, and whether or not they could stomach whale meat. It hardly seemed like they had not seen each other for months.

"It must be quite the story if it requires you reading it so far from civilization."

She closed the book, somehow embarrassed by her choice. "I needed fresh air," she said. "I see you've returned safely from school. How was your semester?"

Harry shrugged and sat down on the rock next to her. "My Latin teacher is evil incarnate," he said. "Perhaps I should have stayed with the other boys in my form instead of skipping ahead."

Harry was ahead of most of his classmates. This was a position that Nora had relished, but it made Harry uncomfortable. He would have rather faded into the background, alone with his books and his maps, allowed to draw his diagrams of automated machines without interruption.

"And life here in Crystal Springs?" he asked. He looked down the hill and toward the fields.

"If it were not for your uncle, I should die of boredom."

"You exaggerate," he said.

"Not at all. Once your uncle and I are successful, I shall leave this place and travel the world over. Dr. Appledore says he will buy me a steamer trunk and an around-the-world ticket."

"I see," Harry said.

"You could come with me," Nora said. Blushing, she hastened to add, "That is, you could also take a trip after you finish school. Is that not customary?"

"I will be happy to return home," he said. "Once and for all." They were silent for a moment, the air around them cold and crackling. "Though if I were to travel round the world, I warrant you would make a fine companion." He regarded her for a moment, and she did not look away.

"If we were to travel to the Arctic, you would surely be the one I chose to go on the expedition with me."

"I wish we could leave right now," Nora said with a sigh. "Though at this time of year there is no daylight."

"I would not mind that. I can just imagine the ice all lit silver by the moon. I love the way the world looks in moonlight." They both sat still for a moment, imagining the crystal stillness of the Arctic at night. It was Harry who spoke first. "I have something to show you." From his bag he pulled a wooden contraption: a thick center with a thinner cross-piece and a small, round bit of metal with hash marks on it, connecting them. "It's a theodolite. Just like the one Peary uses."

Nora was not quite sure what a theodolite was, but didn't want to admit any gap of knowledge on the Henson-Peary expedition. "It's nice. Where'd you get it?"

"My father." He held the device up to his eye. "He's a member of the Peary Arctic Club. They helped to fund the expedition and whatnot."

He said it so quickly Nora couldn't quite believe what she had heard. "But that's wonderful! Do you think that you will meet them when they return?" A more exciting idea was forming in her mind. "Will they come here? Your father should invite them to the hotel. What an honor that would be!"

"Perhaps," he said, not eager to engage in this subject. "My father says he sent along cases of Dr. Appledore's Crystal Water. He's running an advertisement that it's the water that will help you complete any expedition—just like Peary!" His voice went up with false enthusiasm. They both knew that the glass bottles would shatter in the temperatures more than forty degrees below zero.

"So, let's have a look," she said.

"I haven't yet figured out how to use this. I know it's supposed to measure angles and distances, but I cannot fathom how to do so, or how to use it for mapping. Do you have any sense of it?"

"Well," Nora said, trying to sound confident. "I've never actually held one, of course, but it seems a fairly straightforward device, the theodolite. From what I've read, that is."

Harry handed her the theodolite, and she held it up, trying to figure it out. They took turns passing it back and forth and looking at the distant mountains. "What would you say, do you think, if you were the first to reach the Pole?" Nora asked.

Harry cocked his head to the side and gave the question careful consideration. "To be honest, I fear I wouldn't have words. It would be too spectacular, and I've never excelled at putting the right words to things."

"I would say, 'I behold the Pole, and now all shall behold me!'"

Harry laughed. Then he held the theodolite up again. "It really is a useless tool unless we know how to use it. Shall we ask Uncle Orlando?"

The two walked down a hill and then around the property to the side door of the Water Castle. Dr. Appledore was still in the library, dozing on a chair. "I told him the fire was too warm," Nora said. She crossed the room and put her hand on his shoulder. "Dr. Appledore?"

He blinked his ruddy eyes open and took a moment to focus on them and recall who they were. "I was composing in my head," he said, "a proof that would awe Newton himself. We cannot overlook the mathematical as we grow our minds. Is our respite already over?"

It was over by nearly a half an hour. "What do you know of theodolites, Uncle Orlando?"

"What do I know of theodolites? You may as well ask what I know of chemistry or what I know of literature. In short, I know all there is to know and not nearly all I need."

"Can you show us how to use it?" Nora asked. Harry held out the tool. Dr. Appledore took it and examined it from all sides. "Why, this is not a typical theodolite. It is one used for expeditioning."

"It's the same type Peary uses," Harry said.

Dr. Appledore slapped his forehead. "Not another young person taken by Arctic fever!" He held the theodolite up to his eye, just as they had. "You see, this is like a protractor," he said, pointing to the metal piece. "And that is how you measure the angle. As for measuring distance, that is a trickier scenario."

They watched him as he held the theodolite first close then far away, turning it round and round.

"Do you know what we need to solve this problem? Licorice. Run to town and pick us up a bag."

Nora's face brightened. She loved candy of all types, but particularly licorice. Orlando loved it, too, but rarely indulged. "What of your diet?"

"Healthfulness will matter less once we find the fountain. I imagine that a strip or two won't harm me. On second thought, why don't we all go? The fresh air will be good for me. Call around for the carriage."

Nora went out to the stables and found her older brother, Solomon, and asked him to bring the small, closed carriage around to the front of the house. They were going to town.

"Well, aren't you the fancy miss?" he asked.

"We are getting licorice," she boasted.

He sniffed. "None for me?"

"Perhaps yes, perhaps no," she replied. She lifted herself up onto a stall door and kicked her feet against it.

"Perhaps I'll toss you into the lake again," Solomon said as he hitched the horse to the carriage.

"Perhaps I've grown too big for you to do so."

"Have you now?" With a grin, he grabbed her around the waist and tossed her into the carriage.

"Solomon!" she cried, sitting up and smoothing out her

dress. She yanked the door closed, then poked her head out the window to say, "You've surely lost any chance at licorice now."

He laughed and drove the carriage up to the door, where Harry and Dr. Appledore were waiting.

For the bumpy ride down, Orlando spoke of his theories about natural philosophy while Nora stared out the window. The carriage ride made her feel a little queasy, and she would much prefer to walk. She imagined that Harry felt the same way.

"Of course in Peary's case he is searching for something that is an end in itself. No new knowledge will come of it."

Nora snapped her attention back to Orlando.

"But he has already gathered so much information on his previous expeditions. Who knows what else he shall find along the way?" Harry asked.

"He is going to map a place that no one has been," Nora added.

"No one has been because there is nothing there of matter," Orlando replied. "It is a journey for the journey's sake, which is not a bad thing in and of itself, and of course we come from a long line of explorers. But they always sought something in the lands they explored."

"Like the fountain," Harry said.

"Precisely. So far as anyone expects, they will find nothing at the Pole but ice and snow."

"They cannot know until they arrive. Perhaps the fountain is right there at the Pole," Nora said, thinking of Nikola's joke.

Orlando gave this some thought. "I will not rule anything

out as impossible, since nothing is ever impossible, but I would call that hypothesis highly improbable."

The carriage jostled to a stop in front of the Wylie's Five and Dime, and the three alighted. A garland of pine boughs hung above the door, and there was a red ribbon on each window. Nora stood by the carriage to wait for them. Harry went first and held the door open for his uncle, and then for her. "Come on, now, Nora, you're letting in the cold."

Nora hesitated. She was not welcome in the store; Mrs. Wylie had said so explicitly. Harry beckoned her from the doorway. She took a deep breath and crossed the threshold.

She did not know what she had expected. Perhaps for the whole place to be sparkling with silver and gold. Perhaps for the ground to fall away beneath her feet. What she saw was nothing but a plain store. There were bins of goods, stacks of fabric, sacks of flour. A glass counter held all the candy and Dr. Appledore was standing in front of it, contemplating his choices.

At the register, Mrs. Wylie stood, her chin jutted forward, staring down her nose at Nora. Nora felt another set of eyes boring into her from behind, and she turned to see Winnie glaring at her. She walked up closer to Dr. Appledore, who was selecting his licorice. The whole place was silent except for Orlando pointing out precisely which strings he wanted. She even heard the clock, ticking away the seconds, each one following impossibly long after the other.

"It's a lovely day we're having, isn't it?" Dr. Appledore asked.

"Yes, sir," Mrs. Wylie replied. "A mite on the cold side, though."

"I thought it would be a treat to bring the children down for candy."

Mrs. Wylie flicked her gaze past Dr. Appledore to Nora, whose hand was in a bin of pencils. Mrs. Wylie sneered and it made Nora so angry she wanted to snap all of the pencils in half and then stomp on them for good measure.

"I suppose that ought to be enough for us," Dr. Appledore said.

"Yes, sir." She pinched closed the paper bag. Nora thought of how Winnie had insulted Dr. Appledore, and knew that Mrs. Wylie must feel the same way about him. She did not understand why Mrs. Wylie was being polite to someone she held in such disregard.

Dr. Appledore paid for the candy, counting out each coin from his pocket. He held the last penny above her hand, which quaked with anger, cupped below his, ready to receive it. His face lit up as if something had just occurred to him. "I understand we share a passion."

"Excuse me, sir?"

"The fountain?" he prompted.

Her face darkened.

"In the end it seems you did not find what you thought you had after all. So we both press on. I wish you the best of luck."

Mrs. Wylie did not reply, and Dr. Appledore, Harry, and

Nora all marched back to the carriage. Once inside, Dr. Appledore gave them each a long string of licorice. Nora looked out the window to the glassed front of the five-and-dime. Mrs. Wylie still stood behind the counter, glaring at the carriage. Winnie was at the window, her face pressed against it and twisted into a menacing sneer.

Nora took a bite of her licorice, and then decided she would give it to Solomon. It didn't taste as good as she remembered.

NINETEEN

It was, of course, not dignified to hide in the closet, and Mallory was ashamed of herself. But her mother was downstairs, talking to her father, and gathering more of her belongings to take away from their home to whatever place she had rented.

It had been such a good afternoon, in a strange way. She'd found she actually liked spending time with Will and Ephraim, playing that silly game of tag she'd played with her parents. She'd come home smiling and ready to tell her dad that maybe it was going to be okay and he really didn't need to worry so much about her anymore. Then she saw the Volkswagen Rabbit in the driveway.

She'd snuck in the back door and up the narrow stairs from the kitchen to the second floor. From there she'd gone to the landing of the main stairs, where she could spy on her mother. Everything about her looked the same as it always did. Her hair sprang up around her head in tight little cords, she wore sneakers with her jeans, and around her neck hung the same necklace she'd worn all of Mallory's life: a little copper key on a silver chain. It was not comforting, though, all this sameness. Instead it seemed to highlight just how wrong things were. Her mother's departure had upended Mallory's world, but it hadn't seemed to have affected her mother at all.

The retrieval of her mother's belongings from the family house was a slow, twisting process. When she had first left she took her clothes, her toothbrush, and a bag of shoes. She'd come back a week or so after that for a coat, her tennis racket, and the French press coffeemaker. That had been in August, and Mallory had tried to imagine where she was going where she might make coffee *and* want to play tennis.

Now she was back for big things, it seemed. They were negotiating furniture and the record player downstairs. Photo albums and souvenirs.

They were not negotiating her.

She reached her arm out of the closet and found an old science book in which she'd begun a picture of a leaf, drawing each vein of its skin. The book was over one hundred years old, and perhaps valuable. The vandalism of it made her feel good, though it was just a sour little secret. She kept working at the drawing. She frayed the edges the way leaves did in the fall, and added a small hole poked out by a stick, perhaps, or chewed by some animal.

Below her the voices rose and fell, breaking the silence of her home with her father. She wished they would just draw a line down the center of the house, dividing it in two, his and hers. The problem was, she didn't know which side she would be on.

Her mother's voice swept up the stairs, but Mallory couldn't make out the words.

"I didn't want to spend eternity with anyone," was her father's reply. "This wasn't my choice."

"But you did choose."

"I chose you, Eleanor. I chose you."

As the voices rose and got sharper downstairs, she knew she couldn't stay inside. Holding her breath so she didn't make any sound at all, she slinked down the back stairs. She paused in the kitchen.

"That was so long ago. Ages ago," her mother said.

"Time doesn't matter so much anymore, does it?"

"Time is all that has ever mattered."

Her father was silent. There was a soft stacking sound as her mother placed her favorite records—Billie Holiday, Etta James, Chuck Berry—into a box.

"We agreed to stop until Mallory was older. You can't do this to her, Eleanor. You can't just leave. I knew what I was getting into, but Mallory—"

"Don't," her mother said.

And Mallory agreed. She didn't want to hear her parents talking about her. She slipped outside and made her way around the house to the old VW bus. After brushing dried leaves from the front passenger's seat, the only seat that remained, she sat down and looked over the moonlit expanse of their yard, up to the black tar of the road.

She used to play in the van with her mother and father. It was where she always hid when they played hide-and-seek, and still they always pretended to search for her elsewhere. It wasn't until Becky Crosby came over in second grade and found her straight off that she realized it wasn't the best hiding place after all.

She remembered one afternoon back when there were still seats in the van. She and her mother had lain across one of the back benches, her father in the other. They looked up at the sagging fabric on the ceiling, and her parents listed off all of the places they would travel to. "Italy, Greece, Malta," her mother had said.

"England, New Zealand," her father added.

"Alaska," she had offered.

"Alaska," her mother had agreed. "There's nothing like seeing the moon over white ice. Ice for miles."

A warm summer breeze passed through the open sides of the van. She could almost feel it on that cool fall evening, but on the inside, she was still shivering.

The front door opened and her mother came out. She stood on the porch with one hand on her hip, the other on top of her hair. She had a scarf around her head, one that Mallory had given her, and Mallory wished that she could rip it off her mother's head and tear it to pieces. She balled her fists until they hurt. Her mother scanned the area as if looking for her, but if her mother really knew her, she'd be able to find Mallory just as easily as Becky Crosby had.

Instead she bent over and picked up the cardboard box she had packed. Out of the top poked an old lava lamp and a ceramic moose Mallory had made in art class. Mallory started to lean out of the van to protest—that was *her* moose—but pulled herself back in like a turtle into its shell. It took a few tries before the engine of her mother's car turned over, but then she was on her way without even a glance in the rearview mirror.

TWENTY

Brynn appeared in the doorway to Ephraim's room like a ghost. He was lying across the bed, struggling through some earth science work. He needed to be prepared for their next lab on electromagnetism. He was tired of letting Will do all the work, especially now that Will actually seemed like a decent guy. The problem was that all the numbers and facts swirled in front of his eyes. All he cared about proving was whether or not the Fountain of Youth existed. All he could think about was saving his father.

So he welcomed the interruption that Brynn offered. "Everything okay?" he asked her.

"I've been thinking about everything we found," Brynn

said, standing on one foot on the threshold. Her other foot was bent to her knee so she looked like a frail, blond crane.

Ephraim bit his lip and wondered if he should tell her about the tunnels below the ground. She would want to explore them. With the maps, maybe they could find their way without getting lost.

"I've read through everything I could find in the library. Nothing explains the light on the house, or the way the house is built, or that picture of Mallory. The only thing we have is that reference to the Fountain of Youth that you found."

"Would radioactivity matter?" he asked, and reminded her what happened in class with Ms. Little and the Geiger counter. "I had the highest rating of anyone."

Brynn sucked on her lower lip. "I'm not sure. We need to talk to Dad."

Their dad, Ephraim knew, could not talk to them. He could not talk at all. The words stayed locked inside where even he himself could not reach them.

"I'm not sure that's the best idea," he said.

"He knows about these sorts of things," she said. "Mom's too practical. She'll try to come up with a reasonable explanation."

"Aren't you trying to come up with a reasonable explanation?" he asked.

"Just because it's reasonable doesn't mean it can't be strange."

He really didn't want to talk to his mother, but most of all he wanted to avoid going into that dark bedroom where his father sat still as stone, breathing, but not really alive.

"Let's just ask him," Brynn said, and reached out her hand.

"Ask him what?"

"About all of it."

Her eyes were wide and dark and he found he couldn't think of a reason to say no to her. Ephraim climbed down from the bed and took her small, warm hand in his.

It won't be that bad, he told himself. We'll go in, she'll explain what's going on, and then he won't say anything, and we'll leave.

Still, his heart beat faster with each step they took, and he felt his stomach twisting with guilt and fear.

When they got into the room, Dr. Winters was there. He moved their father's limbs and then made notes on his pad of paper. He might as well have been moving a doll or a machine for all that their father reacted.

"This is a bad idea," Ephraim whispered to Brynn.

Dr. Winters looked up. "Oh, hello there, Brynn and—" He paused. "Ethan."

"Ephraim."

"Right," Dr. Winters said. "Just finishing up here. We're making great progress, aren't we, Ben?"

Their father didn't reply.

Ephraim looked at Brynn and shook his head, but she stood firm and resolute.

Dr. Winters put his things away and nodded to them on his way out of the room.

"Okay," Brynn said. "Let's go." She pulled a small chair right up next to the bed. Ephraim stayed back by the wall. Their father was propped up with pillows. The covers were pulled up to his waist, and then turned back so that a perfect strip of sheet was revealed. His hands were folded in his lap.

"Hi, Dad. It's me, Brynn. Ephraim's here, too. We have some things we want to ask you about. First of all, have you noticed the way the house hums and sometimes glows blue?"

Ephraim wished that she hadn't jumped right into the heart of things. In the end, it didn't really matter. Their dad's eyes moved from side to side as if he were reading. His fingers twitched on the bedcovers. That was it.

"Plus Ephraim says that there's a high level of radioactivity here. We found a bottle for radioactive water, but I don't think that's enough to change the ratings. And then we found this picture and there's a girl in it that looks just like Mallory Green, but it's over a hundred years old."

"She says it's not her," Ephraim interjected.

Their dad made no response.

"I think there could be some sort of scientific explanation." She tucked her hair behind her ear and waited for an answer that did not come.

"Brynn," Ephraim whispered. His whole body was getting hotter and hotter as if he had a sudden fever.

She pretended not to hear him. "Of course I'm not going to rule out anything mystical, but you said that most magical things can be explained. Like how you told me how a rainbow worked and how you could never really find the end of it, so that's why people could say there was a pot of gold there."

Ephraim jammed his hands into his pockets. He, too, had received this lesson. His father had taught each of them about refraction, sitting on the beach watching the sunset. "The sun's already gone," he explained. "We're seeing the light as it bends toward us." His dad had grinned widely, so pleased that nature played tricks. He'd wrapped his arm around Ephraim and tugged him close to his body, as if sensing that for Eprhaim, knowing that the sun wasn't really there only made him sad.

His dad's hands sat limply one over the other, just where Dr. Winters had put them. Ephraim tensed his jaw.

"Anyway, I know that you took some pretty big science classes in college, so I thought maybe you might have some ideas." She reached out and put her hand on top of their father's.

Ephraim's hand shot out and grabbed Brynn by the shoulder, pulling her back and tilting the chair up. "Stop it," he hissed.

"What?" she asked.

She blinked her wide eyes at him, but he couldn't stop himself. His voice rose. "Just stop it. He can't answer you. He doesn't understand."

"He does—" Brynn began.

"He doesn't. He can't." His hand was still on her shoulder. He saw it there and saw how hard he was gripping her, and, shamefully, he let it go. With his voice low, he said, "He can't do anything. He can't feed himself. He can't read a book. He can't paint. He can't even go to the bathroom by himself. So don't expect him to explain anything to you."

"Stop," Brynn said.

"You stop. Stop fooling yourself."

"He's in there! He can hear you."

"He can't. He can't," Ephraim cried, shaking his head. "Just leave him alone, okay? Just leave him be!"

Brynn stood and ran from the room, leaving Ephraim alone with his father. He sat down in the chair that Brynn had vacated. He felt small and mean when he thought about how he'd treated her. He wasn't sure if Brynn was right, if, somewhere deep inside, their father was there and could see and hear them.

That's when he realized his father was watching him. He moved his lips like he was working a cherry pit in his mouth, but no words came out.

Ephraim's heart sped up. "Are you there?" he asked.

His father's eyes ached with sadness, and Ephraim felt certain that he had watched the whole scene that had just played out. That he had heard and understood every word.

"It's okay, Dad. I'm going to save you."

TWENTY-ONE

After Mallory's mother left, the little diesel Rabbit hatchback chug chug chugging along, her dad stood on the porch, in silhouette, watching the car disappear around the bend in the road. He would be thinking, Mallory knew, about what was causing the car to make that high-pitched whine, and how he could fix it. But it wasn't his responsibility anymore.

He'd stayed on the porch for at least ten minutes after the car was gone. Then he walked down the path toward the Volkswagen bus and poked his head in. She should have known he knew exactly where she was.

"I'm running into town," he said.

Mallory stayed stretched out on the seat. "All right."

"You going to be okay?"

She hesitated, thinking that she could ask him the same question. "Yes."

"I won't be long," he promised.

"Okay."

"I love you," he said, and stared at her with his bright green eyes.

She turned her head so her cheek was against the vinyl of the seat and looked down at the leaves that shivered on the floor of the bus. "I love you, too."

After he left, Mallory stared at the ceiling of the bus. There were cobwebs and more leaves stuck to the ceiling fabric. The bus had always been old, but it seemed to have passed over a threshold and now it was disintegrating. There was no way to stop it from losing all its pieces into a heap on the ground.

It reminded her of the tunnels, the cool, dank air down there, the walls weeping with water. They, too, were falling apart. Ephraim thought they proved something, and maybe he was right. Or maybe Will was right and it was all part of the sham that the Appledores had going to sell their water.

Maybe, maybe, maybe. It seemed that all she had was maybes and uncertainties.

She crawled out of the van and went back into the house, resolved to put this to rest once and for all. It was time—well past time—for her to do her own research. When she'd told Eprhraim the stories, she'd just been passing along the lies. Now she was going to prove the stories were false. Her parents had been lying to her all along. They may have had the best of intentions—to entertain her, to make her feel like she had a special place in Crystal Springs—but they were lies just the same.

She marched into the house. Her logic was simple and straightforward, as she believed that simple and straightforward was always the best way to think. *Where do stories come from?* she asked herself. They come from books. Maybe her parents' philosophy was correct, and every answer she needed was between the pages. All she needed to do was find a story or two that matched the ones her parents had told and she could prove that it was all made up, woven together from tales they had read along the way.

The trouble was that the house was overrun with books. There were travel books for their planned adventures, thick novels with battered covers, art books with detailed illustrations. None of these, she felt certain, would have what she needed. Anyway, most of them were already filled with her drawings.

She needed to go up to her parents' room. She had not been in it since her mother left. When she was younger, she would creep through their door in the morning and crawl between them in the bed. Her father's face would be rough with stubble and she'd rub her hands over it like sandpaper on wood.

She pushed open the door. The room was totally dark. All the shades were pulled, and no light got in. It smelled different, too, not like the lavender her mother had used when washing the sheets because she said it would help them sleep at night. "An old trick I picked up in Ireland," she had said.

Mallory edged her way to the window and let the shade go

up. It recoiled around the rod with such force the snap made Mallory jump. She had enough light from the moon now to see around the room. She moved to the one small bookcase. It, too, held several novels, the fantasy kind that a lot of the boys at school read.

There was a leather-bound copy of *Frankenstein*. She pulled it off the shelf and began to read the dense prose on the yellowed pages. She read for pages and pages and found nothing about monsters, only ice and snow. The narrator was looking for the North Pole, just like Peary and Henson had been. It was a strange coincidence, and yet also perfectly natural. One doomed quest after another.

A thump behind her made her freeze. Turning her head slowly, she saw that it was just her cat, Orville, who must have been sleeping on the bed. He slinked his way over to Mallory, rubbed himself against her knees, and then began mewing.

"Shh," Mallory hissed.

This only made Orville mew more.

She put *Frankenstein* back on the shelf and saw a copy of *Grimm's Fairy Tales* and a book of folklore. Those seemed her best bets, and she stacked them in her arms.

Mallory wanted to keep exploring, to see what other books there might be, but she didn't know when her dad would return. She had spent too much time reading *Frankenstein;* nearly an hour had already passed since her father had left, and he rarely left her alone for longer than that. So she tucked the books under her arm and pushed the cat ahead of her with her foot.

It was on her way out that a photograph caught her eye. She had never seen it before, and she thought she had seen every photograph of her parents in the house. Her mother was standing in a wide expanse of snow wearing what looked like leather pants and a huge furry coat, which was strange since her mother was always saying that wearing fur was a selfish, soulless act. Mallory picked up the photo to get a closer look. It was black and white, but still she could see that her mother's eyes were bright with excitement.

When Mallory put the picture back, she noticed a book behind it. The scant light hit the silver on the edges of the pages and glinted. Without thinking, she grabbed it and then hurried out, shutting the door behind her, but leaving the blind open: her father loved the moonlight.

February 12, 1909

Nora held her hand on the glass plate that sat on top of a small table. Dr. Appledore pressed a button, and a wheel below the table began to turn, like a sewing machine, only louder. The table shook a bit from the wheel, and then Dr. Appledore stopped the machine. "There we go," he said.

"But nothing happened. The table shook and there was noise, and that was all."

"Nothing you noted," Dr. Appledore replied. "Busy yourself, and I shall show you in a moment just what I've done."

Nora looked at the map on the wall and traced her finger along the path she believed Henson would take with Peary. "They are going to send a party to search for Dr. Cook," she announced. Dr. Frederick Cook had been the physician on earlier dashes to the Pole, but Peary and Cook had a falling out. Dr. Cook sought the Pole himself but got lost, and was feared missing. "Do you think they will find him?"

Dr. Appledore did not answer. He hummed to himself as he worked and almost danced from one end of the lab to the other. More than once Nora had to step out of his way. She would have to write to Harry, she determined, to see what he thought of Cook's fate.

"I got to thinking," he said from the far side of the lab. "If people have been searching for this water for hundreds of years, why haven't they found it? Perhaps it is simply that they did not have the tools to understand? Therefore, and now you will see the cleverness of my reasoning, I looked to the latest developments of science."

Dr. Appledore was prone to long rambles. Nora tried to pay attention, because he was a very wise man, and if she ever expected to go on an exploratory expedition like Henson, she, like he, would need to be very well learned. At times, though, her mind wandered. Now she thought of the ice and snow and how, although there was a group of them, that much empty space must make them feel lonely as they rode their sledges into the endless white day. And to be Cook, lost and alone amongst the snow—that would be maddening. It puzzled her that this very solitude seemed to be what Harry was looking for in the journey.

"Really I ought to have begun with radioactivity. We are just beginning to understand its uses. Why, the Curies discovered two new elements! It simply proves how much there is yet to learn and discover. There could be scores upon scores of new elements, each one with its own distinct properties. Any one of these could be the key."

Nora stacked Orlando's chemistry books into a pile. If he was correct about how much there was yet to discover, they would need a whole library just of books about science.

"What we need to determine is the radioactivity of the

water. We can check it as it is now, and then posit what it might have been in past years, or in other areas. Do you follow?"

"Yes," Nora replied.

"From there we can introduce further electromagnetic rays and test their effects."

"That's what you had Nikola build for you, right? A machine to send electromagnetic waves through the water?"

"Indeed!" Dr. Appledore said, looking pleased.

"He said you were changing your approach from discovery to creation."

"It is all discovery, my dear. Discovering the pieces. Discovering their potential." He glanced back toward the sink and then said, "Ah, good. Done!"

He held a glass plate out to her. Now developed, it showed the bones of a hand.

"I'm not sure what that has to do with the water."

"Nothing, it turns out. It is an X-ray machine, another idea of Nikola's. The electromagnetic waves bounce off your bones to produce a picture. It is useless to us, I'm afraid, but I thought perhaps you might like to see the inside of your hand."

"*My* hand?" Nora took the plate from him and looked at the bones of her hand, the way the small pieces fit one into the other. There were people, she knew, who would consider this demonology. They would claim that Orlando was working in areas from which he should shy away. "I'd like to take it home to show my mother," she said. "I think she would enjoy it very much."

"Of course, of course! Now then, let us proceed with our experiments in radioactivity. Fetch me the water."

* * *

After dinner Nora's family moved into the sitting room, where her mother read to them from the new novel *Anne of Green Gables*. It told of a young girl in Canada, wrapped up in stories. They had been reading it together for several days, and had to catch Nora up on what had happened so far. "She's so very much like you, it's like you've been here with us all along."

Nora's mother was a small woman, but she had a large presence, and the fire cast a giant shadow behind her on the walls. Her long hair was pulled up at the crown, but then fell down around her shoulders in tight curls. Nora's own hair was plaited tightly, and she wished she could wear it free as her mother did.

She sat next to her sister, Mary, who was three years younger and could barely keep her eyes open. Little John and Solomon sat at the edge of the room, near their father, who was mending a leather halter, and pretended that they were not interested in this story of a girl. But they all listened as their mother's voice rose and fell, following the mood of the story.

Anne and her friends decided to reenact a scene from a poem they had read in school, "Lancelot and Elaine." Elaine was a fair lily maid, sent down the river on her funeral flat. Anne didn't want to play Elaine at first, for fear her red hair meant she could be no lily maid, but her friends convinced her. They wrapped her in a shroud, said their farewells, and raced down the bank of the river to meet her at her final resting spot.

Only the boat sprung a leak and soon Anne found herself clinging to the pile of a bridge in a most undignified manner.

"That's our Nora, all right," Solomon said.

Nora hushed him. "How will she get out of there?"

"Well, let's see, shall we?" Her mother went on reading. Gilbert Blythe, Anne's sworn enemy after he mocked her hair by calling her "carrots," came rowing along in his boat and helped her to safety. Nora couldn't help but picture Harry going to save Anne. It was just the sort of thing he would do, to simply show up right when she needed him. Anne, though, refused Gilbert's apology and offer to be friends.

"But she can't do that to him!" Nora cried. "He just saved her life."

Her mother, who had read the book already, gave a wry smile as she closed it. "Perhaps there is more to their story."

"Then you must keep going!"

"It is time for sleep, my dears."

"Mother!" Nora cried.

"It is too late as it is. You need to be back up to the Water Castle early."

"But how will I know what happens with Anne and Gilbert?"

Her mother smiled. "It's the one way I have to make sure you will return home to visit me."

When the others were in their beds, she found her mother and showed her the glass plate. She did not know why she had not shown it to her brothers and sister, but it seemed somehow more special sitting next to her mother, their sides pressed together. "It is my hand. The bones of it," she explained.

"To see the inside of your hand—what a wonder! Next he will be showing you the contents of your stomach, or of that very large head of yours."

"It is not so large," Nora said.

"But it is full of knowledge. I am very proud of you," she said, and wrapped her arm around her daughter. "Now go and get yourself some sleep."

She climbed back into the bed she had left behind. She had shared it with her sister, who was always pleased to have Nora back, but still kicked her in her sleep, keeping her awake. Her mother brushed her hair from her face and whispered to them both, "Good night, my loves, my sweets."

In the morning, Nora woke early. She'd had a thought in the night, when kept awake by her sister's kicks. She went to the shelf and took down a leather-bound book. She tucked it into her satchel, and then let herself out the door. The morning air was frosty compared to the warmth of the house. As she shut the door, she glanced at the fire with longing.

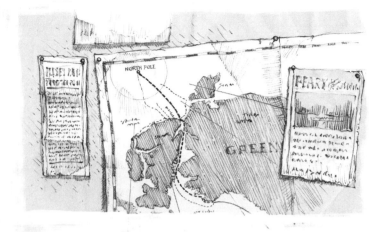

TWENTY-TWO

Ephraim, Mallory, and Will walked three abreast down the sidewalk. "We'll go to the Wylie Five and Dime first for supplies, and then we can go to the library," Mallory suggested. "In case we need to do more research."

Ephraim knew this was aimed at him—Mallory and Will had long since finished their research—but he didn't mind. It was a beautiful fall day with a bright blue sky and the air not too cold yet. A group of younger kids played soccer in the field by the gazebo, and people strolled down Maine Street stopping to chat with one another. With the nodding and saying hello to everyone they passed, the three were making slow progress.

"My mom says she can't believe this place hasn't become

a tourist destination like Bar Harbor or something," said Ephraim.

"We like it this way," Will said.

"Crystal Springs has never really liked outsiders," Mallory said.

Ephraim wasn't sure where this put him. He was new to town, but his family had the grandest house on the biggest hill in town. Still, both the Darlings and the Wylies had been there longer than the Appledores.

"My dad says there used to be a lot of trade and tourists, like with our store and the hotel, but now there are too many secrets in this town and people don't trust each other anymore. It's been getting worse and worse every generation since the fire."

They walked past the bakery that spewed out heavenly smells. All three breathed in deeply. Ephraim stared at the elaborate cakes in the windows. "We could probably use a snack," he said. "To fortify us."

Will agreed. "I'd kill for a Needham right about now," he said, rubbing his stomach.

"What's a Needham?" Ephraim asked as he kicked a pebble and sent it skittering down the sidewalk.

"What's a Needham?" Will asked. "What's a Needham? Honestly, Ephraim, the amount of things you don't know astounds me."

"It's a chocolate made with coconut and potatoes," Mallory explained.

"Oh, come on. I'm not that gullible."

"I'm afraid you are," Will said. "But in this case she's telling the truth. Come on, I'll show you."

He pushed open the door to the bakery, setting chimes ringing. Ephraim felt like he'd walked into a historical reenactment. The floors were wide pine slats, the counter marble, with a glass case. An older man behind the counter raised his hand in greeting. "Well, here's something I never thought I'd live to see. An Appledore, a Wylie, and a Darling walking into my bakery together."

"Hi, Mr. Small," Mallory said.

Will slid onto a stool. "Ephraim has never had a Needham."

"Never?" Mr. Small asked.

"They aren't really made with potatoes, are they?"

"Sure are," Mr. Small said as he brought three of the chocolate treats out of the case. He put one in front of each of them. "The first Needham is always on the house. For his friends, too."

"Thanks, Mr. Small," Mallory said. She let her backpack slip off her shoulder and fall onto the ground with a thunk. It was heavier than usual, weighed down by the silver-edged book that she'd found the night before. She had intended to show it to the boys first thing in the morning, but something kept stopping her. She told herself it was because she didn't want to give Ephraim false hope, but part of her knew it was more about not letting herself believe.

Ephraim sniffed the Needham. "Potatoes?"

"This is Maine, son. You work with what you've got. Now go on, give it a try." Mr. Small leaned on his elbows on the counter and watched as Ephraim took a small bite.

He couldn't taste potatoes, only chocolate and coconut that seemed to fall apart in his mouth. "That's amazing," he said.

Mr. Small sat up and slapped the counter, a wide grin across his red face. "Amazing! In all my years at this bakery, you know I've never had one unsatisfied customer."

Ephraim tried to savor the rest of the Needham, but ended up finishing it in two bites. He would have asked for another one, but Mallory stood up and said, "We're off to the Five and Dime. We've got a project to do."

"The Wylie Five and Dime?" Mr. Small mused, shaking his head. "As I live and breathe."

"Thank you," Ephraim said, wiping his lips on a small white napkin. "I'll be back, that's for sure."

"I know you will."

As the three left, Mr. Small watched them with a bemused expression.

"That was weird," Ephraim said when they got outside.

"I thought you liked it," Will replied.

"I did. I wasn't talking about the Needham. I was talking about Mr. Small. He couldn't quite believe that we were all there together."

Will and Mallory exchanged a glance. Neither wanted to tell Ephraim that in their twelve years of being in the same town, seven years in the same class, they'd never had a real conversation until he'd arrived. Finally Mallory said, "There's generations of bad blood."

"We're practically revolutionaries," Will said, secretly hoping that news of this revolution wouldn't make its way back to his father.

They crossed the street over to the Wylie Five and Dime. Mallory nodded her head to her great-uncle Edward and his friend Edwin—Edwin asleep as usual. "Hey, Uncle Eddie," she said. She wasn't really his niece—more like a cousin at many removes. But they were both of Darling heritage, so they considered themselves family.

"How's my favorite niece?"

"All right," she said. "We're working on a school project and need to get some supplies."

He stood up as if he were unfolding his body and pushed the door open for them. The bells jangled. They went over to a small display of school supplies.

"So how are we going to do this?" Will asked. He'd never been a fan of group projects, preferring to just do the work himself.

"Well, like Ephraim said, we're trying to show how the stories could each be right, and how they fit together. So maybe we do a map and show each of their routes with dates."

"But that would show that Cook got there first," Will said. "Not that I mind, but—"

"But they might have gotten to different places. Isn't that part of it? So we show who found what when. And we can have little parts of their journals and logbooks and stuff, too."

"And newspapers," Ephraim said. "I found a clipping in the house."

"Perfect," Mallory said as she reached for a piece of blue poster board.

"We're going to need some glitter," Will said. "For the ice."

They gathered all the supplies they could think of and carried them back to the counter, where Marie, the shop clerk, and Uncle Edward were talking. Marie reached out and tousled Will's hair. "Hey, Willy, what's new?"

Will frowned. Ephraim gaped. He could not believe that someone had just touched Will's head and lived to tell the tale.

"Ah, come on, Willy, you're still my little cousin, even if you're a giant now. How's your dad?"

"He's fine." Marie and her family were another set of people on his dad's list of those who had done him wrong. Generations before, a cousin in a different branch of the family had gotten the store, while his side of the family had gotten the house. Will's dad was convinced they'd gotten a raw deal.

"You know you're always welcome for Thanksgiving. Tell him that, will you?" She looked at Mallory and Ephraim. "It seems like it's a time for forgiveness, I would say."

"Sure," Will said without conviction. Marie asked him to Thanksgiving every year. He had never been.

"Good." She looked down at their stack of supplies. "Explorers project?"

"Yep. We've got Cook, Henson, and Peary, and we're going to show all the sides of their stories," Mallory explained.

"What about Ootah?" Uncle Edward asked.

"Who?" Mallory asked.

"Who?" Uncle Edward echoed. "You all have been working on this project for how long—same project I did when I was your age, by the way—and you don't know who Ootah was?"

"Now, don't go stirring up trouble," Marie said.

Uncle Edward rubbed his hand through his hair. "Ootah was the Eskimo—"

"Inuit," Marie corrected.

"The Inuit who went with Henson on that last jag. It was the two of them together that first stepped foot on the Pole, with Peary coming behind to plant the flag and claim it for his own. No party for Ootah, no parade. He stayed in Greenland when it was all over and now most folks don't even know his name. How's that for a how-do-you-do?"

The three children exchanged a glance.

Uncle Edward shook his head in disappointment. "Year after year I keep waiting for a student to do his research on poor old Ootah or any of the other three that went with them, but no one does."

"You leave those kids alone, Edward," Marie said. "You come in for your coffee?"

He gave them one last look, then turned and fixed himself a cup of free coffee. The children remained frozen, watching him until he went back outside.

Marie began ringing up their supplies. "Don't worry about

him. He just likes to stir up trouble. Anything else you need today?"

"No thanks, Marie. See ya," Mallory said, and they left the store, saying good-bye to Edward and the still-dozing Edwin on the way out.

Will and Mallory led Ephraim to the library, a stone building guarded by a lion. They found a table toward the back, lit by a lamp with a stained-glass shade that cast a multicolored glow across their work.

Mallory spread out a map of the Arctic. "I thought we could start by marking their routes on the map. If we have dates we can put on, that would be better."

"But Cook didn't believe Peary's dates, and Peary didn't believe Cook's," Will said.

Ephraim tried to concentrate but he was thinking about the water again. He knew it was down there somewhere. Why else have all those tunnels if not to hide a secret? Will said they were carrying water up from the lake, but if that's all they were doing, then they only needed one tunnel.

"Ephraim?" Mallory asked.

"What?"

"Ephraim, you aren't paying attention at all! We're trying to plan our project here."

"I've been thinking about the tunnels," Ephraim said.

"Of course you have," Will said.

"I think we need to go back in. There's something we're missing. We're looking at it from the wrong perspective."

"What are you talking about?"

"We're trying to find it."

"*You're* trying to find it," Will said.

"It's like what we've been talking about with who was first at the North Pole and how trying to figure that out gets in the way of what really matters. What I'm trying to say is, we are not explorers!" He looked around at them triumphantly.

"That's your big revelation?" Will asked.

"I mean we're looking for something that's already been found." He pointed to Mallory's map. "It's like we're *going* to the North Pole, not *discovering* it."

"Where are you going with this?" Mallory asked.

Ephraim wasn't sure exactly where he was going. "We don't need to think about it like explorers. We need to think about it like people who already found it. We don't need to plan an expedition. We need a map. If someone found the water, where would they hide it?"

Will straightened his stack of note cards. "I'm really starting to like you, Ephraim, but I think you're getting obsessed with the Fountain of Youth. I mean, that's kind of in your blood as an Appledore, but, well, there's nothing there. Take a clue from your ancestors: if there really was a Fountain of Youth here, someone would have found it a long time ago."

Mallory sighed and reached down into her backpack. "I think there's something I need to show you."

TWENTY-THREE

After Mallory showed them the silver-edged book she'd found, they forgot about their project and went back to the Water Castle. The house glittered and shimmered in the afternoon light almost as if it were waving a welcome to them. Ephraim led them up to Brynn's room, the library, but she wasn't there.

Mallory's discovery was a logbook, with all the work the Darlings had done on the house, from the laying of the first stone. She'd opened the book to an entry dated February 1889:

> Began work on laboratory for Doctor Appledore to study known medicinal qualities of water as well as what he called energy anomalies in the area. Harold Appledore is

skeptical but approved the work on 2 February. Work
commenced 7 February. Work completed 16 April.

"If there's something going on here, the answers will be in
that laboratory," Ephraim said, taking the house plans from a
stack of Brynn's research and unrolling them onto the desk.
"I've been all over this house. I've found rooms that shouldn't
be there and enough old junk to start a museum, but I haven't
seen anything that looks like a secret laboratory," he said.

"This could have been part of the hoax, you know," Will
said. He was sitting on the windowsill looking out over the
town.

"The only way to know for sure is to find it," Mallory said.
"I'm as suspicious as you are, but don't you want to know the
truth?" It was what she ached for, to know 100 percent for
certain what the real story was. She thought it was all a lie her
parents had told her, but there was still one tiny little sliver of
her that believed. If only she could know, one way or the other.
Will, though, just shrugged.

"We found a guest book and all of these famous scientists
came here. Nikola Tesla and, well, I can't remember the rest of
their names, but Brynn told me they were a big deal." Ephraim
scratched his head. "If the Appledores were explorers on a
quest for the Fountain of Youth, why all the scientists? Why
a laboratory?"

"Either they were testing something or manipulating it,"
Will said.

"What do you mean 'manipulating'?" Ephraim asked.

"Well, if I wanted to find some magical water, and I kept coming up empty, I would see if there was some way I could modify what was already in existence to make it stronger."

"'I shall find a way or make one,'" Ephraim said. "Maybe you're a Peary fan after all."

"Hardly," Will said.

"So you're saying that someone could have been doing experiments to try to change the water so that it would make you live forever. This Dr. Appledore was trying to create the Fountain of Youth?"

"Maybe," Will said. "It's just a hypothesis."

"We have to find that lab." Ephraim picked up the logbook as if he could shake the information out if it. "All we need is some sort of clue." He let the plans roll back up and noticed a yellowing piece of newsprint beneath them. His eye was caught by a photo of a large fire, impressive even in black and white on yellowing newsprint.

```
September 8, 1909
Crystal Springs, ME: A fire ripped
through the world-renowned Crystal
Springs Resort and Recuperation
Center, damaging nearly all of the
buildings and bringing three to
the ground. The fire began after
midnight in the spa. From there
```

it spread to the hotel. Though it was close to the home of the proprietors, the Appledore family, the large stone structure known familiarly as the Water Castle remained largely unscathed.

It is believed that the fire began with faulty electrical work in the hot baths, but arson has not been overruled.

The article went on to interview firefighters, who had taken nearly half an hour to get up the winding road, guests of the hotel, and staff. The Appledores were not questioned. One name seemed to swirl around the story; no accusations were made, but Ephraim could feel the suspicion even decades later: the Wylies.

Ephraim glanced up at Will, who stared back at him. "What?" Will asked.

Ephraim hastily refolded the paper. On top, just below the title, was a headline that went across the whole paper: "PEARY DISCOVERS NORTH POLE ON 8TH TRY." "Nothing. Just found something that might be useful for our research project." He held up the newsprint with the headline. "Another newspaper article. Maybe we can stick it on our poster."

"Cool. Speaking of—" he began.

"That can wait," Mallory said.

"I want to do well on this project."

"Please," Mallory said. "The three of us? Who in that class could even come close to what we're going to do?"

Ephraim couldn't help but be pleased for a moment that she'd included him, but quickly refocused on the matter at hand.

"If there is a lab," Mallory said, "then someone else at least believed that something was going on here. I'm not going to say that it was, just that you aren't the only crazy person to believe the story."

"We have to find it," Ephraim said. "We'll find it and then we'll see what we know."

"You need to check the tunnels," Brynn said from the library doorway.

Startled, they all turned to look at her. Ephraim began shuffling the papers on the desk, hoping she wouldn't be upset that they had invaded her bedroom.

"That's what those lines are, right? Tunnels?" she asked as she crossed the room to the desk. She pointed to the lines on the house plans. "If I were going to build a secret lab, I'd build it underground."

Ephraim nodded. "She's right. We need to go back into the tunnels. It's the only place that I haven't explored completely."

Mallory continued examining the plans of the house. "There used to be a lot more buildings, you know. The hotel and the cottages. It could have been its own building."

"What would be the point of having a secret lab if it was

right out in the open?" Ephraim asked. "Brynn is right. Underground tunnels are the perfect place to hide it."

Will picked up a small ceramic elephant that had been placed on the windowsill and stared outside. From up here he could see all across the town. He was pretty sure he could even pick out his house, miles away. His dad was always talking about "the riches" and "how the other half lives"—and not just about the Appledores. About anyone who had a little bit more than they did. Like life had given them the worst lot it possibly could and they had done nothing to deserve it, while others had everything good and wonderful packaged up and delivered at their doorsteps. But they had been wealthy once—Will knew this from his grandfather's stories. They'd been in Crystal Springs first, before the Appledores or anyone else. Somewhere they'd gone off track and Will found it harder and harder to blame that on anyone outside his family. From up on the hill, everything blended together, and he couldn't see the lines his dad was talking about.

"We'll look," Will said. "But if we don't find it, then you need to just drop it, okay? That'll be the end of it and we can get back to work on our project?"

Ephraim bit his lip. It was a big promise, but he was sure they would find something—at least enough to keep them looking for more. "Okay," he agreed.

As they walked outside, Brynn took Ephraim's hand. "What do you think we'll find down there?" she asked. "Do you think it will explain the blue light and everything else?"

"Maybe, Brynn." Ephraim wasn't sure if he should tell her that he hoped to find a cure for their father, a way to unlock the cage that held him. He didn't want to get her hopes up if it didn't work out. One look at her pale face, though, so much more serious than it had been before they'd moved, and he could tell she was looking for the same thing he was.

They went in through the door in the bottling house, leaving it propped open with a small stone. Ephraim had borrowed Price's headlamp, and used it to shine on the path in front of him. They walked back the way they had come, but then came to an intersection.

"What's down there?" Ephraim asked.

"I told you: I've only ever been along this one path. You know when you watch movies about people exploring and searching for treasure and stuff—they always find the skeletons of the people who came looking before. I don't want to be that skeleton."

"We won't," Ephraim said. "We're going to be the ones that finally find it."

"If we leave something here, like a marker of some sort, it will help us find our way back," Mallory said as she dug into her pockets. She pulled out a pencil and put it on the ground with its point in the direction from which they had come. "We won't make any turns. Just down as far as we can go and then back." It was the same system she had used with her parents when they had gone hiking: they'd made little guideposts out of rocks and sticks.

Ephraim said, "That's a great idea!"

Will, though, kicked the ground. In his mind, these tunnels belonged to him, and he didn't like the idea of other people exploring them.

"If you don't want to go," Ephraim said, "you can just stay here. You'd be easier to see than a pencil."

Ephraim hadn't meant it as a dare, but Will took it as one, clearing his throat and saying, "I'm going. I'm going."

They walked single file: Mallory, Ephraim, Brynn, then Will. Brynn clutched the hem of Ephraim's shirt. At first it seemed just like the path in the other direction—stone floor, stone walls—and Ephraim feared it would merely lead outside on the other side of the house.

The ground sloped downward, slight at first and then more severely. The air around them became cold enough for them to shiver. The tunnel got smaller and smaller so that they were crouching and then crawling, the dirt roof brushing their backs.

Eventually, they got to a point where they could go no farther.

"Maybe the tunnel collapsed," Ephraim said. "Or maybe— maybe this is it. Maybe this is the spring, or where the spring used to be and it dried up or it turned and—"

"Or maybe it's a false tunnel that was put here to confuse people. It's a trap and we walked right into it," Will interrupted.

"Let's just go back," Mallory said.

They couldn't turn around, so they crawled backward until they could nearly stand.

"If it *was* a false tunnel, then there must be something to hide," Brynn suggested. She hadn't spoken the whole time they had been underground—had barely made a noise.

"Exactly," Ephraim agreed. "Something really good."

Will grunted.

When they got to the pencil, Will bent over to pick it up.

"Wait," Ephraim said. "We still have the other direction to go." He was not ready to give up yet. He was even more sure that they were going to find something, and soon.

"We'll do the same thing. Down as far as we can go, and then back."

"There's not anything there," Will said.

"You don't know that. Maybe you just don't want anything to be there," Ephraim challenged.

"What's that supposed to mean?"

"Nothing," Ephraim said, but he was thinking of the article about the fire. If they found the Fountain of Youth, then it would show that the Appledores—or at least some of them—had been telling the truth all along, and the Wylies had been wrong.

Mallory swung her flashlight down the other tunnel. "Let's just go," she said.

This path was monotonous. The floor was flat, the walls smooth, the ceiling a foot above their heads. They walked without tripping over rocks or packs of dirt. Just walked and walked and walked.

None of them spoke, and the damp air closed in around

them. Mallory was in her own head, thinking of her parents and their fight. Even out in the van, she'd been able to hear the rise and fall of their voices, the entreaties and the accusations. She wondered what had happened to change the love between them. She didn't notice the air getting cooler and dryer, or the slight decline of the floor.

They walked and walked. And then they came to the end. Even with his headlamp on, Ephraim walked right into the wall. "Oomph," he said, just as Mallory walked into him.

"Oh," she said, clearing her throat. "I'm sorry."

"This can't be the end," Ephraim said, a crack in his voice.

"We can go back and try another path," she said.

"I guess." But Ephraim had been certain that this was the way to the lab. The lab would lead them to the magical water, and the water would cure his father. A straight line. Now, though, they were at a dead end.

He hung his head. It was this act of self-defeat that showed him he had been right all along. Or, at least, partially right. His headlamp shone on a flat panel on the wall with a tiny, key-shaped hole in it.

TWENTY-FOUR

From the moment she saw the keyhole, Mallory knew the key was around her mother's neck.

She got a ride home from Ephraim's mom, and the whole trip back to her house in the Appledore-Smiths' cinnamon-scented SUV, Mallory hoped against logic that her mother's Rabbit would be sitting in her driveway. Even if her parents were having another fight or if her mother was packing more boxes into the tiny trunk, that would be okay as long as she could see the key.

Ephraim's mom steered the car past the garage and pulled to a stop in front of the house. Mallory's mother was not there.

Ephraim's mom waited until Mallory pushed the door

open and went inside before she turned around by the old gas pumps and drove away.

"Where have you been?" her dad asked. He sat in a chair in the living room.

"I went to see Ephraim."

"Up at the castle?"

"Yes," she said. "His mother drove me home. I think I would like to go see Mom." She braced herself for her father's reaction to this news. She feared he would see it as a betrayal, but she couldn't explain the real reason she wanted to see her mom.

"I think that's a great idea. How about this weekend?"

"I was thinking maybe tomorrow, actually. It's Field Day at school, so maybe I could go to see Mom instead." She had never before lied to her father, and she didn't like the way it tasted in her mouth: sour, bitter, and dry all at once.

"Field Day?" He raised his eyebrows and Mallory knew he knew she was not telling the truth.

"Yes."

"I suppose I could give your mother a call and see if she's free."

The phrasing struck Mallory: *your mother*, as if he himself no longer had any connection to her. She began to wonder if going to see her mother was a bad idea. It's not like she could just ask for the key and then be on her way. Her mother would want to talk about their feelings. Worse, her mother might try to explain why she had left home.

She had to do it, though, because if there was a chance, however slight, that something behind that door might help Ephraim's father, then she wanted to help find it. At least she could fix one family.

They went in the morning. Her dad drove them out of Crystal Springs and through two more towns until they reached a small house. Her mother was renting an apartment above the garage.

He turned off the truck, and Mallory feared he was going to go in with her. Instead he twisted in his seat so he was facing her. "This means a lot to your mother," he said. "That you wanted to come."

"I know," Mallory said.

"But I know it might be confusing for you. Or difficult. Or maybe you'll have fun. Whatever happens, though, we can talk about it if you want. Or not, if you don't want." He rubbed his hand hard against his head. "And you can call me to get you whenever. Even if I'm elbow deep in a six-cylinder engine, I will come and get you."

"Thanks," she said. Then she took a deep breath and got out of the truck.

Her mother was waiting for her on the landing and ushered her in with a huge hug. Mallory felt the key press against her shoulder. She wished she could reach up, grab it, and run back to the warmth and diesel smell of her father's truck.

"I always hated Field Days, too, you know."

The comment slipped by Mallory, who was taking in the

apartment. The door opened right into the kitchen, which had black-and-white tiles, black counters, and white cabinets with black handles. Her mother had added red accents: dish towels and a vase with white lilies.

"Are you hungry?"

"I just had breakfast."

"Of course."

She took Mallory by the hand and led her into the living room, where they sat on opposite ends of the couch and said nothing. There was a big picture window that looked out over the driveway. Her mother had filled it with plants, some of which Mallory recognized. "You took those plants," she said.

"Yes. Did you want them? You can bring them home with you."

Mallory wasn't used to the urgent tone in her mother's voice, an eagerness to please so intense that it sounded more like panic. "No." She shook her head.

"I shouldn't have taken them anyway. I'm going on a trip soon. There'll be no one to water them."

"It's fine," Mallory said. "Keep them."

Mallory shifted her weight on the couch. The apartment had everything a home should have: couch, coffee table, plants, and such. On the wall was a series of photos her mother had taken on various trips: Paris, Dubai, New York City, Kyoto, the Grand Canyon. But something was missing so that it did not quite feel whole.

Her mother reached out and pulled Mallory closer to her.

Mallory was enveloped with her smell, something so familiar she hadn't even realized it was there until it was gone. "Sometimes it's like looking in a mirror with you. You look just the way I did when I was little."

She said it like she was sad about it, like when she looked at Mallory she saw all that she could have been and all that she had lost. Mallory's face was muffled against her mother's skin, so she didn't say anything. She thought of the little girl in the picture, and imagined this whole line of girls leading from that turn-of-the-century version up to her, all looking exactly like her. She thought about all that those girls had seen and experienced, and wondered if they were any happier than she was. Then her mother sighed, let Mallory go, tugged at the tails of the scarf in her hair. There was a hint of tears at the corner of her eyes.

"How's school?" she asked.

"Okay. I'm doing a project on Matthew Henson."

"The explorer?"

"Yeah. Why?" Mallory asked.

Her mom smiled. "I did some research on him, too, when I was about your age."

"They probably assign him to us because he's black."

Her mom brushed her cheek. "Or maybe Mr. Wright recognizes your indefatigable spirit and your intelligence and thinks that you would relate to Henson."

"Maybe," Mallory said. "Anyway, it's kind of interesting, although who knows if they were even the ones who made it first."

"Of course they were!"

"Ephraim Appledore is doing Robert Peary—"

"Appledore?" her mother interrupted.

"Well, Appledore-Smith, I guess," Mallory said, thinking of how Ephraim always corrected people.

"I'd heard they'd gone back to the Water Castle. I didn't realize they would be going to school with you."

Mallory knew that if they started talking about the Appledores and the Water Castle now, they might never get off the subject, and she wouldn't be able to ask about the key that glinted on a chain around her mother's neck. She should have known better than to even bring it up. "Yeah, he and Will Wylie and I are going to present together. Will's doing Frederick Cook."

Her mother frowned, and Mallory realized she had again stumbled into bad territory: the Darlings had never liked the Wylies, and vice versa.

"We're doing radiation in science class," she said to change the subject. "Ms. Little brought in a Geiger counter. The readings were way high. And one day we went and saw the Van de Graaff machine to talk about electromagnetism and Ephraim got shocked." She couldn't seem to stop herself from talking.

"Wowzers," her mother said.

This familiar word made Mallory happy and sad at the same time. She looked around the apartment and realized what was missing. "You don't have any books!"

"I've left those for your father."

Mallory wasn't sure how her mother could live without books.

"I want to travel light," her mom said as if to answer the question Mallory had not asked. She twisted her fingers together. Mallory noticed the space on her left hand where the gold wedding band used to be. Now only a slight indent remained.

"Is there anything you want to ask me? Anything at all?"

There were any number of things that Mallory wanted to ask about why her mother had left, and how it had been so easy for her to leave Mallory behind, but she wasn't sure she wanted to hear those answers. Anyway, she was there for a purpose, and so she asked, "Where did you get that key around your neck?"

Her mother's hand went up and grasped the copper key on the thin silver chain. "Oh," she said, her eyelids fluttering as she looked away. "I just found it somewhere."

"Up at the Water Castle?"

Her eyes darted toward Mallory, then just as quickly she looked away. "No. Not at the Water Castle. Why do you ask that?"

Mallory could see just the edges of the key peeking out on either side of her mother's closed fist. "Can I have it?" she asked.

The key was still in her hand. "What would you like it for?"

Mallory tried to act like she wasn't very interested at all. She knew the words to say that would make her mother rip the key from her neck and hand it to Mallory: I want to keep a piece of you with me. But she was not that desperate yet, or that cold. "I think it's pretty. And mysterious."

"You'd like to wear it?"

"Yes."

Her mother hesitated for a moment, then lifted the key from around her neck.

"You know it doesn't open anything, right?"

"Of course it doesn't," Mallory said, as breezily as she could with the key so close to her own hand. "It's just for show."

Her mother passed the key to Mallory, who slipped it on. The warm metal of the key burned her skin with hope.

TWENTY-FIVE

After Mallory's mom gave her the key, it seemed to relax them both, and the visit went fairly smoothly. Her mother had bought some beads, and they made bracelets together. Mallory made one for Brynn and one for Ephraim. She also made one for Price, though she doubted she would ever give it to him. She started working on one for Will.

"Where do you think you'll go?" Mallory asked. "On your trip?"

Her mother's face brightened. "I haven't decided yet. I was thinking Turkey maybe. I've never been there. Or Alaska."

"Alaska, but I—" Mallory stopped herself. That had been her trip of choice back when they'd been daydreaming in the van.

"What?"

"Nothing. Alaska sounds nice."

"It's not really the best time of year for Alaska, but that does make it more affordable. I've got a call in to a travel agent."

Mallory's parents were the only ones she knew who still used things like travel agents. "Sounds like fun."

Her mother was very curious about the Appledore family, so Mallory told her all that she thought was important. She explained that Ephraim's dad had a stroke, and that's why they'd come back to the house, for him to recuperate.

"Just like old times," her mother murmured.

"What do you mean?" Mallory asked.

"You know, Mallory. People have always come to Crystal Springs to get better—to the Water Castle especially. The Resort and Recuperation Center may be gone, but that doesn't mean the magic is."

Mallory concentrated on slipping a bead onto the string so her mom couldn't tell how interested she really was. "But that was never really true. I mean, it wasn't magic but just, you know, the fresh air and everything."

Her mother sorted through the beads in the pile and picked out one as bright and green as Mallory's father's eyes. "It was the water, actually."

"But what did they think was so special about the water? I mean, it's just spring water, right?" She hesitated and then added, "Will Wylie says it just came from the lake."

Her mother scowled. "The Wylies were always causing

trouble." She picked up three brown beads and placed them on the string next to the green one. Then she sighed. "The truth is that most of the water that your—" She paused. "Most of the water that Harold Appledore bottled and sold did come from the lake. That water was good and healthy. Why, look how healthy people in Crystal Springs are. Have you ever gotten a cold?"

Mallory shook her head.

"The flu?"

Mallory shook her head again.

"But there was other water that was stronger," she explained. "That was the Fountain of Youth. That was the water that could make people live forever as long as they kept drinking it."

"As long as they kept drinking it?" Mallory echoed. She had always been told that it slowed aging, but never that you had to keep drinking it.

Her mother looked at her closely, and Mallory felt as if she were being measured. Finally, after a long pause, her mother said, "That's the legend anyway. Angus Appledore never found it, and neither did anyone who came after." She picked up Mallory's hand and laid it on top of her knee while she tied the bracelet she had made around Mallory's wrist.

"But you believe the story?" Mallory asked.

Her mother let both of her hands rest on top of Mallory's, warm and soft as a fleece blanket. "Yes," she said. "I do."

Soon after, her mother drove her home, but didn't come inside, and Mallory thought that was for the best. She didn't want to hear another fight. It was three o'clock. Mallory picked up the phone and called Ephraim. "I have the key," she declared.

Ephraim had to wait for his mom to be free to go and pick up Mallory. He called Will, who of course said he didn't want a ride, and told Ephraim that he'd meet them at the intersection in the tunnel. Ephraim would never want to be alone down there, but, aside from not wanting to deviate from the path, Will liked it.

For the whole car ride to Mallory's house, he had to deal with his mom making comments like, "I suppose it is about time for you to take an interest in girls. Price had a girlfriend when he was in fifth grade."

He glowered, but he didn't bother to explain that Mallory was just a friend. A colleague.

The car ride back to the Water Castle was just as tense with Dr. Appledore-Smith asking Mallory all sorts of questions, like what her favorite subject at school was. Mallory answered gamely, all the while stealing glances at Ephraim, who was ramrod straight with anticipation.

"It's nice that you two are spending so much time together," Dr. Appledore-Smith said.

Mallory saw Ephraim squirm and immediately knew what his mother thought was going on between the two of them. The moment was awkward and embarrassing, and Mallory responded in the worst possible way. "I made you a bracelet," she said, holding out the blue and green beaded circle to Ephraim. "Thank you," he said. He slipped the bracelet onto his wrist and found the beads warm from being crushed in her palm.

"I also made one for Brynn. And Price."

"Well, that was very nice of you," Dr. Appledore-Smith said.

As soon as the car stopped, the two were out of it and around the house, running toward the old bottling house. Ephraim thought for a moment that he ought to have told Brynn and brought her along, but now that they were on their way, there was no going back for her. They scurried down the stairs, Ephraim with a flashlight in one hand, and hurried down the tunnel. They barely stopped for Will, who was sitting on the ground right where the two paths crossed. He jumped up and trailed after them as they sprinted all the way to the door.

Mallory lifted the key from around her neck. It went in about halfway and then stopped. "Oh," she said, and they all deflated. Then she pushed a little harder, and it slipped into place. She turned it and they heard the click of the lock unlatching. Mallory leaned forward, and the door squeaked open.

August 14, 1909

Each summer the Appledores took a photograph of the entire family with their staff. Harry was nowhere to be found, so Nora was dispatched to find him out in the fields. She was already dressed in her best clothes, a ribbon tied tightly in her hair that tickled her neck with each step. Her pinafore was stiff and bright white, and she worried about the dirt from the road.

She was nearly at the end of the property when she saw him. He waved to her, then ran to catch up.

"It's nearly time for the photograph," she said to him.

Harry looked confused for a moment, then said, "I forgot that was today!"

"You'll have to change your clothes," she said, appraising his muddied riding pants.

He nodded, unconcerned. "Have you heard the latest?" he asked.

"The *Jeanie*'s about to set sail with coal for Peary's return," she supplied, tugging at the neck of her dress.

"Which means they could be home at any moment. They might have already reached the Pole."

"Or," she cautioned, "they might have failed and are settling in for the winter before they make another dash next spring."

"I prefer to think they've already been there. That they have already stood on the spot and planted the Stars and Stripes into the icy ground. Why are you so cranky?"

"These clothes are uncomfortable," she said.

"They don't exactly suit you, it's true."

"What do you mean by that?" she demanded.

He looked down at the ground and rubbed his head. "Only that you tend to wear clothes that are more practical. Sensible. Don't be cross with me."

Nora let the comment pass. It was too lovely an afternoon to get angry. Cool, but the sun shone on their faces, Peary and Henson may have reached the Pole, and Nora and Harry were both as content as they had been in a long time.

A figure leaped from the bushes, and Harry stumbled backward. Winnie Wylie.

Nora turned around to help Harry to his feet.

"Where are you going with her?" Winnie asked.

"Nora and I were going for a walk," Harry replied, having regained his composure.

"Are you now? Does your mother know who you are walking with?"

"I do not suppose it is much my mother's business. Or yours."

This took Winnie by surprise. Her face darkened. "You should sooner walk with a turnip."

"And conversation with you would be so much the better?" Nora asked. "Have you made such strides in comprehension and expression since I left school? Why, Mrs. Brown was at her wit's end with you. I'm glad to hear she has helped you—"

Winnie was upon Nora within a second, tackling her to the ground and slapping her about the face. The blows were not very hard, as Winnie was not especially strong, but still the hits stung, one after another, and Nora couldn't help the tears from forming in her eyes. She struggled under the other girl's weight, unable to fight back.

Harry was frozen for a moment, not sure of what he was seeing, but then he yelled, "Stop it!" and pulled Winnie off Nora. She rocked back so she was sitting in the dirt. He helped Nora to her feet. Her cheeks were red, her lip cracked. Her white pinafore was now a dusty brown and the right strap was torn completely. She seethed at Winnie, but Harry stood between them.

"Have you no decorum?" Harry asked.

"Have not you? Walking with her? Why are you walking with her when any number of nice, proper girls would give an eye to walk with you?"

Harry shook his head. "Go home, Winnie," he said.

She did not move, so Harry took Nora by the elbow and guided her around Winnie.

Once they were well past her enemy, Nora shook free. "An ignorant little wretch," Nora cried, wiping at her lip. "The apple doesn't fall far from the tree, that's for certain. A rotten, stinking, festering apple full of worms and brown mushy spots, just like her mother. Jumping on me in the middle of the road, and she has the gall to question my place? How am I to be in the photograph now? Look at me!"

"I think you look nice. More like yourself."

Nora stopped and glared at him. "Dirty and beat up?" she demanded.

"Feisty," he replied. Then, blushing, he said, "Let's cut across the field. We'll get back faster."

She looked at the muddy field. "I suppose I cannot dirty myself any more than she already did."

As they walked in the grass, she felt her heartbeat slowing, and her shoulders letting go of the rage that tied them together.

Harry cleared his throat. "You asked me once what I would say if I discovered the Pole, and I thought of my reply."

"And?"

"A place once found cannot be undiscovered. I hope we serve you well."

"Lovely," she replied, for it was, and as such suited his personality.

"And what of your project with my uncle? What will you say when you find the Fountain of Youth?"

"I'm sure Dr. Appledore will have words enough for both of us."

He laughed, but then his tone grew more serious: "And will you drink it and live forever?"

Nora leaned her head back and looked at the sky. "I should like to see the whole of the world. I should like to see beyond this world."

"So you would?"

"Think of all the places you could go! You could discover one thousand north poles."

"But then each would have little meaning."

An eagle flew overhead, and they both watched its path.

"So you would not drink?" she asked.

He started shaking his head before she had even finished asking the question. "One life is enough for me; that is the natural order of things."

She was disappointed. He had to want more than what was around him. "What if I tied you up and forced you to drink it?" she asked, and he raised his eyebrows in alarm. "What would you do with all that life?"

The eagle was joined by a second, and they circled round and round above Nora and Harry. "It looks like those eagles are dancing," he said.

"I suppose," she replied.

She expected this meant he wasn't going to answer her question, but then he said, "Sometimes you don't need to go out and find adventure. If you stay put, the world will grow and change around you. I'm not afraid of what is new. I think I would like to see the changes that come." He looked up at the eagles soaring. "I should like to go up and fly in an airplane, like the Wright brothers. I should like to see what other inventions are in men's heads ready to explode upon the world. But I can see it all from right here in Crystal Springs."

The eagles finished their circular dance and lighted down

upon some trees at the edge of the pasture. Harry was just like those eagles, she thought, willing to circle round and round that same plot of land year after year, while she would soar along in the air drifts as far as they would take her.

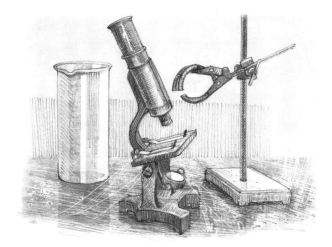

TWENTY-SIX

The laboratory was covered in dust like the first snowfall. Motes hung in the beam of Ephraim's flashlight, which lit up strange shapes as he swung it around the room.

"There's a light switch," Mallory said as she pushed the top of the pair of buttons. Two of the overhead lights crackled on, making a pale yellow glow.

The floor was made of stone and was crooked and cracked from the earth shifting beneath it. A long lab table in the center of the room had a black top just like the lab tables in their science class. The surface was pockmarked from chemicals. The Bunsen burner on the lab table was put away just as Ms. Little always taught them to, its cord coiled like a snake.

"It's like someone closed up for the night and never came

back," Will said. He ran his finger along the table, leaving a trail behind it. He crossed the room to look at a device that he recognized as a microscope though it had only one lens for looking through. A cobweb stretched from the lens to the plate. He put his eye up to it, but the mechanism was too cracked and dusty to work.

Mallory picked up a model of a head with lines dotted over it. It had black lines where its eyes should be, as if it were sleeping or dead. "What do you think this could be?" she asked. "Some kind of mannequin?"

"I have no idea." Will took it from Mallory and turned it round and round to get a better look. He ran his fingers over the lumps and ridges. It didn't seem scientific enough to belong in a lab—maybe it was some kind of old-fashioned hat holder. He was more interested in all of the instruments. He found a small table that had a glass plate on top and a wheel below. When he pushed a button it made a creaking noise, but nothing else happened. Lifting up the glass plate, he saw some sort of tube and decided it might be a type of imaging device. He would have to look in his *Encyclopedia of Scientific Devices* when he got home. "This is hands down the coolest place I have ever been." This was science history. Was there something in here, he wondered, that he could use for the World's Science Fair? Perhaps he could re-create an experiment using these old instruments and compare it to new data.

Mallory picked up something that looked like two wooden bars glued together. She recognized it from her research. "This is a theodolite," she said. "They used it to map the Arctic. This is going to be awesome for our project."

Ephraim hadn't moved since they'd gotten into the lab. He had his hands on the table to steady himself. The realization that they were *there* nearly toppled him. They were in the room and the answer was here. Somewhere in this stony, dusty room was the cure for his father. "They were working on something. Dr. Appledore or whoever it was *was* working on something. We were right! There's something going on here," he whispered.

"Or someone else thought there was something going on here," Mallory said.

"Just because they were looking doesn't mean they found it," Will added as he examined the other instruments on the table: a mortar and pestle that had a faint white residue, a distilling contraption with six different bottles.

Ephraim ignored the pessimism of his friends and moved over to a set of shelves filled with tiny jars of chemicals neatly marked with handwritten labels.

Mallory saw a familiar-looking map and crossed the room. It was a map of the far Northern hemisphere and on it was plotted the route of the final Peary mission. Dates were noted in handwriting that looked familiar to her, though she couldn't quite place it. "Guys, you have got to see this." She began carefully taking the map off the wall. "This will be perfect for our project. Someone was keeping track of the journey. It looks like they stopped just before Peary's expedition finally reached the Pole."

"Maybe that's because he never reached it," Will said. He had moved over to the bookshelf, where he was squinting to read the titles.

Ephraim picked up one of the bottles; its cork stopper was askew and blackening around the edges. "Maybe one of these is what we need."

Mallory looked up. "Don't touch them, Ephraim! Chemicals act funny when you let them sit for a while."

"But one of these is probably the answer." He reached toward an amber-colored bottle.

Mallory slapped his hand away. "Don't touch the chemicals."

Will read the labels and then held up one of the bottles. "This one says it cures obesity, constipation, and jaundice. Oh, and this one says it will clean out your blood, liver, and stomach," he snickered.

"So?" Ephraim asked. "Maybe somebody working down here was sick."

"None of these cures really worked. People would believe anything because they didn't understand the science of it. So other people who were looking to make a quick buck would just slap a label on it and call it good." He put the bottle down carefully.

"What are you getting at?" Ephraim asked.

"It's like that radium water you found. After the Curies discovered radiation, people thought it would cure anything. So some guy started selling radium water even though there was no evidence that it was any good for you."

"Are you saying that you think there's more radium water down here?" Mallory asked. She scanned the bottles with alarm.

"Why was it stupid for people to believe the radium water would help them?" Ephraim asked. "Mallory said that sometimes radiation can have good effects. People didn't know—"

"That's exactly the problem," Will said. "They didn't know. They didn't have all the facts, but they jumped right in anyway. This one rich guy drank so much of it he lost his jaw." He sighed. "I'm saying that wealthy people looking for a quick fix may not be the most reliable scientists."

"Whoever built this wasn't just some wealthy guy," Ephraim said. "He was a scientist. Maybe he discovered something new, some new way to use radioactivity—or something else entirely. Something else to explain the Fountain of Youth. Or create it, like you were saying. Look at all this stuff. This is the real deal."

"It does look authentic," Will said, and indeed it did. But just because someone was a scientist didn't mean that they'd found the Fountain of Youth. "I'm trying to be realistic. You've got your hopes up so high—"

"Why is it so hard for you to believe that there could be some truth to this? Just because it hasn't been found or proven yet? Isn't that what science is all about?"

"Yes, but people have been looking for the Fountain of Youth for ages and there is no evidence of it."

"That we know of. Maybe the person who worked in this lab found it."

"And never told anyone?"

Ephraim shrugged. "It just seems to me that things usually feel impossible until someone figures it out. And then they are amazing."

Will picked up the sculpture of the head again and looked at the dotted lines. "But the fountain is mythology, Ephraim. It's like a whole different subject in school. I mean, Ms. Little is never going to do a lesson on the Fountain of Youth, right?"

"A lot of science was explained by myth and magic before it was understood," Mallory said as she picked up a book from the desk in a puff of dust. She opened it up and read what was inside. "'Laboratory Notes of Orlando P. Appledore, as recorded by E. Darling.' Huh."

"What?" Will asked, grateful for the subject change.

"Darling," she said. "That was my mom's maiden name. It's the family that was the caretakers. This person was probably related to me." She flipped open the book and saw pages and pages filled with notes. In the margins were diagrams, sometimes of things that looked science-related, other times more like the pictures she drew in books: people and nature. She ran her fingers over the pages, feeling the slight rise of the ink. She thought of that girl in the picture, the one who looked just like her. Maybe this was her book. Maybe they were more alike than she had known.

"Can I see?" Ephraim took the notebook from Mallory and began looking through it. There were notes about temperature and pH, color, saturation: whole tables of them. The details, though, were faded and difficult to read in the slight light of the laboratory. "The answer could be here in this book or in this room. Something new. Something amazing. We just have to be willing to see it," Ephraim said.

Will shook his head. "But don't you see? You're missing the fundamental point of science. You can't have any ideas before you start. That's bias. You have to see what you see and then make sense of it."

"You have to have some idea, don't you? Or else how would you know where to look? Anyway, it seems to me that science shouldn't be saying 'No' and 'That's impossible.' I mean, science is about discovery, right? Just like Peary and everyone looking for the North Pole."

Will pursed his lips. Ephraim was right, to a point. "I guess I can read it over. See if there's anything in there that looks legitimate."

Ephraim didn't want to give up the book to Will, but he knew that his own scientific skills were nowhere near strong enough to make sense of the notebook. Will was their best chance at making sense of it, and therefore their best chance at helping his dad. "Okay," he said. "Let's go, for today."

Ephraim was the last one out of the room, and he turned off the lights. As he did, he noticed a thin bar of light, no thicker than a dime but nearly as tall as a door, by the bookcase. He stared at it, wondering what it could be.

"Coming, Ephraim?" Mallory called.

"Sure," Ephraim said. When he shut the door to the lab, he made sure to leave it open a crack.

TWENTY-SEVEN

Ephraim's mother had her arms up to her elbows in the sudsy water of the sink. They were cleaning up after another mediocre dinner: spaghetti again, this time with a sauce his mom called carbonara. Ephraim hadn't minded much. His attention had been fixed on that thin line of light. Where was it coming from?

"So," his mom said, taking a pot out of the suds and rinsing it before handing it to Brynn to dry. "I think we've all noticed that your father isn't improving quite as we'd hoped."

The pace of Price's dish-clearing slowed and he hesitated between the small table in the kitchen and the sink. They'd given up eating in the formal dining room, as it was too vast and hollow. "I think he's doing okay."

Their mother shook her head. "Dr. Winters isn't pleased either. He's recommending another specialist, down in New York, so . . ." She left her unfinished thought hanging.

Ephraim scraped out their bowls into the compost bin as she spoke. He was thinking that light could be coming from two places: outside or another room. Either way was intriguing to him.

"So?" Price prompted.

"If that's where your father needs to be to get well, then that's where we need to take him."

Brynn carefully dried a slotted spoon. "So we'll be moving down to New York?"

This finally got Ephraim's attention. "What?" he asked.

"I don't know," their mom said. She placed her soapy hands on the edge of the sink.

She couldn't possibly want them to move, Ephraim thought. Not now. Not when he was so close.

"I'm going to give the other doctor a call tomorrow. Dr. Winters sent him your father's records. We'll do a consultation and see what he thinks."

They didn't need to go anywhere, Ephraim thought. The answer was right here. All he needed was the time to find it. "When would we go?" he asked. "If we went?"

She picked up a pan and dunked it into the water. "Nothing's settled yet. I just wanted to let you know so that you had it on your radars."

Nothing's settled. So he still had time. That was all he

needed to hear. But he would have to act quickly to save his father. The light, he was sure, the light was the key.

Ephraim waited until the house was dark and still, except for the faint humming that always surrounded them. He slipped from his bed still fully clothed and padded down the stairs. The half moon cast a silver glow over everything and washed out the colors around him. He put his hand on the warm wood of the banister and slipped down the stairs to Brynn's library. The door squeaked as he pushed it open and she sat up in bed. "It's me," he whispered. "Ephraim."

"What are you doing here?" she asked. "Is everyone okay?"

He hurried across the room, dodging piles of books that looked like strange creatures in the shadows. He sat down on the edge of the bed. "We went back into the tunnels today. We got into the lab."

"Without me?" she asked.

"It happened really quickly. Listen, I saw something. When I was leaving, the lights were off—"

"The lights?"

"Yeah, there's electricity down there. Anyway, the lights were off but I saw this line of light over by the bookcase. There's got to be another secret passage."

"Okay. That sounds possible." She rubbed the heel of her hand into her eyes.

"So let's go."

"Right now?"

"The answer's down there, Brynn. We just have to find it. You should have seen this lab. All the devices and chemicals—even Will said it looked legitimate."

"Why can't we go in the morning?"

"You heard Mom. We don't have much more time."

Brynn rubbed her face some more. "I don't know about going into the tunnels at night."

"It's dark either way," he said. "Come on."

"Let's get Price."

Price, Ephraim knew, would not believe them. He wouldn't concede it was even possible that there was something magical or mysterious here. "I don't know, Brynn. We haven't told him about any of this yet."

"I'd just feel better if it were all three of us."

What she meant was she'd feel better with Price there to look out for them, and maybe Ephraim did a little, too. "Fine." He sighed. "Go up and get him and meet me by the back door."

She stretched and then, dropping her arms, hesitated, as if she were going to change her mind after all. "Brynn, please. I know you've thought about this, too. If there's something special about this house or the water here, it could make Dad better. We're doing this for Dad."

She threw off the sheets. "Okay," she said. "If Price will go, then I will, too."

TWENTY-EIGHT

In the dark of the tunnels, the three children fell into stride. Even their breath seemed to come in unison. Ephraim led the way, followed by Brynn, then Price, who had come along reluctantly. Brynn had tugged him by the hand to the back door. His hair stuck up at odd angles and he'd looked at Ephraim with confusion and contempt as Ephraim had tried to explain everything they'd found. "Let me just show you," he'd finally said.

The tunnel air felt cooler than it had earlier that day. Their feet scuffed along the paving stones.

Now here they were, back at the door, which was still propped ajar. Ephraim pushed it open and then reached in to turn on the lights. They all blinked to get used to the sudden brightness. Ephraim hadn't noticed the smell of the lab before, acrid and acidic. "We found the key and finally got in today."

"This house just gets weirder and weirder," Price said.

"It's amazing," Brynn said, spinning around.

"I told you," Ephraim replied, heading straight for the bookcase. He ran his fingers along the edge. "There's cool air blowing in!" he exclaimed. "Help me move this."

Price took one side and Ephraim took the other. Grunting, they slid it along the stone floor.

"Oh," Brynn said softly.

Moving the bookcase had revealed a small opening, about two feet wide and four feet tall. Inside the hole was a steep staircase. Another secret of the Water Castle revealed.

Ephraim started up.

His fingers brushed through cobwebs as he steadied himself on the stone wall. He could see, but barely, the light a pale gray.

"What's up there?" Price called.

"Nothing yet," Ephraim replied. He heard his brother start up the stairs behind him.

"The hum—it's stronger here," Price said.

"I know," Ephraim agreed. But he kept climbing. They could see only a few stairs in front of them and a faint glow in the distance.

The humming grew even louder.

"What do you even expect to find?" Price asked.

Ephraim considered the question. Maybe Price would

believe him. They were climbing up a secret staircase in their strange old house. If someone was going to believe in magic, this would be the place to start. "This house has secrets," Ephraim said. "Strange secrets."

Price laughed. "You don't believe that, do you? I thought you were just playing along with Brynn."

Ephraim felt his body stiffen. "Look where we are."

"I'm telling you, people used to live for this kind of thing. There were raids by American Indians and wars and stuff. They needed places to hide."

"The American Indians didn't raid here," Ephraim said. He wished that Price had stayed behind, that Brynn had never woken him. At least the hum was getting louder, which made it harder to hear Price as he marveled at how Ephraim could still possibly believe in something as silly as magic. It wasn't magic, though. It wasn't mythology, like Will said. It was science, and it was real.

Ephraim noticed that there were shelves cut into the sides of the stairs. He peered in at one, saw a collection of lanterns, and wished for a match. The pitch of the hum went up, and the boys could feel it in their bodies. "I don't like that humming," Price said. "We should just get out of here."

"Are you scared?" Ephraim challenged.

"No," Price retorted. "I'm just thinking that, well, maybe we're coming up on the electric center, you know. Mom said this place had a generator. I don't want to stumble into some hundred-year-old electrical device. We could be fried like potato chips."

Ephraim smiled to himself. For the first time in their lives, Price was scared and he was not.

Still the hum rose in pitch and volume.

A few steps more and there was another shelf. This one held beakers and test tubes, all empty. Maybe these stairs were for storage. And maybe, just maybe, the cure was hidden in the stairs.

"We have to get out of here," Price said, and tugged on Ephraim's shirt.

Ephraim went a few more steps, and that's when he saw the wooden crate.

"Ephraim, come on."

Peeking into the crate, he saw bottles of water.

"Ephraim, now," Price insisted.

Ephraim grabbed the crate and followed his brother back down the stairs.

"What happened?" Brynn asked. She was holding a book in each hand.

"Price freaked," Ephraim said.

"I didn't." Price glared at his brother.

"What's that?"

"I found it up there." He looked down at the top of the crate. It was printed with the logo for Dr. Appledore's Crystal Water. "Probably nothing."

He slid the cover off the crate and counted three bottles. He lifted one out to examine it. There was a label on the side of the bottle that he could barely make out. He blew on it to get some of the dust off it.

The label was a simple white rectangle. The script in which it was written was nearly impossible to read.

Fountain of Youth
Crystal Springs, Maine
The cure for all that ales ye

Ephraim read the label twice, then looked at his siblings and grinned.

TWENTY-NINE

Ephraim lay in bed contemplating the bottle he had taken from the case. Brynn had pointed out that *ails* was spelled wrong. But *ails* wasn't the word that had hooked Ephraim. *Cure* was.

Any number of things could be in that bottle. Maybe it was just lake water, as Will insisted, and it was a big sham attempted by his ancestors. That was the idea that was easiest for him to dismiss. The bottle had a different label from the Dr. Appledore's Crystal Water he'd seen.

So maybe it was the real thing. But what made it special? There were a lot of chemicals down in that lab. Had someone long ago added some to the water like the Radithor? As Mallory had pointed out, even if the chemicals had been safe before, after sitting around for so long they could be very, very dangerous. He didn't want his father to lose his jaw.

He flipped onto his side and looked at the bottle in the moonlight. Price had told him he was being ridiculous, that there was no such thing as the Fountain of Youth. If Price was correct, though, then why was the crate hidden away in an underground staircase behind a bookcase?

There was something special about that water. Ephraim was sure of it. He could almost hear Will talking in his mind, quoting his grandfather: "My Pepe always said, *sure* ain't squat." Though Will used a more colorful word. It meant that you could believe something, but it didn't make it true. He needed proof. Explorers went in search of what they believed existed. But he was not an explorer, he reminded himself. He was a scientist now. He needed to keep thinking differently.

His mind turned over and over. All he needed was a piece of evidence and then he would know 100 percent no doubt about it that the water was the cure he sought. Evidence. He had learned in his science class the best way to test a hypothesis was with an experiment. As soon as he thought of the word *experiment*, he knew what he would do next. An experiment needs a subject, and the only possible subject he had was himself. It was dangerous, of course, but the end result was a possible cure for his father. And, though he would be loath to admit it, part of him was eager to get a taste of that water. If it was magical, maybe it would change him, too. Maybe he could become more like the people of Crystal Springs. Maybe he could be something less ordinary.

He slipped out of his bed for the second time that night and retrieved one of the bottles. He held it in his hands for a moment before twisting the top. Rust had sealed the metal top to the glass, but after a struggle, it twisted free. He wiped the mouth of the bottle on his shirt.

If he was right about the water, drinking would make him immortal. No, not immortal. Mallory had said it just slowed things down. So what would that mean? Would he be stuck in his twelve-year-old body forever? Given a choice, twelve was not the age at which he would choose to stay or even to linger. But he did not have a choice. He had to save his father and this was the only way to do it. Dr. Winters had said that he wasn't progressing the way he was supposed to be, and now they were even talking about leaving the Water Castle. No, he had to act, and he had to act now.

He took a long, cool drink. It tasted okay, a little metallic maybe, but not poisonous. He couldn't feel any changes in his body, but that didn't mean anything: he wasn't sick. He was young and healthy, and so the effects on him would not be immediate. All he needed to find out was whether or not it was dangerous. He figured if he made it to the morning without getting sick, he could judge it to be safe.

When he climbed back into bed his unsettled mind turned toward his father. Would he be grateful that Ephraim had saved him? Or would he be resentful that he'd stay the same while his wife and other children aged on beyond him? Maybe his father would keep aging, though. Maybe one sip would be enough to cure him without affecting him permanently.

Ephraim squeezed his eyes shut. The repercussions spun on and on and on and they were too big for him to contemplate.

It didn't matter, he told himself. It didn't matter because he needed his father back. He needed his father to laugh and sing off-key and to draw. He needed his father to say things like, "You know, I was a bit of an odd duck when I was your age, too." He needed his father to put his arm around him and say, "Don't tell Brynn and Price, but you're my favorite middle child, you know. Absolutely."

The father in his memories became the father in his dreams. Nothing strange or fantastic, just the two of them sharing the couch at their home back in Cambridge, feet to feet, each reading a book and sharing the best parts. It was so normal that Ephraim didn't even realize it was a dream until he woke up in the oversized bed, the heavy duvet weighing down on him.

He remembered the events of the night before all at once and sat up straight in bed. He ran his hands along his body. Everything felt fine. In fact, it was possible that he felt a little better than normal, though he knew that could just be wishful thinking. He was not dead or sick, though, and that was enough reassurance for him.

Along the hallway he went, and down the stairs to his parents' bedroom. His dad was awake and propped up on the pillows, his head turned to the windows. If he heard Ephraim, or noticed him coming in at all, he didn't show it.

Ephraim walked slowly, careful not to make a sound, to the far side of the bed and into his father's line of vision. "Hi, Dad," he said softly. "I told you I was going to save you, and now I have the cure."

Ephraim's father's lips were moving without sound.

"It's this house. This place. There's something magical about it. Or maybe scientific. I'm not sure. I just know what I found and that it's going to help you."

Still his father did not respond.

Ephraim hesitated. What if he hadn't waited long enough to test the water's effect on himself? It could be eating away at him as he spoke, sprinkling tumors and cysts around his insides. No, he couldn't think that way, he told himself. He needed to be smart and rational like his sister. He needed to be brave and decisive like his brother.

"I dreamed about you last night. We were reading together like we used to do." His voice cracked and he couldn't talk anymore.

He held the bottle out to his father, and helped him to drink.

And then, nothing.

Or rather, not the something that Ephraim had hoped for. His father sputtered on the water, seeming to choke. Ephraim pulled the bottle back and his dad watched him with wide eyes, panicked.

"I'm sorry," Ephraim said. "I'm sorry, but you have to drink it."

He tried again, and this time, some went down. He watched his father's throat working as he swallowed. Then his father coughed and spit some of the water out.

"Ephraim!" Ephraim turned to see his mother in the doorway, red-faced and confused. "Ephraim, what are you doing?"

September 3, 1909

Nora spread the newspapers out on the table and used Dr. Appledore's elephant figurine to hold down the curling edge. She read the headline again and again: "COOK REPORTS HE HAS FOUND THE NORTH POLE."

Frederick Cook had been presumed dead. Missing in the best-case scenario. Now he was back and insisting that he had reached the Pole before Peary and Henson, who had not been heard from in months. Some had hoped that Peary would find him on this latest mission.

Yet here he was back and claiming victory.

Nora could not believe it. Could not fathom how he had been gone, lost in the wilderness, and then to survive that long. To survive that long was simply impossible. It made more sense that he had hidden away somewhere safe and warm. Then, just when Peary had succeeded (for she was certain Peary and Henson had made it), he emerged from hiding and claimed the Pole for himself before Peary could make his announcement.

Nora folded the paper. She had to find Harry and let him know. He would be headed back to school soon, and she hoped he was not tucked away in his rooms preparing to leave. She ran through the house, checking rooms until she discovered him back in the library, where he had gone to look for her. She arrived breathless, and he spoke before she could. "You've seen it!"

"Yes," she said, still breathing hard.

"I suppose I ought to be glad that anyone has found it," Harry said. "And yet—"

"Yet there is nothing to be glad about."

"A shame, really," Orlando Appledore said. Both children jumped. Dr. Appledore had been sitting so still in his shiny leather chair that neither had noticed he was there. "He worked so hard and for so many decades. Yet science does not always reward fortitude." He reached out to pick up the poker and prodded the fire. "Cook worked for Peary, you know. He was the doctor on several of his expeditions. He wanted to write about it, and Peary would not let him. Such is the way. Such is the way of exploration and such is the way of hubris."

And then Dr. Appledore's mind, momentarily distracted by the news of the day, returned to the thoughts that ruled his waking and sleeping life. "Herodotus thought it was in Ethiopia, you know. That's what he reported. The Ethiopians lived for many years, and he ascribed this longevity to a fountain," and here he began to read from the book in his lap, "'wherein when they had washed, they found their flesh all glossy and sleek, as if they had bathed in oil—and a scent came from the spring like that of violets.'"

He put the book down on the table next to the newspaper and stared at it. "They were certain they had found it. Just like Ponce de Leon. Just like Cook, for that matter. Yet had they? We do not live forever. We do not come close. Perhaps that's for the best." His gaze turned to the fire, which seemed to mesmerize him. "Sometimes we seek and seek and seek for so long that we convince ourselves we have found something that is not there to be found."

"That's true," Nora said. "Cook has provided no proof."

"He says it will follow him back to New York. He left it with a friend in Greenland," Harry explained.

"If you had made the greatest discovery of our day, would you not keep the proof close to you?"

"True," Dr. Appledore agreed. "As close as skin."

"Harry!" the voice of Mrs. Appledore called from outside the library. She saw the room as the world of Dr. Appledore and would not enter. Harry frowned, but went to his mother.

Nora picked up the paper and began to reread the article, seeking any bit of information that might prove the tale to be a falsehood.

Dr. Appledore jumped to his feet, startling Nora, who dropped the paper to the ground. "My word! Eureka!" he exclaimed. "To think I nearly forgot. To the lab, dear."

As they walked, he explained himself. "You see, as I was taking my bath last evening, it occurred to me. I was following in the footsteps of Archimedes, in the way he discovered the concept of water displacement. It seems so self-evident now, that of course the volume of the object would displace the water. Yet, for the ancient Greeks, it was a wonder."

"Dr. Appledore—"

"'Eureka,' Archimedes is claimed to have cried out. 'I have found it.' And so have I. Or nearly."

Nora took the copper key from her neck and unlocked the door. "Dr. Appledore, what have you found?"

Dr. Appledore rushed into the laboratory. From his desk he took a rolled piece of paper. "I worked all night on this." He spread out a map that was covered with interlocking circles. In some of the circles, numbers were written. "We've tested and manipulated all the waters above the land, and found nothing. Thus, by clear deduction, it must be an underground spring. Perhaps it once had an outlet, but no more. Of course, this means a much wider area for us to search. We must have an organized approach," he said. "The numbers will tell us. We're getting close, Nora. We're getting very close."

The map looked to her like the work of a madman. The circles, drawn in his shaky hand, overlapped in no discernible pattern. She looked at his face, wrinkled and careworn. His eyes were bloodshot. She wondered if he had slept at all. "These circles will tell us?" she asked.

"Of course, my dear, of course. We must take many measurements. Carefully, carefully. It will take much work, but eventually—"

"Perhaps you would like to sit down, Dr. Appledore."

"Sit? Now, when we are so close?"

"We mustn't get too overexcited."

"We can never be sufficiently excited! Do you not understand how close we are?"

She did understand. She understood as she never had before. She put her hand down on top of the map and felt the fragility of the paper. All his hopes and dreams were wrapped in this map, and she could tear it as easily as she could roll it up and tuck it safely away for him—more so.

"I am merely arguing that we should proceed rationally. With care and diligence."

"I just said that, did I not? Honestly, Nora, if I cannot rely on you to pay attention, why, I, I—" He opened his mouth and closed it. "Why, I fear I have lost the thread of my discourse."

"A seat, Dr. Appledore," she said gently. "Perhaps by the fire."

Yes, she understood. She understood from the wavy lines of his drawing, his rheumy eyes, and the way his attention waxed and waned. She understood from the way Mrs. Appledore avoided him. It wasn't disgust, Nora realized, it was pity.

This project was as doomed as Henson and Peary's.

He began rolling up the map roughly. "We'll start in the morning. I've put an order in through the catalogs. Of course, that will take days to reach us, but we can begin with what we have."

Nora took the map from him. "If it's there to be found, then we will find it."

"Of course it's there, my child. Why else would I have looked so long?"

She put his hand on his. "Indeed," she lied.

THIRTY

Ephraim called a meeting after school in which he explained what had happened the night before.

"It was stupid," he said. They sat on a crest in the lawn of the garden, their backs against the base of a large sculpture. "*I* was stupid." He held the bottle in his hands. He'd brought it out to show them.

"It wasn't stupid," Mallory lied.

"You had a good reason for believing," Will said.

"My mom said she doesn't know what to do with me," he said. She had cried when he'd told her how he'd planned to solve the mystery of the fountain and save his father. She'd held him so tightly that he wasn't sure if she would ever let go; maybe they would be frozen there like the statues on the lawn.

Price had told Ephraim that he didn't know why he was even surprised anymore. "Ever since Dad got sick, all you've done is made a mess of things. Grow up, would you?" And then Price stopped talking to him altogether, which was even worse.

He wasn't sure what Brynn thought, but she had been avoiding him, and he didn't think that was a good sign.

"Can I see the bottle?" Will asked.

Ephraim handed it over. "It's just water," he said. "Just plain old stupid water."

Will spun it around in his hands. "I've been looking through the notebooks. I haven't found anything. They seem to go in one direction and then another. There's lab notes from experiments. There are strange conversations recorded. Nothing is really complete, but I'll keep looking."

Ephraim thought he should tell him not to bother.

Mallory had the copper key around her neck, and she pulled it from side to side on the chain. "People get better from strokes," she said. "On their own, I mean. Over time they just get better."

"A little. But not all the way." Ephraim tugged on the laces of his sneakers. "It's best if they get treatment right away, and my dad was alone for hours after the stroke. My mom told us not to expect too much."

"Anything is possible," Mallory said. She tried to make her voice sound hopeful, but it just fell flat.

"It all made such perfect sense when I was thinking about it. We'd get the water. We'd get it to my dad. He'd get better and we could go home. Simple."

"Your judgment was clouded," Will said.

Brynn would not have made this mistake. Or Price. Or Mallory or Will. Only Ephraim. And that was the real problem, he was starting to see. He thought that this place was magical because everyone seemed so smart and talented. There had to be something happening to them, he had reasoned. The truth was, he just didn't measure up. He couldn't save his father; he might not even pass sixth grade.

"It's like he has this big hole in his brain. I just want him to be whole again," Ephraim said.

The words *hole* and *whole* reverberated in Mallory's head, reminding her of her own fractured family. Whole and hole. They had learned about homophones in elementary school, but now the near-opposite words that sounded so much alike were painful and profound. "I know what you mean," Mallory said.

"Me too," Will agreed.

The sun was fading and the air cool, but none of them moved, their circle providing just a small slice of warmth.

THIRTY-ONE

Mallory could hear her father downstairs puttering around in the kitchen. He was probably making himself a baloney and cheese sandwich, something that Ephraim's father could no longer do, and would probably never do again.

She pulled a book from a stack on her desk, tucked it under her arm, and headed down the stairs. He was sitting in the armchair, the sandwich sitting on the small table next to it. The Patriots were playing the Giants on television.

"You really are a bachelor now," she said.

He smiled, but she could tell that her joke had stung. "Are you hungry?" he asked.

"I made myself some mac and cheese earlier," she said. "I ate it in my room."

"What are you doing up there?"

"Working on my explorer project," she said. Ephraim had found a scrapbook of articles about the expedition—gathered by the same E. Darling who had kept the science journal, and, she assumed, created the map. She had been going through them.

"Ah, the great explorer project," he said. "Due soon, isn't it?"

She nodded. "Next week. Who did you do?"

"What? Oh, we didn't do that project way back in the stone age."

"But you must have. Uncle Edward did it. Mom, too."

"Oh?" He stared fixedly at the television. "I guess I forget, then. Mustn't have been anybody as exciting as Henson." He picked up a sandwich and took a bite. It wasn't like her father to forget these things, but she figured these weren't regular times. "Did you need something, honey?" he asked.

"Actually, I wanted to show you something. I drew a picture of you," she said. "Do you want to see it?"

"There's nothing I want more in this world."

She flipped open the book to the drawing. He muted the television and took the book from her.

"It's beautiful," he said.

"Thank you," she replied.

"I didn't know you still liked to draw."

"I kind of hide it," she admitted.

He grinned. "By drawing in books, I see." With his thumb in the book to mark the page, he looked back at the cover. "*Properties of Electromagnetism?* Well, at least it's something I'll never need."

She decided not to tell him about the dozens of other books she had defaced.

"I'm glad you're still here, Dad."

"Mallory, I'm not going anywhere. Ever. Wherever you go and whatever you do, you'll always have a home to come to."

"Because of the Water Castle," Mallory said.

He shook his head. "That's not what ties me here. That's Eleanor's duty. It was her family that made that promise." He rubbed his palm on his forehead. "I'm here for you. I may not always stay here in this house but wherever I am, that's a home for you. Do you understand?" he asked.

She nodded her head.

"So are there any other pictures hidden in here?" he asked.

He slid over a little and she squished into the chair with him. When she was little, she'd been able to slide in right beside him, but now the space was tight. She felt the flannel of his shirt against her skin. Even though he had showered after work, he still smelled like oil, and she breathed deep.

He flipped through the pages and stopped on her picture of the tree. "It's really lovely, Mallory," he said.

"Thanks."

"If you want to take some classes, or need supplies—"

"You don't need to buy me things."

He turned the page and revealed Price's face. Mallory reddened. "You got his likeness very well."

There were no more pictures in the book, Mallory knew, but she liked sitting in the chair with her dad. She closed her eyes and tucked into his chest.

"Brushing up on a little chemistry?" he asked.

She fluttered her eyes open and saw notes in the margin of the book. "I didn't write that," she said.

"Well, if you had, I'd send you right off to MIT. That's advanced stuff. And some Latin, too." He pointed to three words: *Nemo can teneo.*

"Can you read it?" she asked.

"There was a time when I was a Latin superstar. Not as good as your mother—" He shook his head. "It's all gone now. Been too long since I used it."

Her heart was beating faster. "It's probably nothing," she said. "I think I'm going to go to sleep."

"Okay."

She climbed out of the chair and took the book back from him. She turned the page and saw more writing. Pages and pages of it, mostly equations. And then, scrawled across a page: "You have to burn the water."

She read it twice, but it still didn't make any sense.

"Show me your next drawing, okay?"

"Sure, okay. Good night."

"Good night," he replied. He leaned his head back and closed his eyes. "I love you," he said.

"I love you, too."

Mallory raced up the stairs, hoping her science skills were strong enough to understand what was written in the book.

THIRTY-TWO

Ephraim could not sleep. He lay on his back and looked at the ceiling, counting the chirps of crickets outside. He rolled over and saw the water bottle sitting on the floor next to his closet. It filled him with shame. He imagined throwing it into the lake or smashing it against the stones of the house. He would get rid of it, that much was for sure. Maybe he'd write a note about how stupid he had been, how you shouldn't believe the stories you hear, and he'd throw it in the river on the far side of town. It would float down to be discovered by some other kids so that they would not make the same mistakes he had.

Once he was out of bed, he realized how futile the idea of sleep was, so he left his room. He walked down the moonlit halls. The house was almost familiar now. He knew where an errant floorboard made the rug pucker up, so he no longer tripped over it. He knew that the door to the bedroom next to his never stayed closed. He knew that the house hummed. And he knew that it didn't mean anything.

He stepped over the floorboard that always groaned and around the door and went to the stairs, pausing at the top of them. He could see the mirror at the bottom, but no reflection in it.

He walked down the flight of stairs and past the library where his sister slept. He kept going to the next door: his parents' room. When he put his hand on it, it swung inward. He could make out the shapes of his parents in the large bed. His mother was curled up like a comma. His father lay in a straight line. The only bright side to his unsuccessful attempt at saving his dad was that his actions hadn't done any more damage to his fragile father.

The doorknob was cool in his hand as he pulled the door shut, trying not to make a sound. He climbed up the stairs, but he wasn't ready to go back to his room, so he walked to the end of the hall to the window that looked out over the garden. He knew that the bumps were sculptures and the fountain. The big hulking shape was the marble bottling house that led to the tunnels.

He hoped the blue light would come again, and the flash, so he could maybe believe in the magic and mystery of the house again. But the light outside was silver and still, like an old photograph and not the real world. He turned and there in the nook was the sculpture that he had seen on his first night in the castle. Orlando Priam Appeldore. Keeper of the flame.

He'd pinned all his hopes, he realized, on a man with a ridiculous mustache.

September 6, 1909

Nora found Orlando slumped over the lab table. There was a case full of glass bottles in front of him. She ran to his side and put her hand on his back, worried that she would feel no heartbeat, no breath. He lifted his head slowly, blinked his eyes, and said, "Eureka. I have found it." He pointed to a wooden box full of bottles.

Nora glanced at the bottles, which seemed very similar to the ones for Dr. Appledore's Crystal Water. "How do you know for certain?" she asked.

He brushed his arm over the map in front of him that was covered with circles. They had been testing soil, with her carefully writing down the numbers he dictated—numbers with no rhyme or reason. "The map and the numbers. There is no other place. You have to burn the water." He lifted one of the bottles. Indeed it was one of Dr. Appledore's Crystal Water bottles, but Orlando had replaced the label with a white one on which he had written in his shaky penmanship:

Fountain of Youth
Crystal Springs, Maine
The cure for all that ales ye

"They never found it because it wasn't there to be found. Don't you see? I had to make it."

Nora shook her head.

"I kept searching and designing theories. Nothing ever came of it. All those scientists we met, Tesla with the contraption he built—none of it mattered. The answer was here all along. Angus knew. Angus built it. This house. The answer is this house."

"Dr. Appledore, I'm not sure I understand."

"It's simple, really. The house makes it stronger. The house burns the water."

Nora put her hand on top of his and helped him place the bottle down on the table.

"*Inveniam Viam Aut Facium.* 'I shall find a way or make one.'"

"Peary," Nora said, recognizing the explorer's words.

"Yes. I was thinking about your Peary so focused on the final destination. Has he considered what will happen when he reaches the Pole? Will it seem a small thing, a tiny spot no different from all the other ice around him? Or will he be overwhelmed by the vastness of it all? Eternity is such a big thing." He laughed at himself, a hollow laugh. "Eternity is a big thing. I might as well say that a grain of sand is small. Yet standing at the precipice, it is unfathomable."

Nora held herself very still. She had never seen Orlando this bad off.

"Do you know of St. Elmo's fire?" he asked her.

She knew that it was something sailors saw, a glow of blue

light on the mast of the ship. "Do you think Peary and Henson saw it?" she asked, trying to follow the line of his thinking, something that was getting harder and harder to do each day.

He waved his hand. "Perhaps. The air would be rather dry up there. An electrical charge builds up and glows blue."

"It's supposed to be good luck."

"I've seen it here," he said. "On the house."

"Yes," Nora agreed. She had seen a blue glow from time to time herself.

"You have to burn the water," Orlando told her.

He was speaking nonsense, and Nora knew she should get him up to bed. There was a book in front of him, the printed words covered over with a madman's scrawl. She leaned over to read what was written there. Orlando slapped his hand down on the book. "You will need to protect it. Protect the secret!"

"Yes, sir."

"Others will want to use it. To profit from it. That's all men want, but this secret is beyond the realms of commerce. You must understand what you are promising. For generations, your family must keep the secret and let no one drink from these bottles, and let no one create any more, no matter what they offer you."

The wildness of Dr. Appledore's eyes made her rock back. "You should get some rest," she told him.

"Promise me."

"Dr. Appledore."

"Promise you will tell no one!"

"Yes, of course. I promise. Now go get your rest."

The light in his eyes faded. "Rest? Yes. Yes, I think I will. Clean up, won't you?"

"Certainly."

He left the room slowly. When he was gone, she gathered his papers and stacked them neatly on his desk. She placed his lab notebook on top of the loose pages. She wound the cord of the Bunsen burner, and cleaned off the distillation tubes.

Nothing Dr. Appledore had said to her made any sense to her mind. She wished Harry were home so she could talk it over with him. She was not certain if Dr. Appledore had truly solved the riddle, or if he was deluding himself. It seemed madness: you have to burn the water. Water by its very nature did not burn. And what was the talk of St. Elmo's Fire? Was he saying electricity was somehow involved? She was not sure if his ravings were the work of a damaged mind—or simply too complex for her to understand.

If he was correct, though, she had promised him a great deal. The monumental nature of it began to overwhelm her. Eternity was the very thing that Dr. Appledore so feared, but that's what she had promised, not only for herself, but also for every generation that followed.

Thinking they should not be out in plain view, even in the secret laboratory, she picked up the crate of bottles and looked for a place to hide them. With great effort, she slid aside the bookcase to reveal the stairs that went up to the roof of the house. It was one of his latest additions to the Water

Castle, one he had not explained to her. She carried the crate up to a shelf and tucked it away. The bottles clinked together.

After a moment's hesitation, she removed one of the dozen bottles. It was warm in her hands, as if Dr. Appledore had been holding it. She carried the bottle with her back down the stairs, thinking of Matthew Henson and how he would not have turned back so close to the Pole. Even if he had heard that Cook had already made it, he would have kept on going and completed the expedition. Even if he were overwhelmed by the vastness, as Dr. Appledore predicted, he would have marched onward.

With the bottle in one hand and Dr. Appledore's book tucked under her arm, she turned off the lights and went out through the tunnels. As she stepped out into the light of day, she smelled the faintest whiff of smoke.

THIRTY-THREE

N o one can know. *Nemo can teneo.*

Mallory put the Latin words into an online translator and that's what came out: *No one can know.* These four words made her heart beat faster. There was a possibility—just a slight one—that they were on to something. Then again, there was the scrawl, as if written by a madman at his wit's end: "You must burn the water." That didn't even make sense: it was impossible to burn water.

Still, she went forward, working her way through what was written in the book. She found chemistry equations. She did not know much about chemistry since it would be another four years before she studied it in school. Still, she read the pages with the notes on them and copied over the letters and numbers as best she could. And then she looked at what she had. She couldn't tell if they were notations about what the scientist had found, or if they were what he hoped to create, but it was definitely some sort of chemical formula.

She tried rearranging it. She had to look things up, like what letters stood for which chemicals. Some of the terms she knew. H_2O was water, and she took that as a good sign. She saw the symbols for uranium and radium, which she figured, if they were in the water of the town, would explain the high radiation readings on Ms. Little's Geiger counter. There were more benign elements in the equation, too: magnesium, chlorine, calcium. Then there were letters she could not figure: *Or.* She thought maybe it was just the word: or, like either/or. But that didn't make sense as she read the equation. She looked at the periodic table online, and it wasn't there. She searched and searched. She even tried reading through a chemistry book that she'd used as one of her journals. Nothing.

Her eyes burned like they'd been kept open for days, and her head throbbed with the letters and numbers on the pages when she finally pushed the book away.

Disappointment and frustration made her agitated, and she paced around her room, not even bothering to hide the sound of her footfalls. She had told her father she wasn't feeling well and needed to stay home. He had swallowed the lie as readily as he had the one about Field Day when she'd gone to see her mom. It didn't make it any easier.

Outside her window, a crow landed on the branch of a tree

and cawed at her. She looked past it. In the distance, looming over the town, was the Water Castle.

The lab. She needed to go back. After checking to make sure her father was in his garage, she rolled her bike out to the main road, then pedaled as fast as she could to the Water Castle. Dropping her bike at the side of the house, she ran around back to the old bottling house, pushed aside the ivy, and went through the door. The stillness of the marble room slowed the beat of her heart and she took a deep breath before descending into the tunnels. It was creepier alone. The walls seemed wetter and her footsteps echoed. She went deeper in, and she thought she heard a skittering noise behind her. She stopped. The noise stopped. Her heart beat and beat and beat like the little drums they used in music class. On she walked. Again the noise started, as if someone were following her dragging a stick on the wall. Whirling around, she shined her flashlight up and down the tunnels.

Nothing.

It's just your imagination, she told herself. All those old stories are bumping around in your head. She rubbed her eyes, took a deep breath, and kept walking. She hadn't slept much the night before, trying to make sense of what she had read. She hummed to herself to cover any sounds.

She remembered the laboratory being closer than this was; she felt sure she should have been there by now. Had she gone down the wrong path? Had it moved? Now she was starting to think crazily. She took longer strides.

Finally, she saw the door in front of her. It was propped open, so she let herself in and turned on the lights. Right away she saw the bookcase moved out of place and the opening behind it.

The shelf of chemicals was her first stop and she read each label, carefully picking up and replacing each bottle, but there was no clue there, no sign of what "or" might mean. A breeze rushed down the staircase and tickled her neck. A hidden staircase in an underground laboratory. There were no clues in the lab, but maybe she would find something up those stairs.

Up and up and up she climbed. There was faint light from up above and in it she could see all the cobwebs, with the spiders in them, large and lazy. She could feel their eyes on her and could only imagine what they were thinking, to have been undisturbed so long and then suddenly there she was in front of them.

As she climbed higher, the air grew warmer. The light seemed to be getting brighter, too, though it was hard to tell, it happened so slowly. She thought she saw the skeleton of a mouse or rat, but didn't look any closer. She just shivered and kept going.

The stairs went on for an impossible distance. Her legs started to hurt. She leaned forward and put her hands on the step in front of her. Another step and the wood broke out beneath her foot, her shin scraping against the splinters. "Ow!" Her voice echoed back around her. She felt tears stinging her eyes, but she was so close. She took a deep breath. Up and up and up she kept climbing. Little by little, the light grew brighter and she found herself nearing the opening. It looked like the top of a slide, with a small half dome that covered the opening to the stairs.

After crawling out, she stood and found herself on top of the Water Castle. She was dizzy at the change and had to brace herself. She blinked against the brightness, then pulled herself out of the hole and stood on top of the slate shingles. *I'm standing on top of the Water Castle,* she thought. It was amazing. She had never been up so high before. It felt like she imagined sitting on the clouds would. The whole town stretched out below her. A cool breeze ruffled her hair. Breathing in deeply, she thought, *This is my town, my air.* For the first time, she thought it was beautiful.

She reached down to rub her sore shin and saw a metal barrel, about as tall as she was and about as far around. It was stamped with the words *Crystal Springs Water Co.* Below, faded, something was written. She shuffled across the roof to get a closer look. She recognized the scrawl immediately, and even though it was hard to read them, she knew what the words said: *You have to burn the water.*

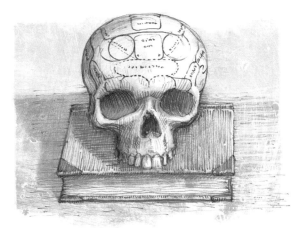

THIRTY-FOUR

I never told my dad that I found these tunnels," Will said as they snaked their way through. After school, Will had asked to come over to see the stairs. Ephraim hadn't really wanted to go back to the lab, but he felt he owed Will at least that much, after he'd tried so hard to help Ephraim's dad.

"Why not?" Ephraim asked.

The tunnels were becoming almost familiar to Ephraim: their musty smell, the way the light made everything seem both closer and farther away.

"I dunno. I guess maybe because it would just add fuel to the fire. Not actual fire, but my dad's being so angry all the time. Like if he knew the tunnels were real, he would think it would be just more proof that the Appledores had cheated everyone, especially our family."

"But I thought you believed him when you were little?"

"I guess I did and I didn't," Will said. "He was wrong about your family."

"Thanks."

"I'm sorry I listened to him."

"It's okay."

The tunnels were making Will talkative again. "It's not. My family has had this grudge against yours for so long. I know it's stupid because it was over a hundred years ago, but my family wanted to sell the water, too. They did okay, but they weren't rich like your family. There was a big family farm, and the five-and-dime, so I guess they were better off than most people. But they wanted more. They were going to open up their own plant. They knew the water wasn't really magical or whatever, but if the Appledores were making money off it, why shouldn't anyone else?"

"Okay." Ephraim didn't know why Will was telling him all of this. It was ancient history.

"I grew up hearing about all those greedy Appledores and how they ruined our family. So maybe I didn't give you a chance at first. That's all. But I'm glad I did eventually, because I'm glad to have, um, gotten to know you. And also we didn't burn the hotel down. My mean great-aunt Winnifred always said that she wishes we had, but my Pepe swears we didn't."

"It doesn't matter anymore anyway." Ephraim tugged at the bracelet around his wrist, the one that Mallory had made for him. No one had ever made him a friendship bracelet before—or a friendship anything, for that matter. And Will was turning out to be someone he could rely on, too, someone who looked out for him. He pulled the bracelet and let it snap back against his wrist, wondering why he'd been so eager to leave this place. It wouldn't be too long before they were leaving. It was what he had wanted since he'd arrived in Crystal Springs, but it didn't bring him any joy.

He pushed open the door of the lab and went inside. The light was still on. "I guess we forgot to turn that off," he said.

Will picked up the skull with the lines on it. "I looked this up online. It's for phrenology," he said. "People used to believe you could determine a person's personality just by the lumps on his head."

Ephraim looked at the skull, at the dotted lines that crisscrossed it. His skull would say he was gullible, foolish, reckless, even. But what happened when you changed? Did your head change with it? It was a ridiculous idea. "I guess that's just more proof that nothing going on down here was real."

Will put the skull down. "Oh, it was real. I mean, they were doing real science down here, they just never found anything. Those lab notes prove that they were definitely testing something, but if they ever succeeded, there was no note of it. Not in that book at least."

"Thanks anyway." Ephraim looked at the books on the shelf, thinking of all the time and energy they wasted in this pursuit.

Will let out his breath, relieved. "I really tried to find something there. I just couldn't make it work. All of my ideas have gone nowhere."

"Yeah, well, mine, too. Those are the stairs. Follow me."

The two boys started climbing up through the dark. Ephraim noticed more this time, like that there were sconces on the wall for candles or torches. Maybe this passageway had nothing to do with the water, but was just a place to hide like Price had said. The tunnels, too, could have been part of some elaborate escape mechanism. Rather than brilliant, maybe Ephraim's ancestors had just been paranoid.

"You find any more stuff for our project around the house?" Will asked.

"No, but I haven't really been looking."

"I was thinking maybe we should dress up as our explorers. Like we could pretend we were at a convention, giving talks, you know?"

Ephraim said, "Sure. That sounds okay. I know where there's a hat I could use." He was having a hard time planning for the project when so much in his life was about to change. He didn't even know if he'd still be in Crystal Springs when it was time for presentations.

"Ephraim?" Will asked.

"Yeah?"

"Are you okay?"

"Yeah," Ephraim said again, but it wasn't true. With his dad lost to him, he didn't think he'd ever be okay again.

They kept climbing. Ephraim thought he felt wind blowing down the stairs and across his face. It smelled both sweet and rotted. They kept climbing. Past the place where Price had started asking to go back. Past the place where he had found the crate. The only noise was the scuff of their feet.

Until, that is, the crack.

The crack was followed by the tumbling.

The tumbling was followed by the scream.

THIRTY-FIVE

M allory knocked her fist hard on the front door of the
Water Castle and called out, "Ephraim!"

After she'd been on the roof, she'd come back down into
the lab and then out through the tunnels to the bottling plant.
She'd sat up on one of the counters in the cool, marble room
and glanced up at the bits of sky that she could see between the
ivy leaves. She was thinking about how the spaces between
the ivy seemed as real and solid as the ivy itself when an idea
came over her. The pieces fell together and for a moment, she
thought she understood the writing in the book. She thought,
but she wasn't sure. She knew she needed to find Ephraim
and Will.

She banged on the door again. "Ephraim!"

Price opened the door and looked her up and down as she stood there panting and wide-eyed. "You okay?" he asked.

"Where's Ephraim?" she asked.

"Don't know and don't care."

"I need to see him."

Price arched his eyebrows and then leaned against the doorway. "You *need* to see him?" he asked. "I don't think anyone's ever needed to see Ephraim before, not in his whole sad, sorry life."

"He's with Will," Brynn said, peeking from around her brother.

"Good. We need to find them right away. I figured it out. Maybe."

"You did?" Brynn asked.

"Figured what out?" Price asked, now standing up straight.

"The water. The cure. Everything."

Price looked from Brynn to Mallory and then back to Brynn again. "I can't believe the two of you are in on this, too. I thought you both had a little bit of common sense. You're as crazy as he is."

Mallory's cheeks burned. She had been called crazy all her life, but it hurt more this time, not because it was coming from Price, but because now she was so sure she was right. All the stories her parents had told her, they hadn't been lies to amuse her. They had prettied it up and made it into a fairy tale, but the essence was true. The house was powerful. The water was magical. Her parents had told her the truth.

"It's not crazy. It's chemistry, sort of. About the water."
She took a deep breath and started over, trying to sound as
sane and reasonable as possible. "It's not all straight in my
head. It's like those optical illusions where you look at the picture and it's a rabbit but it's also a woman. Most of the time I
just see the rabbit, but sometimes I see the woman, and sometimes, for just a second I can see them both, and I can see
how it works."

Price slouched against the door frame, but at least he was
listening.

"Okay, listen, have you heard the stories about this place?
About the water?"

Price gave a half shrug. "Yeah, sure. I mean, that's how
these people made their money, right? Selling the water?"

"Exactly. They told people it was special and that it could
cure them."

"Yeah. It was stupid. And Ephraim was stupid for believing it and almost gagging our dad."

"He was just trying to help," Brynn said softly.

"Maybe they were exaggerating, but every legend has a
little bit of truth, right?" She kept going before they could
challenge her. "What if the stories about the water are
kind of true? I mean, it would explain a lot about Crystal
Springs."

"Like what?" Price asked.

"Like how people here are smarter and stronger. Even you,"

she said. "Ephraim told me about you setting the pool record. You were a good athlete before, but now you're great."

"I guess," Price said, grinning.

"So it seems possible that the water actually causes mutations, making people smarter and stronger. Like maybe there's something in the water. Something that's only here in Crystal Springs." She held up the book she'd been analyzing. "I think there might be some new element in the water, something that no one else has known about."

"It sounds like X-Men," Price scoffed. "And I'm not a mutant."

"Okay," Mallory said. "I know it sounds far-fetched, but just bear with me a minute. Let's say there is something in the water. And let's say it really does affect people. What if they found a way to strengthen it?"

"How?" Brynn asked.

Mallory slumped. "That's the part I'm not so sure about. But here's what I know about this place. First, there's a high level of radioactivity here. Did Ephraim tell you about the Geiger counter?"

"He mentioned something once."

"Ms. Little measured all of us and everyone was higher than they should be. Everyone, but especially Ephraim. Ian said something about radiation giving us superpowers, which I thought was stupid at the time, but now maybe he was on to something. Anyway, I don't know if the radiation is coming from the water or if it's part of what makes the water stronger, but I think it's part of it."

"If the water is radioactive, why don't we all have cancer?" Price asked.

"I don't know. Maybe there's something in the water that protects us, too." She shrugged. "But there's also the house itself. You've seen the blue glow and the flashes, right?"

Price nodded. "Sure."

"Okay, well, those flashes are like lightning bolts, right? Which means electricity must be being discharged. That's what lightning is. It's like with the Van de Graaff generator. The whole house is getting charged with electricity somehow." She thought about the generator and how the band inside spun around while electrons were sprayed onto it, building up a charge. She wasn't sure how the house was building up a charge. There had to be something special about the way that it was built. She widened her eyes. Another cog slipped into place. "The frame of the house! It's all metal, with the stone placed around it. It was a big deal at the time. My dad said they did it because Angus Appledore was afraid of fires."

"Fat lot of good it did him," Price said.

"The metal could hold the charge. I'm not one hundred percent sure where the charge is coming from, but it could just come from the atmosphere, or even the earth, since the house is built right into the bedrock."

Brynn nodded. "So the glow is the air being charged?"

"Right," Mallory said. "And the flash, that's just like

lightning, except instead of going from the cloud to the ground, it's going from your house up."

Price did not look convinced, but Brynn said, "I guess it's possible."

"I wish I could be more clear. But you take that new element that's only in the water in Crystal Springs plus the radioactivity plus the light—it all has to add up to something, right?"

Price stood still in the doorway. Mallory looked to Brynn for support, but Brynn was staring down at her shoes with a furrowed brow as if she were still working through Mallory's explanation.

"I'm not sure how it all goes together, but I know it does. Will's the one who really understands this stuff. So let's go find Ephraim and Will and show them this book I found and see what Will says. If it makes sense to him, then maybe you'll believe it?"

"We don't even know where they are," Price said. "They could be anywhere."

"They're in the tunnels," Brynn said. "Will wanted to see the stairs."

"Why didn't you say that before?" Mallory asked.

"You were telling your story," Brynn said.

"Come on, let's go."

Mallory tried to run, but Price took long, loping strides across the yard to the bottling house as if he couldn't be bothered. They descended the stairs in single file. "This is a total waste of time," Price said as they started down the path. "I could be doing weight training for swimming, you know. I've got a big meet next weekend." He kicked a stone so it skittered down the tunnel.

"Come on, we're almost there," Mallory cried over her shoulder. "The sooner we get there, the sooner you can get back to whatever it was that you needed to be doing."

"I was in the middle of a set of pull-ups when you pounded on the door with your story about crazy-serum," Price said. "That's what's really going on here. That's what's in the water. It's crazy juice and you've all had your fill."

Just as they reached the intersection and were about to turn toward the lab, they heard the scream.

THIRTY-SIX

When the stair snapped under Ephraim's foot it sent him tumbling backward. Almost immediately he ran into Will, and the two of them bounced down the stairs like children's marbles. They landed in a heap with Will's back pressed against the bookcase. Ephraim's head and body ached with each movement he took to extricate himself from Will. "That was awful," he groaned.

Will didn't answer.

Ephraim turned, and there was Will with a large piece of wood sticking out of his thigh. His face was ashen, lips pinched together. Blood spread out from around the wound.

Ephraim didn't know what he was supposed to do. Pull the board out or leave it in? Apply pressure or elevate it?

He knew he needed to stanch the bleeding, so he pulled off his sweatshirt and tried to wrap it around the splintered shards of wood. Will sucked in hard. "I'm sorry," Ephraim said.

Will's lips were white and he seemed to be biting at the air to get it into his lungs, like a fish. Ephraim reached around him looking for something, anything. His hand wrapped around a glass bottle.

It was one of the two bottles of water left in the crate that he and Price had found: the magical water that had no magic.

"Please," Will murmured.

Ephraim looked at the water and back at Will. His mind flashed through the decision process, deciding in less than a second that the water hadn't hurt him or his dad, so it must be okay for Will, who was pressing his dry lips together. As he held the bottle to his friend's mouth, though, he tried to remember from all the movies and television shows he had watched if you were supposed to give someone water when they were injured. Maybe it made things worse. He wasn't sure and he had just sent his friend tumbling down the stairs.

The blood was soaking through his sweatshirt and he thought he could feel it on his hand. Wooziness began to overtake him and he felt himself swaying from side to side. It was like he was outside his body, though, or sleeping deep inside it, unconnected to what his eyes were seeing.

His hand started to fall away, pulling the bottle with it. Will weakly pressed Ephraim's hand back up.

Ephraim had never seen blood like this before. He had

never seen a face turn so white with pain. Even his father's stroke, by the time he saw it, was neatened up and contained.

This was raw. This was real. And it was all his fault. "I'm sorry," he said. "I'm sorry. I'm sorry. I'm sorry." The words came faster and faster, running together.

Will just shook his head and kept gulping from the water bottle until it was nearly empty.

"Ephraim!"

"Will!"

Ephraim turned his head and saw his brother and sister and Mallory rushing into the room.

"What happened?"

"We were climbing and the stair broke and I fell and then we fell and—"

"Brynn, run back to the castle and call an ambulance," Price interrupted.

"No one calls the ambulance in Crystal Springs," Mallory said.

"Don't tell me: they heal themselves magically," Price said.

"No. It'll take an ambulance at least a half an hour to get here. We can be to the hospital by then."

"Mom's not home," Brynn said.

"Where is she?" Ephraim asked.

"She went for a walk down to the lake. She said she needed to clear her head."

"She won't be back for at least an hour," Price said.

They all stared at one another. Even if Mallory called her

dad, it would take him fifteen minutes to get to the Water Castle. The way Will was bleeding, who knew if they had that long.

"Can you walk?" Price asked Will.

He shook his head, his jaw clenched tightly.

"We're going to have to carry him," Ephraim said. He looked around the lab for something to make a stretcher out of, but there was nothing.

He looked at Price. Price hooked his arms under Will's shoulders. "Get his legs. Carefully."

Ephraim and Mallory each took a leg and they carried Will back out through the tunnels, which seemed to have stretched and grown more unleveled since they'd come in. Will gritted his teeth as each step jostled him and brought him new pain.

"Steady now," Ephraim said. "We'll have you out of here in no time, Will."

When they reached the stairs, they all stopped.

"We can't—" Price began, looking up the steep, rickety stairs that led into the bottling house.

"We have to," Ephraim said.

"They're too narrow for us both to carry his legs," Mallory said.

"I'll do it." Ephraim carefully took Will's leg from Mallory. He stared into Will's flinty eyes. "This is going to hurt, but then it will be over."

"I know."

"On three," Ephraim said. "One, two, three."

Price went first, backing up the stairs, and Ephraim did his best to keep Will steady, but still they seemed to jar him with each step. By the time they reached the top, all three boys were sweating, and Will's lips had gone gray.

When they got out into the sun, Ephraim and Price exchanged a glance. "We'll have to take him ourselves," Ephraim declared.

"I'll drive," Price said.

"You know how to drive?" Mallory asked.

"Sure. I mean, I *have* driven. Anyway, it's an automatic. It's really just steering." He tried to sound confident.

The three lurched across the lawn to their parents' SUV. They laid Will across the backseat, and Ephraim sat on the floor, holding his sweatshirt tightly against the wound. He would not move his hand, not ever, as long as keeping it there kept Will alive.

"Where's the hospital?" Price asked, his voice thin as piano wire.

Mallory, who sat in the front seat chewing on the inside of her cheek, had to force herself to think. She had been there; she just had to remember how to get there. "Maine Street," she murmured. "Out of town."

Price dropped the gearshift into drive. The car shot forward, and Price slammed on the brakes. Will rocked, almost falling into Ephraim, who tried to hold him still. Will screamed and the sound echoed around the inside of the SUV.

"Keep it steady, Price, will you?" Ephraim demanded.

"I'm sorry, okay, these aren't exactly ideal driving conditions." He took his foot off the brake gently, and then eased down on the gas pedal. They started bumping down the driveway. Will pinched his eyes closed. "It's okay," Brynn said. "We'll be on flat roads soon." Her voice sounded just like their mother's when she talked to her patients on the phone: calm and confident. "Just a little bit longer. Just hold on a little bit longer."

He nodded and then, immediately, passed out.

September 9, 1909

When he heard about the fire, Harry booked himself on the earliest train to Portland. He had barely had time to pack a bag. In the station, he had grabbed a bite to eat and the *New York Times*. As the train jostled along, he read the article in the newspaper, the one he and Nora had been waiting for: "PEARY DISCOVERS THE NORTH POLE AFTER EIGHT TRIALS IN 23 YEARS."

On the trip north Harry read the article so many times he scarcely needed to look at the words anymore. Peary telegraphed that he had reached the Pole on April 6, nearly a year after Cook had claimed to have been there. Why, then, Harry wondered, had Cook waited so long to make his announcement, whereas Peary had telegraphed as soon as he had reached a station? He would have to talk to Nora about it, but he felt sure this was more proof that Cook had been mistaken, and perhaps even deliberately misleading people.

At school Harry had been reading in the *New York Times* of people who had questioned Cook's account, and he had those articles to share with Nora, too, though he was much more interested in speaking with her about Peary's success— and Henson's.

The train shuddered to a stop in Portland. Making his way through the station, the people all bustling about him, he stopped at a newsstand to pick up the local paper. He took a seat on the second train of his journey, which would carry him to Crystal Springs. With a release of steam and a loud groan, the train started up and he spread the newspaper out in front of him. The front page had two stories, one on Peary, and one on the fire.

The article described the fire, and what had been done to combat it. He could imagine the people of the town forming a chain to send water up the hill from the lake. Even with the property ablaze, Harry felt certain that his father would never confess to the tunnels underground.

He read the article once and then a second time. All fingers were pointing toward the Wylies. One of the firefighters said a lantern was found tipped on its side in the packaging plant. One of the guests reported seeing a man running through the woods shortly before the alarm was sounded and Solomon, Nora's brother, swore he had seen Mr. Wylie at the scene before anyone else from town arrived. No one made any direct accusations, but the meaning was clear. Harry could not help but feel a twinge of sympathy for Winnie.

When he arrived at the Water Castle, the smell of smoke hung in the air. From the front of the house, it looked as if nothing had happened, but when he walked around to the back where the hotel had stood, all he saw was a pile of rubble with embers still glowing. The packaging plant, where bottles were packed into cases and shipped far and wide, was gone, too, along with the stable and another outbuilding. The back of the Water Castle was singed black but the stones, and the metal frame—chosen by Angus because of his fear of fire—had kept the house safe. The bottling house, too, encased in glass, still stood. That was all.

Townspeople busied themselves with the family's workers, sifting through the remains for things that could be saved. Harry scanned the crowd for Nora. Though he was home for a family tragedy, all he could feel was grateful that he would be able to share Peary's discovery with her. They could speculate together on what Peary had found there, what he had seen.

His father stormed past him in a fit of rage and paused only long enough to say, "Your future went up in those flames."

To Harry, this felt like a liberation rather than the doomsday promise his father meant it to be.

Then his father was on his way, running to catch up with a business associate.

Nora grabbed him by the arm. "I'm so glad you're home," she said. Soot smudged her cheeks.

"You've heard the news?"

She shook her head. "None of that matters anymore. Come with me." She led him to the library.

He took the newspaper article out and put it on the desk. "I feel certain he made it before Cook. Why, Cook's story was already falling to pieces and now Peary is coming back with actual proof."

"Harry, listen to me. Dr. Appledore is missing."

"Uncle Orlando?"

"No one has seen him in two days."

"They don't think he was in one of the buildings?" Harry asked, his eyes widening.

"No. People saw him after the fire. Solomon said he saw him heading down the road out of town. No one stopped him. It was madness here. You cannot imagine the scene, the smoke and the flames." She let herself fall down into Orlando's leather chair by the fireplace, which was cold, the skeletons of burnt logs on the grate. "This is my fault. I should have been watching him."

"You were his assistant, not his caretaker."

"You don't understand. The day of the fire he was in the strangest state." She looked to the door to make sure it was closed. "He said he found it, Harry. He was sure he had found the water. The way he spoke, it was like a madman, but there was honesty in his eyes, assuredness. I cannot explain it."

"Why would he disappear after finding the water?"

"I cannot say. The discovery did not seem to make him happy. Rather it seemed to frighten him. He asked me—" She pushed her hands down on her skirt. "He made me promise that I would tell no one about the water, where it was or how it was done."

"How it was done?"

"That's the strangest part," she said. "He told me you have to burn the water."

"You don't think he set the fire, do you?"

"No," she said firmly. "He was quite clear that no more

water should be made. I do not think that the fire was what he meant by burning the water." She buried her head in her hands. "But then, I understood little of what he meant that day. I promised, though. I promised to protect his secret forever."

She stood and walked across the library. She removed a panel from the wall and retrieved one of Dr. Appledore's hand-labeled bottles. "Do you think it is possible?"

"Peary has made it to the Pole," he said. "Peary and Henson. I believe anything is possible."

She nodded. "Then I must drink as well. If it is real, then I must know."

"You needn't make this decision right now," Harry told her, placing a hand on top of hers. "Wait until things are more settled. Perhaps Uncle Orlando will return and things will make more sense."

"I don't believe he is ever returning," she said. She gripped the bottle tightly in her hands. "I see why he was so distraught. It is a thing too large to contemplate, this idea of eternity. But I must know. Don't you see? I must know."

"I understand how you feel."

"Still, it scares me."

The two were silent, staring at the bottle in her hands. It looked unremarkable. Just a simple bottle with clear water inside.

She lifted her eyes and stared into his as she unscrewed the top. "Will you drink with me?"

THIRTY-SEVEN

"You're a lucky boy," the doctor said to Ephraim as he put down the little light he'd been shining into Ephraim's eyes.

Ephraim sat on the exam bed, his legs stretched out in front of him. A nurse had put a bandage across a scrape on his cheek, and another on his elbow. Other than that, he'd been fine.

"How many steps would you say you fell down?" the doctor asked.

"I don't know."

"The stairs go all the way up," Mallory said. "From the basement to the roof. And the house is four stories." She sat in one of the plastic chairs near the bed in the emergency room. Price sat in the other with Brynn in his lap.

The doctor raised his eyebrows. "Miraculous. You should have at least a broken bone or two. Thank your lucky stars."

Mallory knew it wasn't lucky stars that Ephraim needed to thank. It was the water he had drunk that protected him.

"How's Will?" Ephraim asked.

"That slice of wood went deep into his leg, and let me tell you the surgeon had quite the job getting all of the splinters out. But no bones were broken. You said you fell into him?"

"Yes," Ephraim said, nodding. It didn't make sense, though. He had held his hand against the wound and he had felt Will grow so weak. It seemed impossible—a wonderful miracle, but still impossible—that Will was going to be fine. "What about all that blood he lost?"

"With wounds like that, the blood is usually not as bad as it seems. You just aren't used to seeing so much of it."

As the doctor snapped Ephraim's chart closed, Ephraim's mother rushed into the room and gathered him in her arms. Brynn practically leaped out of her chair to join them. Price, too. Mallory was left alone. She watched their mother, the tears in her eyes and her wild hair. Mallory balled her hands into fists and pressed them into her stomach, trying to replace one ache with another.

"When I got home and saw the car gone, I couldn't fathom what had happened. Then the hospital called. Ida down at the grocery store drove me here. We came as fast as we could."

"He's okay," Price said to his mother. "We're all okay."

She held Ephraim back and looked at him more closely. "Look at you. You're all banged up."

"He's fine," the doctor said again. "Nothing but bumps and bruises. Both boys came out of this about a hundred times better than could have been expected."

"He's okay? Will's okay?" The voice came from a man in the doorway wearing jeans and a wool shirt.

"Are you Will's father?" the doctor asked.

"Yes. I'm Rene Wylie."

"Come with me," the doctor said.

Rene Wylie started toward the doctor and then he took in the Appledore-Smiths. "You the Appledores?" he asked.

"Yes. I'm Emily Appledore-Smith." She extended her hand, but Rene didn't take it.

"You'll be hearing from me," he said. It didn't sound like any sort of a party invitation.

"It was an accident," Mallory said from her chair.

"Sure you'd say that," he replied, without even looking at her. "A hundred years of indentured servitude, sure you'd say that."

Mallory reddened and looked down at the floor, willing herself not to say anything to Mr. Wylie.

"Let's go see your son," the doctor said. "He's doing very well. Amazingly well. These children did everything right."

Rene Wylie looked at them all, at Ephraim in particular. "Sure. Right after they pushed him down the stairs."

The doctor put his hand on Rene's arm and led him away, as if sensing that this whole thing could get very ugly, very quickly.

Dr. Appledore-Smith looked at Ephraim again. "You fell down stairs? What stairs?"

"In the basement," Ephraim said.

"Basement?" she asked.

"It's a long story," Ephraim said.

She ran her fingers through his hair. "I want to talk to the nurse who admitted you. You could have a concussion."

"I'm fine."

"Let me just go and see. I'll find out about Will, too. You stay here." She looked at Ephraim, Brynn, Price, and Mallory in turn. "All of you."

Her sneakers squeaked as she left the room.

Mallory ran up alongside Ephraim. "It was the water," she said.

"What?"

"That's how come you weren't hurt when you fell down all those stairs. And you gave Will the water, too, right? I saw the bottle."

"It was all I had."

She took him by the arm. "Dr. Appledore figured it out. I found this book with equations—that's what I did all day. And it's real. On the roof, they burned the water. You saved him with that water."

"Please, Mallory, don't start with that," Ephraim said.

"It's the truth. It's all written down in this book."

"You aren't making any sense. Anyway, I don't need that story anymore," Ephraim said. "I don't need a make-believe world and imaginary solutions. Wild made-up stories won't make me feel any better—or cure my dad. I just have to deal with it. I would think you'd understand."

Mallory felt the words as punches. "It's real," Mallory said. "Just think about it. Think about that fall, and—"

"No," he interrupted. "No, Mallory, I don't want to think about it anymore."

The room fell silent, the only sound the beeps and dings that came from the hall outside, and the incessant tapping of Price's foot on the floor.

After several moments, Mallory said, "I think we should go see Will."

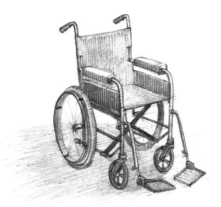

THIRTY-EIGHT

Will lay in his hospital bed and fiddled with its controls, raising his back and then lifting his feet. It was just like the beds in the infomercials, the ones for old people. The sheets were bright white like those he sometimes saw hanging from Mrs. Andrews's clothesline—never at his own house. He had a tray that swung out and over his bed, and so far he'd gone through two cups of Jell-O and one of ice cream. All in all, life in a hospital did not seem so bad except for the smell: disinfectant on top of something unknowable and unnamable.

The mustard-colored curtains were pulled far to the side, and through the window he could see the fog approaching in a big gray mass. He imagined it surrounding the whole hospital, trapping them in. He decided that would not be so bad either.

He heard the door swish open and turned his head, expecting to see another doctor who would marvel over how he was healing so quickly. Instead he saw his father. He held his hat in his hands as if he were at a funeral, and his face was red and splotchy. "You're okay," he stated.

"I'm a miracle," he replied. It was what the doctors and nurses kept saying.

His father looked him over, eyes scanning him like a robot. "You sure you're fine?"

"Yeah."

"No thanks to that Appledore kid," Rene said. He sat down on the chair next to the bed. "What were you even doing up at the Water Castle? Haven't I told you to stay away from that place?"

Will glanced at the monitor that ticked out his vital signs. "He invited me."

"And you went? Talk about walking into the lion's den."

"Dad." The pillows behind his back were slipping down, and he tried to rearrange himself so he was sitting more upright. The movement hurt the wound and he winced.

"You know if it weren't for that family, our situation would be totally different. They're dangerous, Will, you know that."

"Actually I don't know that," he said. "I only know what you've told me."

"That's all you need to know," he said. "Trust me, you've had a target on your back since those people came to town whether you knew it or not."

"Dad, please—"

"They're going to take care of all of this. Finally and once and for all—"

"Dad, stop, okay? Just stop." As Will got angrier, his wound seemed to pulse with pain. "Ephraim fell. The stair broke."

"Because they aren't careful people. They think they just float above the rest of us, can't get their feet dirty, can't be bothered to look down. Well, not this time, Will. This is their fault. We'll sue them and finally get what's ours."

"It was an accident, Dad. Ephraim's my friend."

"You think about it a little and you'll see what I'm saying." He twisted his hat in his hands. "And then we can move forward."

Moving forward for his dad would really just be staying in the same spot. Still angry. Still bitter. Never getting to that place where everything was free and easy, because such a place didn't exist. "I think I need to rest."

"All right. You've been through a trauma, I know. So you just rest and I'll be here."

"You can go."

"I don't mind. This chair is comfortable and I can just watch the TV. Bruins are playing the Maple Leafs."

"I'd rather just get some rest," Will said. "You can watch the game at home."

His dad stopped twisting his hat and looked at his son. Will felt like his dad was really seeing him for the first time ever. They held each other's gaze for a moment. "All right, then.

Doctor says they can let you go tomorrow. I'll be by first thing in the morning." He hesitated and then he pulled something out of his back pocket. "I brought you one of those books you like. Isaac Asimov." He dropped the book on Will's nightstand, then he tugged his ball cap back on his head and left the room.

Will wished his dad would stop and turn around, that he would come back and they could start the conversation over again. They'd talk about what had happened and how Will felt—not about the Appledores. His dad didn't stop though. Will looked over at the cover of the book: an orange background with a robot raging at the sky. He'd been wishing his whole life for the same thing, he realized, for his dad to be someone he was not. In that moment he realized that wish was never going to come true, no matter how many times he made it.

This realization brought on an unfamiliar tightening in his throat, a heaviness in his body. He knew that he was about to cry, and decided he would let himself do it, but only for a minute. His face squinched up and he blinked his eyes, but he did not allow any real tears. It was a shaking sob and then he was done.

He closed his eyes, thinking he might just rest after all, but then he heard the door opening again, and two sets of feet. Mallory and Ephraim stood at the foot of his bed, two pale faces and two pairs of wide eyes.

"You're really okay?" Mallory asked.

"So they tell me."

"I'm sorry, Will. I'm so, so sorry." Ephraim's voice squeaked.

Will shrugged. "It's not your fault the stair broke."

"I wasn't watching where I was going or holding on to the railing or anything."

Mallory studied Will. She noted his ashen skin and the dark circles under his eyes. She also noted that from behind those dark circles his eyes shone brightly and that there was something regal in the way he held himself, sitting there among all the pillows.

"Why are you looking at me like that?" Will asked.

"Like what?" Mallory replied.

"Like you're measuring me with your eyes. Everyone who comes in here, it's like they're scanning me for errors."

"How do you feel?" Mallory asked.

"What do you mean? I fell down a mammoth flight of stairs and got a piece of wood jammed into my leg, how do you think I feel?"

"Tired, aching?"

"My leg is burning up around where the wood went in, and yeah, I guess I'm a little tired."

"I'm sorry," Ephraim said again.

"If you apologize one more time I'm going to climb out of this bed and clobber you."

Ephraim stared at the brown and white tiles. The room suddenly felt crowded with all of the people and their guilt. "Can we go for a walk?" Will asked.

"You can walk?" Mallory asked.

"The doctor told me not to yet, but you can push me."

Mallory and Ephraim helped Will into a wheelchair that was tucked into the corner. Mallory took the handles and navigated him out of the room. They walked down the hall, their feet making a padding noise that accompanied the swish of the wheels. They passed a series of closed doors, each with a name written on the outside and a chart hanging up.

They left the ward and went into an open mezzanine with a wide set of stairs going down to the main entrance. There were potted plants around the edges of the stairs and the whole area looked more like a grand hotel than a hospital.

Mallory couldn't help but imagine shoving Will, wheelchair and all, down the grand staircase. She was sure that he would be just fine even if he fell out of the chair and tumbled head over feet, down and down and down. She gripped the handles more tightly.

"Your father thinks I pushed you," Ephraim said.

"My father thinks a lot of things."

"He doesn't think much of me and my family." Ephraim scuffed his feet along the shiny tiled floor.

"Don't worry about it," Will said. "We're friends now, right?"

"Yeah," Ephraim agreed. He smiled at Will, but then the smile faltered. He'd finally found some real friends, and then because he was so clumsy, one ended up in the hospital. And now his family was probably moving away, anyway.

Mallory gripped and regripped the handles. They walked to the end of the floor to a set of windows that looked out over

Crystal Lake, now totally covered in the fog. "It's like something out of a scary movie," Ephraim said.

It did look very much like the settings of the zombie movies that Mallory liked to watch, though she realized she hadn't watched one in a long time. Her own story had been holding her attention lately.

Will rubbed his temples. "Are you feeling okay?" Mallory asked.

"Yeah," Will said. "Just tired."

"Well, that makes sense. Your body is doing a lot of healing. Remarkable, superhuman healing."

"Sure, I guess," he said. "The doctors seem impressed."

She nodded. "Do you *feel* different?"

He started to say no, but then, there was something different, a little solid core of strength. "I guess, maybe. I told my dad that I didn't want to hear any more of his trash talk about the Appledores. I'm not sure if he listened, but I told him. That felt pretty good."

Mallory glanced at Ephraim, then back at Will. "So maybe you're feeling a little invincible?"

Ephraim caught on to what Mallory was hinting at. "Stop it, Mallory."

"What?" Will asked.

Mallory spun the chair around so Will was facing her. "If there was an element—a new element that no one has ever heard of—could it have properties that could mutate people?"

"I guess anything is possible. Sure."

"Mallory, come on," Ephraim said.

"I found a book. A science book with notes in it and I worked at it all day. I think they discovered a new element. And then I went to the Water Castle. There's a special water barrel on the roof and—"

"Mallory, please. He just wants to rest."

Will, though, looked at her with a gaze both curious and sure. "A new element?" he asked.

"Yeah. *O-R*."

Will smirked. "*Orlando.* Of course he named it after himself."

"You don't believe her, do you?" Ephraim asked.

Mallory sat down on a bench next to Will's wheelchair. "There was something in the notebooks about the different elements that made up the water. I saw *O-R*, but I just read it as *or*, like they weren't quite certain. But then I thought, what if that's an element, too? I don't understand it all, but it's a possibility, right?"

He shifted his body and winced. "If there was another element, who knows what its properties could be." A new element. That would surely be worthy of the World's Science Fair. "My father told me scientists studied the radioactivity here once. They could measure it but couldn't see it doing anything. So they let it go."

"But maybe they just didn't see it."

"Right. If there was a new element, it wouldn't even occur to them to look for it. So they didn't see anything." Will looked at Ephraim. "It's just like you were saying—something new, something undiscovered. But he found it. Orlando Appledore found it."

Ephraim shoved his hands deep into his pockets, feeling the watch there. "There's no way he found a whole new element. I mean, scientists today do experiments way more advanced than anything in that lab, and Orlando is the *only* one who figured it out? Let's face it. It was just a silly story." He started walking away from them. How could they finally believe once it was clear that there was nothing special about the water?

"Orlando Appledore said you had to burn the water," Mallory continued. "There's a water tank up on top of the house, right where the blue light is. You know the house has a metal frame, right? Well, I think it builds up a charge and releases all that electricity right at that point. It's like that water barrel is being hit by lightning."

"If the element was able to make people healthier, then that kind of energy could amplify it."

Amplify. That was the word she hadn't been able to think of. The water had a special radioactive element and then the electricity pumped it up even more so that someone could drink it and live forever if they wanted to. Orlando didn't *find* the fountain, he *made* it.

"Will," she began.

"If you're right about this, it changes everything."

"Of course." Mallory leaned in closer. "The thing I can't

figure out is why it saved you and Ephraim, but didn't do anything for Ephraim's dad."

"I'm not sure," Will said.

Ephraim heard them talking about him and his father, their heads bent close together, but he didn't care. They could fall back on silly stories, but he was moving forward. He looked out the window. He was pretty sure he was looking toward Crystal Springs, but the fog was too dense to tell. If it was Crystal Springs, and his dad was on the other side of the fog, Ephraim hoped he was sleeping peacefully.

"Maybe because Ephraim's dad's stroke affected his brain, not his body? There are still so many questions. I need to get a sample. I need to see it up close. The implications—" He stopped himself. What *were* the implications?

If Mallory was right, then in the moment that Ephraim had given him the water Will's whole life had changed.

If it was real, what did it mean for him? What was happening to him? He looked up and down his body, searching for any change. Would it mean no World's Science Fair? He couldn't draw attention to himself like that. Would it mean no moving out and going to college? He could be a scientist, but he would have to do it alone, working away in some secret laboratory like Orlando Appledore had.

He shook his head. He was getting ahead of himself. He didn't know if Mallory was right, yet. He wouldn't know for sure until he could get a sample of the water back into his lab above the garage. He would look at it under his microscope and run tests and see what was really going on. He had to believe he could figure out the mystery. Orlando Appledore had spent his whole life trying to find the formula; Will just needed to be able to understand it.

"I'll help you," Mallory said.

"I know," he answered. He lifted his eyes to meet hers and forced a smile.

THIRTY-NINE

Before she started the car, Dr. Appledore-Smith turned and looked at each of the children: Brynn, Ephraim, Price, and Mallory. She made sure they were all buckled in. Then she sighed and put the car in reverse.

Brynn had a book to read. Price retrieved a tennis ball from the glove compartment and began to squeeze it. Mallory and Ephraim looked out opposite windows at the trees and cars passing by. The truth was bursting inside of her, and she wanted to lay it all out for Ephraim, to make him understand and believe, but she knew he wouldn't, not right now.

"A set of stairs from the basement, you say? The first thing we're going to have to do is have your dad come over and take a look, Mallory. I didn't even know there was a basement."

"I'm sure he'll come," Mallory replied.

"All that matters is that you are okay. Each one of you."

Okay. It was a little word and, Mallory realized, all relative. Three of them had drunk the water: Ephraim, his father, and now Will. It saved Will and Ephraim but it certainly didn't make them okay. What would the water do to them? How long would they live? And *how* would they live? It's not like they could just keep going to sixth grade forever.

She was starting to realize how little she knew. She'd always heard about the water, but the details from the stories were hazy to her. Her mother said people had to keep drinking the water or its effects would wear off. But how much and how often? Did they need to drink every day or every year? Did it make a difference that Will had drunk nearly a whole bottle?

All the questions awed her. She wasn't sure she could make the choice to drink even if she had all the answers. It would mean she could see so much more of the world outside of tiny Crystal Springs. She certainly wouldn't be able call her life boring if she were immortal.

Mallory still had the key around her neck and she tugged it back and forth on its chain. The necklace pulled into the back of her neck, a tiny little weight. When her parents had told her the stories, they had been full of magic and wonder. She hadn't realized how heavy and complex the reality could be.

She thought about how Will had never wanted the stories to be true because then it would mean his father had been right. But he'd gone along with them, steady as a ship on flat sea, to find out the truth. He would keep on being steady, she knew, keep working to find out all of the secrets of the water no matter how scared he was.

She didn't think she could be so calm. She didn't think she could make the choice to drink the water. Will hadn't had a choice. That seemed impossibly unfair to Mallory since Will was someone who liked to have choices and to know all the facts before he made his decisions.

She would keep his secret. That much she could do for him. It was her job now, she realized. Maybe it had been all along. Maybe her family wasn't just the caretakers of the house, but of the water, from E. Darling, who never told what Orlando had found, right down the line to her. She glanced at Ephraim. He would keep the secret, too, once he believed. Their families were all knotted together still, as they had been for generations.

Orlando . . . what had ever become of him? Was he still drinking the water? He could be living among them. Or perhaps he had left Crystal Springs far behind, moving from one place to another as he grew tired of each, a vagabond for eternity.

She turned to Ephraim. "I'm going to give the book to Will," she told him.

"That's a good idea," Dr. Appledore-Smith interjected. "It will keep his mind occupied. I've found that bodies heal more quickly when the mind is being exercised as well."

Ephraim, though, shook his head. "I think we can get him some books from the library. Ms. Little will know what he likes."

Mallory chewed on her lip. "I just think that Will is the

kind of person who likes to *understand* things and to make up his own mind."

"Except that sometimes it's easy to get confused and it's hard to tell the difference between what's real and what you wish would happen," Ephraim told her.

Mallory glanced toward the rearview mirror and saw Dr. Appledore-Smith's gaze shifting away from them. "Yes," she said. "But that doesn't mean you shouldn't try to find out." It was all Mallory had wanted. This whole time they had been searching for the water, what she really wanted was the truth. Now she had it. The whole truth, not just the pretty version her parents had told her. The facts were there. They had to finish what they started: they had to make sense of it. She couldn't understand why Ephraim would want to back away when they'd come this far.

She knew Will would want to see the book, to study the water. If anyone could figure out the whole mystery, and maybe even how the water could be used to help other people, it was him. She wasn't going to just let this go. "Maybe we can get together later. I'd like to finish our project."

"Oh, I'm sure Mr. Wright will give you an extension," Ephraim's mom assured them.

"Once Will is feeling better," Ephraim told Mallory. "Maybe we can have a group meeting. Maybe."

As Ephraim's mother turned down the driveway of Mallory's house, Mallory wanted to drag Ephraim from the car, to sit him down and explain it as best she could. She would explain and explain and explain until believed. He had to believe. Then she caught sight of the Volkswagen Rabbit out front. It was both familiar and strange, and Mallory felt her heart beating faster. As they drove closer, Mallory saw the silhouette of her mother sitting out on the old porch swing, rocking back and forth.

Did her mother know what she had found out? Mallory wondered. Was she there to help make sense of it all? Maybe her parents didn't really know the whole story. Maybe they had heard the tales passed down from parent to child, too. If that was the case, Mallory wasn't sure how much she should tell them.

"Do you want me to go in with you? I can explain what happened to your dad," Ephraim's mom said.

"No, thank you."

"Are you sure?"

"Really."

"I should go in. He's going to have a lot of questions."

Mallory fumbled with her seat belt. "Really, it's fine. I can explain it to him. I have a lot to explain."

Ephraim's mom looked up to the porch and saw Mallory's mom on the swing. "Oh," she said. "Well, if you're sure, I would like to get Ephraim home and into bed."

"Mom," Ephraim said. "I'm fine."

Mallory looked at him, and he just as quickly looked away, knowing what she was thinking.

"You tell your parents to call me if they have any questions. They have the number."

"Thanks for the ride," Mallory said, her fingers hooked onto the door handle, and she pushed it open.

She told herself to walk, but she found herself running with a hitch in her throat toward the porch. Her mother stood and came down the steps where they met, Mallory nearly crashing into her mother and knocking her down. Her mother put her hand on the back of Mallory's head, pulling her close, just as she always had.

"Ephraim's mom called us," her mom said. "She said she'd bring you home, but your dad went there anyway, and I waited here just in case. Are you okay?"

"Yes," Mallory sobbed. "It was Will and Ephraim. We found these stairs from the lab and they were climbing."

"From the lab in the tunnels?" Her mom touched the space on her neck where the key used to be.

Mallory blinked. Her mother had never mentioned the lab or the tunnels before. She *knew*. She knew about the lab, but she hadn't told Mallory about it. Why? Just how much did she understand about the water?

"Are they okay?"

"They fell all the way down, but they're fine," she said, watching her mother's reaction. "They both—" She was going to tell her mom that both of her friends had drunk the water, but she stopped herself. She still wasn't sure she could trust her mother, after she had left—and all the secrets she had kept when she'd been around. Mallory wanted to know what her mother knew before she revealed her own hand.

"If everyone is okay, why are you crying?"

Mallory wiped her eyes. "I wasn't until I saw you." The words came out wrong. It wasn't sadness she had felt upon seeing her mother; it was relief.

Her mother, though, just smiled. "Some days, some moments are like that."

Mallory pulled back. "I thought you were going to Alaska."

Her mom leaned against the porch railing. "I decided to wait until the summer. Alaska's supposed to be beautiful then. Imagine, twenty-four hours of daylight."

Mallory frowned at the dried leaves on the ground. "It's overrun with mosquitoes in the summer."

"Then I guess we'll have to bring bug stuff."

Mallory lifted her eyes. "We?"

"Oh, Mallory." Her mom sighed. "I messed up. Your father and I, we need some time apart. We've always been this way. But you—as soon as I started planning that trip, I knew I couldn't go without you."

Mallory was crying again, and embarrassed. So she wrapped her arms around her mother. She knew her mom couldn't fix everything. Mallory had so many questions about the water and what her parents knew, but she was too tired and overwhelmed to put them into words. There would be time for that later, anyway, once she and Will and, hopefully, Ephraim could talk about what they wanted to do. For now, though, Mallory's mother could hold her and tell her that whatever it was, it was going to be okay. In that moment, that was enough.

FORTY

E phraim's mom had waited while Mallory ran across her lawn toward her mother. Ephraim watched them meet on the steps and embrace and he guessed that after a day like that, anyone could be forgiven.

As they drove away he kept watching Mallory. Would she miss him when he was gone, he wondered, or would this story just fold into the rest of the tale about the town, a little blip in the families' intertwined legacies? He hoped that she would miss him. He felt pretty certain that he would miss her.

Driving back through town to get to the Water Castle, Ephraim watched the now-familiar sights go by. The white church that had bells that chimed on Sunday mornings, clear all the way up to the Water Castle. The town hall was open only a day and a half each week. There was the library, its lion seeming to cry with the mist that dripped down his face. The bench outside the Wylie Five and Dime was empty; Edward and Edwin must have gone home because of the weather.

When he'd arrived a few weeks before, Ephraim never would have thought he would have gotten used to this place. Now they were going to leave and it would be like they had never come, like nothing had changed.

"What's happening with Dad?" he asked.

His mom lifted her hand and brushed at a stray hair. "It's still up for discussion, but don't worry about it now. One crisis at a time." She gave a nervous laugh.

"Whatever you need to do for Dad," Ephraim said, "we'll help you out wherever we need to go."

Price turned around in the front seat and looked back at Ephraim. He looked confused at first, but then he nodded. "That's right, Mom. Whatever you need."

"And I'm sorry about today. About adding to your stress."

"Thanks, boys," their mom said.

As they wound their way up the hill, Ephraim looked back over the town that still looked to him like something right off of a postcard. Now, though, he realized, it was the kind of postcard he would tack up on his wall, not shuffle to the bottom of a drawer.

There was nothing special about the town, nothing magical, and that was just fine. The funny thing was, if anyone had been transformed by Crystal Springs, it was him. Price had always been an athlete and Brynn had always been smart. He was neither of these things. He had never really been sure what he was. But now he was someone who'd been on a wild adventure. He had put himself on the line to try to save his father. Maybe he hadn't succeeded, but he had tried.

He had come to this new town, and he had made friends, and they had done all sorts of things he never would have imagined before. No one back in Cambridge would believe that he'd been crawling around in dark tunnels, or climbing up stairs with no destination. Maybe, he decided, growing up meant letting go of the stories, letting go in general, letting yourself fall just to see if you could catch yourself. And he had.

They drove up the winding road and the Water Castle came into view. Steel gray against the paler gray sky. It looked regal, but you could also sense the years of memories inside of it. He peered up to the roof and caught a glimpse of something metallic. Maybe it was the water barrel Mallory had talked about. Maybe it was nothing.

His mom pulled the car right up in front of the house. Ephraim climbed out of the car and said, "I'm going for a little walk."

"Ephraim, I really think you should head up to bed."

"Just for a minute, Mom, I promise. I need some fresh air after being in that hospital."

She hesitated but said, "Okay."

He walked around back to the bottling house. He wanted a moment alone, and it was the most private place he could think of. After letting himself in the ivy-covered door, he sat down on the marble floor. The gray day and the ivy over the glass made it seem like he'd walked into an antique photo. He could almost imagine how it had been once, the workers in crisp white uniforms filling each bottle with water, rolling it down the line. It had been state-of-the-art at the time, that's what Mallory had told him. This whole place had been alive once.

He leaned over with his head between his knees and saw a crack in the marble. He ran his hands along it: a whole chunk was loose. He pulled at it the way he and Price used to dislodge stones on the rocky beach they'd visited as children, wiggling it like a loose tooth until it popped out. Beneath it was a dark space, but something glinted.

Ephraim hesitated. He was tired of secrets. Tired of mysteries. Tired of hidden staircases and secret rooms. Someone had hidden whatever the glinting thing was, and maybe it was better that it just stayed a secret.

There was no denying, though, that he felt a familiar twinge. The twinge of hope. The twinge of possibility. So he stuck his hand down into the hole.

As soon as his fingers closed around it, he knew what it was. Still, he pulled it out: a water bottle marked with the same label as the others he had found:

Fountain of Youth
Crystal Springs, Maine
The cure for all that ales ye

Tied to the neck of the bottle was a small scrap of yellowing paper. After loosening the knot, he unrolled it. The letters were hard to read in the dim light and he had to hold it close to his eyes: *For Harry, in case you change your mind.*

The bottle was nearly empty.

He knew he should just put it back into the hole, cover it up, and forget about it, but he held on to it for a moment, reaching into his pocket to feel the watch he had taken from the wardrobe. He'd carried it around all this time, but never really given much thought to the inscription. Who was Harry and who had left the note? Who else had believed?

He pictured a man wearing the fur-lined hat Brynn had given him in the storage room. Maybe the woman who had left the bottle wore the peacock feather hat. They were gone now, but had been real and alive before. Maybe that was all that mattered. You had your time and you did the best you could with it.

Outside, a crow called and another answered. It was nearly dinnertime, and he knew he ought to go in and help. On his hands and knees, he placed the bottle back into the hole and slid the marble into place.

He walked across the lawn just like countless people had done before him. Appledores and Darlings and hotel guests and even Wylies—their footprints were gone but their spirits remained.

The setting sun was starting to peek through the clouds, making the whole sky like luscious ink. "Painter's sky," his dad had always called it. Against the backdrop of pink clouds, two eagles circled round and round. He had seen them before, as they had a nest in one of the trees that bordered the field. He had never seen them flying like this, though, circling up and up and up as if daring each other to go higher. He stopped on the edge of the lawn to watch them until they were little more than tiny brown dots against the fuchsia.

Ephraim wondered if his father could see them. Maybe he could set him up in a chair by the window. Would he really see them, or know what they were? It was worth a try. If they moved to New York, then he would take his father to museums and roll him in a wheelchair up to his favorite pictures.

Rounding the front of the house, Ephraim looked upstairs to his parents' room on the second floor. He did it every time he came up to the house, and every time he expected to see his dad standing there. But he didn't expect to see his dad this time. It was just force of habit.

The light was bad, and at first the window just seemed dark. Once his eyes adjusted he saw that the curtain of the window was pulled aside. Ephraim blinked, thinking the figure was only a trick of his eyes. But no, he was right about what he had seen: the silhouette of his father. He was looking out toward the eagles that rose and fell with the air currents.

Ephraim stood still for a moment. It couldn't be. It had to be someone else, but Ephraim would recognize his father anywhere. Maybe they had found a way to prop him up. It was some new medical trick of Dr. Winters's: Ephraim imagined his father's body wedged into a stand as a mannequin, and it made him shudder. He wanted his father to be himself again, not forced into some fake version of it.

The pink sky softened the edges of the Water Castle and made it less imposing. He could feel its warmth. The house had sheltered generations, and now it was his home, at least for a little bit longer.

His father's head turned toward him. Ephraim squinted again. It couldn't be. It was impossible. Yet there his father was, looking down at him from the window. Ephraim held up his hand in a small wave.

And his father waved in return.

AUTHOR'S NOTE

The idea for this book did not start with the Fountain of Youth but rather a house. And perhaps not the house you'd expect. The first real image I had for the book was a brown house, its front yard littered with garden ornaments and old cars in various states of disrepair. In Maine, where I live, such houses are common. These homes always intrigue me. I wonder if the people had planned to fix the cars at one point in time, or if they were saving them for some reason. The inside of the house was just as clear to me: every available surface covered in books. I had a friend growing up whose house had books stacked in every room. There were bookcases in the kitchen and bathroom, all full to bursting. This was a family of readers: people who loved books. Just like Mallory's family. Once I had the house, a town sprung up around it. I had this idea of a stranger coming into town and meeting Mallory. And in that town, strange things were happening. People were smarter and stronger and they seemed to live longer.

I was living in Poland, Maine, while I wrote most of *The Water Castle*, just a few miles down the road from the Poland Springs headquarters. On their grounds was Preservation Park and a hotel. Soon after moving to Poland, my husband and I went for a hike on the overrun trails. We followed the signs to "the Source" and found a small building. We couldn't go in, but the glass sides afforded us a view of a tiled room with a well in the middle. Two mannequins sat in wicker chairs while a third mannequin served them water in crystal glasses.

Later, we were able to go into the bottling house. I was surprised at how different it was from my idea of today's manufacturing plants. Just as it was described in this book, the floor and walls were made of marble. Black-and-white photos showed white-clad workers filling bottles of water. We also visited the Maine State Building, which shared the history of Poland Springs. In the eighteen hundreds, Hiram Ricker, who had suffered from digestion problems for many years, went out to the fields to supervise his laborers. After drinking the water from the spring on the property, he was cured. Though the family had long drunk from the spring when ill, Hiram's recovery marked the first time the family believed the water was truly medicinal. The Ricker family, which owned the land, opened an inn near the bottling plant that would eventually grow into a grand hotel, the Poland Spring House. They began selling the water in 1859. At the same time, they marketed the resort as a place to come and enjoy the countryside—and drink the restorative water.

The resort and water business were at their peak just as science came into its own in this country. You can see this in the advertisements. A full-page ad in the *New-York Daily Tribune* in 1893 proclaims the "marvelous cures" of the water from Poland Spring, and boasts of the "rare and mysterious properties in the water, which are beyond the power of man or science to explain." Yet to bolster the claims, the ad goes on to quote doctors who confirm the medicinal properties of the water. The purveyors claimed it had been proven to aid with everything from diabetes to malarial fever to scrofula (a form of tuberculosis) and gravel (an old name for kidney stones). This tension between the wonder of miracles and the scientific claims of doctors interested me and became the heart of my story.

It might seem strange now that people once believed in the power of the water. It would be easy to mock them as naive or gullible, just as Will chided those who believed in the cure-alls of the time. However, it is in our nature to want quick and easy fixes. As a culture we celebrate youth and fear mortality—that is why the legend of the Fountain of Youth is so strong. Makeup promises to keep our faces looking youthful, while every day it seems a new food is heralded as a way to fend off aging. And so the fountain—water that can give life—wound its way into the story. A question that interests me—one that Mallory struggles with at the end of the book—is if such an elixir truly exists, would we want to drink it? Would you?

But what about the Water Castle itself? I have visited many preserved buildings and historic homes that have been restored to a certain time period and opened as museums. These places always fascinate me for their glimpses into the past. Several years ago, though, I was able to see a magnificent old home that was still in use by the heirs of the original family. How strange it was to eat off dishes older than my grandparents and to sleep in an oversize bed and think of how many other guests had slept there. The final piece fell into place: a building from the past put into modern use. This Water Castle is based on this house: a large stone building with rooms upon rooms, beguiling architecture, and mysteries at every turn. I am so grateful to my distant cousin who let me work in the house. I sat at the desk I imagined to be Orlando's and typed out the words that you read. As far as I know, the house has never glowed blue, there are no tunnels or laboratory underneath, and, certainly, there is no barrel of life-extending water on the roof.

TO LEARN MORE

If you are interested in any of these topics, go to your school or public library and ask for help to research them. Your librarian will be able to guide you to books, magazines, databases, and websites with great information.

To get you started I recommend Matthew Henson's own account of the expedition: *Matthew A. Henson's Historic Arctic Journey* (Guilford, CT: Lyons Press, 2009).

Also recommended: "Robert E. Peary's 1908–09 North Pole Expedition Web Log" (http://www.bowdoin.edu/arctic -museum/activity/northward-journal/). Of course, Peary did not keep an actual Web log—there was no Web at the time. This blog was created based on the journals of Peary, Henson, and others on the trip.

If you are interested in electricity, the Theater of Electricity

from the Boston Museum of Science website (http://www
.mos.org/sln/toe/toe.html) has detailed information about how
the Van de Graaff generator is constructed and how it works.

Here are some places you can visit (virtually or in person):

- Peary-MacMillan Arctic Museum at Bowdoin College in Brunswick, Maine (http://www.bowdoin.edu/
  arctic-museum/).
- Thomas Edison National Historical Park (http://www
  .nps.gov/edis/index.htm). This is where I went to see
  what a turn-of-the-century chemistry lab would look
  like. Apologies to Nikola Tesla, who would surely be
  offended by my choice to visit his rival.
- The Museum of Science, Boston (http://www.mos
  .org/). Be sure to catch the Tesla presentation!

ACKNOWLEDGMENTS

While we often imagine writers as solitary creatures, no book is ever truly the work of just one person. I would like to thank the following people for their support, whether it be in guiding my research, reading early drafts, providing child care, or giving me moral support: my agent, Sara Crowe; my editor, Mary Kate Castellani; Nicole Ellul; Beth Andersen; Ed and Audrey Blakemore; Laura Burnes and the Burnes-Pikcilingis families; Larissa Crockett; Eileen Frazer; Joseph Frazer; Jim Garner; Benjamin Levine; Lindsay Oakes; Susan Tananbaum; Genny LeMoine; Monica Wood; the 2009 Debutantes; the Maine KidLit group; and the Westbrook High School Writing Club. Special thanks to Nathan and Jack Blakemore, who accompanied me on my research trips, put up with less time playing trains, and always told me that I could do it.